STALKED BY SHADOWS

Lucy Jarrett is terrified. She's convinced that somebody is watching her, following her, lurking in the shadows. The phone calls are real enough, even if the caller never speaks. With the recent murder of another young woman, DI Tom Mariner must take Lucy's fears seriously.

However DI Mariner's team is stretched to the limits, when Nina Silvero, the widow of a former police officer is brutally murdered in an attack that could hark back to her husband's past misdemeanours. Someone, it seems, is out for revenge...

STALKED BY SHADOWS

STALKED BY SHADOWS

by

Chris Collett

Magna Large Print Books
Long Preston, North Yorkshire,
BD23 4ND, England.

British Library Cataloguing in Publication Data.

Collett, Chris
    Stalked by shadows.

    A catalogue record of this book is
    available from the British Library

    ISBN   978-0-7505-3445-1

First published in Great Britain in 2009 by Piatkus

Copyright © 2009 by Chris Collett

Cover illustration © Girts Gailans by arrangement with
Arcangel Images

The moral right of the author has been asserted

Published in Large Print 2011 by arrangement with
Piatkus Books, an imprint of Little, Brown Book Group Ltd.

Magna Large Print is an imprint of Library Magna Books Ltd.

Printed and bound in Great Britain by
T.J. (International) Ltd., Cornwall, PL28 8RW

For Joe and Beth

CHAPTER ONE

PC Ralph Solomon was facing a dilemma. Ten minutes ago he'd picked up a call to go to the home of one Nina Silvero, to check that there was nothing amiss. Apparently a friend of Mrs Silvero, who was aged sixty-one and a widow, had contacted the station concerned that she had not turned up to an appointment for that afternoon. Since then, said friend had been ringing Mrs Silvero's house continually and been unable to raise anyone. Finally she had contacted the police. There could, as far as Solomon could see, be any number of reasons why Mrs Silvero had not kept that appointment, not least that she had wanted to avoid a woman who was clearly a busybody. Now, in the early evening, after nightfall and in a blustery breeze, Solomon happened to be in the area so had been asked to go and check over the house, and that was what he was doing. The March winds came in gusts, rattling the street lights and rustling the emerging leaves on the horse chestnut tree in the corner of Mrs Silvero's front garden, all of which reminded Solomon of *The Munsters*. It was a nicer house, though – detached, with a mature garden. Solomon had been brought up on a council estate not two miles away, where his parents still lived, the only African-Caribbean family in their road, and this was the kind of house his mother had aspired to.

As he walked up the drive, across the pool of light cast from the hall, and around to the side of the house, he could see the promising glare that he guessed was from the kitchen. Solomon's substantial stomach rumbled loudly and he optimistically envisaged a short and apologetic conversation with Mrs Silvero, during which she would confirm his theory about the neurotic friend, and he'd be on his way, back to the station for R&R, a thick bacon sandwich and mug of strong coffee, very soon. After a weekend off it would be nice if his first night back was an uneventful one.

Solomon rang the doorbell and was rewarded by the prolonged and satisfying peal of a bell inside the house. But there was no movement behind the frosted glass. It didn't mean anything of course. The old dear could have gone out anyway, just not with her over-anxious friend. Crouching down, Solomon could see nothing through the spring-flap letterbox except a long and empty hallway, with its perfectly centred carpet runner, though he thought he spied the corner of a couple of letters immediately below him on the mat. Similarly the lounge, though only partially illuminated by the residual light from the hallway, viewed through the front windows looked perfectly normal, the furniture and ornaments all intact and in place. Solomon walked round to the side of the house, coming to a seven-foot-high wooden side gate that blocked access to the back garden. It was, of course, bolted from the inside; and this was his dilemma.

Solomon had scraped by his medical a couple of months ago and was neither slim nor athletic. Should he take the undisturbed nature of the house as proof positive that all was well with Nina Silvero, or should he try to heave his considerable bulk over the wooden gate?

Lucy Jarrett looked down from the computer screen, picked up her pen and scored a line through the last item on the Post-it note stuck to her diary. It was after six and she'd completed everything on the list she had intended to do this afternoon. Not bad for a Monday. Clicking the mouse, she logged off and closed down the computer. She should have been satisfied with such a productive day. She could count on the fingers of one hand the number of occasions when she had previously cleared her in-tray, and those harked back years to the time when she was newly qualified. But, instead of satisfaction, all she felt was the bubble of anxiety that rose in her stomach like in-digestion, because now the only remaining option was to go home.

The sole person left in the office was the contract cleaner, an efficient woman of Eastern European origin who spoke little English, except to say hello and goodnight. And now Lucy must go out into the dark alone. The feeling was disconcerting. For once in her life, she, a grown, mature woman, who had always been so absolutely in control, was afraid. And afraid of what exactly? A feeling; no more, no less. She got her coat on and, calling out goodbye to the cleaner, went down the stairs. The lobby was empty. On impulse she took out her mobile and speed-dialled Will. She had no idea what he'd be up to but–

'Hey, babe.'

He made her smile instantly. A few months off his fortieth birthday and he still insisted on talking like a fifteen-year-old. Occupational hazard, she supposed. Even he admitted that his was the kind of job that rendered him the eternal teenager. 'Hi. 'What are you doing?' In the background she could hear the thrum of an acoustic guitar over the random clatter of drums.

'Setting up. We go on pretty soon.' It was a couple of hours by her reckoning but he was telling her this was a bad time. 'You OK?'

'I'm fine.' *Just needed to hear your voice.*

'I'm just leaving work.'

'It's late.'

'What's new?'

She heard a yell in the background to which Will responded, turning away from the phone.

'You should go. I'll talk to you later,' she said.

'Sure. It's all happening here. I'll call you.'

'When? What time?' Lucy knew as soon as she'd said it that it was a mistake.

'I don't know.' His voice had hardened, almost imperceptibly. 'Does it matter?'

Yes, she wanted to say, it does. 'Of course not, have a good–' But he'd already, abruptly, ended the call and now she had no more delaying tactics in her armament. Pocketing the phone, she took a deep calming breath. Pull yourself together, woman. In ten minutes you'll be home and tonight it may not even happen. She used to be irritated by media commentators who made Birmingham sound like the knife- and gun-crime capital of Britain, but now, after dark, even for her, the city took on a menacing feel.

Cautiously she emerged from the building and quickly crossed the almost empty floodlit car park, buffeted by the gusts of wind that swept across the open space. The few remaining vehicles all seemed empty and there were none that she recognised, but the park was also used by shoppers for the main street and customers for the nearby video store and cashpoint. She couldn't ever remember seeing the same car twice. Her own car was in the middle of the compound, parked under a light, and fumbling for her car keys Lucy felt suddenly exposed; she'd been so busy on the phone she hadn't thought to have them ready. Panic began to bubble up inside her. At last she got the door open, threw herself inside and slammed shut the door, locking it again immediately. Her hand trembled as she sought out the ignition, eventually finding it and revving too hard as the engine started. She paused at the car-park entrance, but her rearview mirror showed nothing behind her. Which way to go home; the short way or the best-lit way? Would it make any difference? She'd play it safe and stick to the main roads.

Pulling out, Lucy drove into the side street and up to the traffic lights with the main road, glancing behind as she pulled to a halt. A car had fallen into line behind her and Lucy tried to make out the driver, male or female. She couldn't. A horn blared, making her jump; the lights had changed. Signalling left, she turned on to the dual carriageway, the car behind her keeping close, but then this was a major road; the main Bristol Road going south out of the city. And, as she accelerated away from the lights, it almost immediately pulled out and overtook her.

Going down the hill, the road behind her was clear, in her rearview mirror she could see the trees that lined the route rolling and swaying in the wind. She kept steadily to the speed limit and a couple of cars passed her on the outside, brake lights flaring as they hit the speed camera zone. Lucy began to relax. Then, as she was approaching the foot-bridge, headlights homed in towards her, hugging her tail unnecessarily closely, and as she signalled and left the main road, heading towards her estate, it did likewise; the same pattern as before. Inside she could just make out the outline of a single occupant. Lucy's mouth went dry and her heart rate quickened. Only headlights, but driving too close, crowding her, urging on her speed in the narrow winding lane, the headlights dazzling in her mirrors, and nowhere to pull over to let him pass. Fear propelled her even faster, until finally, turning into the estate, she glanced into the rear-view mirror again. The road was completely empty. Relief washed over her. It was going to be all right. And, by the time she pulled into her driveway, she wondered if it was all in her imagination.

Glancing across as she got out of her car, she could just about make out her neighbour at number sixteen, hunched as always over his computer. She waved to him but he didn't respond, staring instead into space, and she realised that he probably couldn't see her at this distance, beyond the half-open slatted blinds. Nonetheless, Lucy took some comfort from seeing another familiar presence so close and lightened her step with relief as she walked up to the house. She started as something nearby clattered, and hastily got her key in the lock, pushing her way in through the front door and stepping over the ever increasing pile of junk mail that greeted her every day. She slammed the door behind her, and switched on the lights, exhaling with relief. The house was all in order, everything right with the world. The phone rang. Will, ringing to check that she'd got home all right and apologise for being short with her. She picked up the receiver. 'Hello?'

For seconds she was mesmerised by the long and raspy exhalation, followed by further laboured breathing, in, out, in, out, before the line went dead. Wrenching the phone line from its socket in the wall, she sank, dizzy and light headed, on to the stairs, her confidence crumbling like dry sand.

'Table fourteen, salmon and lamb!'

Stephanie Rieger dumped down the dirty plates with a clatter, her plan for a five-minute break from beating her relentless route back and forth from the kitchen temporarily thwarted by the chef's efficiency.

'Come on, Stephanie love, they're getting cold!'

18

'I've only got one pair of hands,' she snapped back, picking up the plates nonetheless and reversing out through the swing doors and into the restaurant. She was run ragged, mainly because her mean bastard of a boss refused to employ anyone else during the week. Switching on a smile, she placed the dishes in front of the table-fourteen customers, and that was when she saw the new punter at table eight. She noticed him at first because he appeared to be dining alone and because he was holding the menu almost at arm's length. 'You should get your eyes tested,' she smiled as she walked past.

He looked up. Not bad looking, clean cut and sharply dressed in suit and tie. Salesman probably. No wedding ring, which didn't mean he wasn't married, of course, only that he didn't advertise the fact. In those few seconds she had him half-naked and making love to her.

'Sorry?' he was saying.

'Get yourself some specs. Your arms aren't going to grow any longer. I'll come back and take your order.' She smiled again.

Coming to her senses, Lucy lunged at the front door and with shaking fingers fumbled the chain into its runner, and shot the top and bottom bolts, before hurrying through to the kitchen to check that the back door was secure. Satisfied that it was, she went

19

from room to room, drawing the curtains and blinds to keep out the night, making sure – making sure of what? That there was no bogey man hiding there? This was ridiculous. She switched on the radio, but turned it off again immediately. That was no good; she had to be alert to any sounds that shouldn't be there.

Up in the master bedroom Lucy changed quickly out of her work clothes and threw on jeans, T-shirt and a baggy jumper. Even as she did so, she kept one eye on the thick velvet curtains as if they might suddenly part to reveal her tormentor on the other side, some ghastly apparition, ogling in at her. Impossible, of course, but she was certain he was out there. How else could he know the exact moment when she'd walked in the door? So far he had kept his distance, but for how long? And what did he want? Lucy's heart thumped and she was gripped by a wave of nausea. A couple of weeks ago she might have got changed and gone out for a run, but not any more; she couldn't risk going out again.

No good calling Will, the gig would be about to start, he'd never even hear his phone. Julie-Ann would be at aerobics; Tamsin would be busy with the family. For a second Lucy considered Martin just across the road. She could ask him to come over. Simply speaking to him would be a comfort. But that would be a mistake. He'd misunderstood her intentions once before – at least that was what she told herself – so she couldn't risk that happening again. Gazing helplessly around the big bedroom, she recalled the day she'd first looked round. On that sunny autumn afternoon it had seemed perfect. After four years in her cramped flat, all the size had seemed such a luxury; with ample room in here for the king-sized bed, and the separate en-suite bathroom with shower and sunken bath. Now all the space frightened her, leaving her feeling exposed and wanting to shrink into the corner of the room and hide. With hindsight it would have been so much better to have simply upgraded her apartment. There she would have been close to other people, and be able to hear their voices and their movements, instead of feeling remote and stranded, and so very alone. It might have been different if Will was here, but most of the time she had no husband here to protect her. The wind gusted, splattering rain against the window, underlining her isolation and shaking her from her trance-like state. She needed a distraction. With some trepidation she switched on her computer and went online. Tonight again her email account was flooded with spam. But these were not the usual penis-enlargement, African-prince messages, they were nasty and personal, including replies to a blog that she'd never posted. As fast as she could delete them, more appeared, taking their place, and in the end Lucy abandoned the machine in despair.

Down in the kitchen she made a sandwich, but within inches of her mouth the salty smell of the cheese made her gag and she had to drop it and run for the downstairs cloakroom, where she retched unproductively, before finally leaning her head against the cool wall, feeling clammy and dry at the same time. After consigning the rest of the sandwich to the bin, she took a bottle of mineral water out of the fridge and went into the lounge, where she switched on the TV, muted the sound and sat rigidly on the sofa, staring at the meaningless images, while her ears strained to catch the slightest unwanted noise.

Gradually, Lucy began to relax. Bang! Something slammed against the window and Lucy leaped out of her seat, crying out with fear. The tapping against the window continued and frantic with indecision she hovered by the curtains, daring herself to look and yet terrified of what she might see. Eventually she forced herself to lift aside the curtain and relief washed over her. A sheet of hardboard, picked up and carried by the wind, lay flapping against the window. Shuddering, she peered into the blackness of the garden. Was he out there?

Tearing herself away from the window, Lucy returned to her sofa-bound vigil. The TV was playing a programme about enormously overweight people being winched out of their homes. The next thing she knew it was after eleven and the water bottle was empty, her head and neck aching from the tension. She climbed the stairs, brushed her teeth and lay down on the bed fully clothed, feeling too vulnerable to undress. Instead she lay on top of the bed, in the foetal position, biting on a thumbnail, listening and waiting, her ears straining to catch the slightest sound; the occasional car going past, local teenagers coming home from an evening out, the volume of their footsteps and voices increasing before dying away, with the distant slamming of doors. The wind howled around the house, bowling over a milk bottle with a clatter, and Lucy heard it roll away down the drive. She should go and retrieve it, but it would mean going outside, and the prospect petrified her.

PC Solomon had decided to take action. Scrabbling up the flimsy planks of the gate, he had managed to get a toehold for his size-thirteen boot on the narrow lock mechanism. Things started to go downhill when he swung his left leg over the top, catching his thigh on a protruding nail, ripping a hole in his trousers and gouging his flesh in the process. But now he was, at least, no longer alone. First off he'd found Nina Silvero. After landing hard on the block-paved patio, his trouser leg flapping, he'd walked round to the kitchen window and peered in. It was what the DIY stores always described as a farmhouse kitchen, pretty big, with ornate pine cupboards and a wooden table in the middle. Among other things on the table was a bottle of wine and a single glass, but no sign of—

It was then that he glanced down to the floor and saw the foot sticking out from behind one of the chairs. It was attached to a leg, Nina Silvero's leg, it seemed reasonable to assume. And it was lying very still. Solomon took off his jacket, wound it around his fist for protection and moved towards the window.

At midnight Lucy started as her mobile trilled on the nightstand beside her.

'Hey.'

'Hey.' She had to stifle a sob of relief.

This time the background noise was chatter and tinny music. Will was in a bar or a club, female voices close by. 'I tried the land line,' he said, 'couldn't get through.'

'I unplugged it. I had another call.' She couldn't keep the tremor from her voice.

Will's voice remained level. 'OK, stay calm. What did he say?'

'Nothing; that's the point, it's just that horrible noise.' She wanted him to say that he would drive home right now and take care of her, but it wasn't Will's style.

'Come on, honey. It's just kids, fooling around. Don't let it get to you.' He wasn't taking her seriously.

'Perhaps I should go to the police.' The idea had come to her suddenly.

'And tell them what? That you've had a couple of crazy phone calls?'

'It's more than a couple, and someone's following me.'

'You're sure about that?'

Was she?

'Well, I can't be absolutely certain, but–'

'Don't you think you're overreacting a little? What can the police do anyway? I mean you haven't actually seen anyone following you, have you? You're tired, honey; you'll feel better in the morning.'

'Yes.' *And how would you know?* A woman, or perhaps a girl, giggled very close to him. 'Where are you?' she asked.

'In some bar.' He was vague. 'We're having a bite before we get back to the hotel. It was a terrific gig tonight. Listen, you try to get some sleep, huh, and I'll see you tomorrow.'

'OK. Safe journey.'

'Sure. 'Night, babe.'

The woman's voice cut in even before he'd switched off his phone. Lucy didn't like to speculate about who she might be. And she could have been mistaken, but she was sure what the woman said was *'Kiss me, baby'*. Maybe she wasn't talking to Will. There were others there; must be. But now a different unease began to nibble at Lucy.

Normally after a gig, Will went straight back to his hotel. Socialising with the band was a recent phenomenon. She glanced down at the white-gold ring on her finger. It had been there for six months now. Was the novelty wearing off already? Before they married, Lucy had been convinced that Will would quickly get bored with her and find someone else more glamorous. But not now – would he? What was happening to her? The last couple of weeks she had begun to doubt everything, even her own sanity.

Lying back on the bed, she recommenced her auditory vigil. Finally, as the sky was beginning to lighten, she heard the whirring thrum of the milkman's float and the clink of milk bottles and only then did she feel safe enough to allow herself to drop off to sleep.

CHAPTER TWO

Mariner couldn't remember how he'd got into this mess, but he knew for sure that he had to get out. Running across a muddy field in the half light, the gunman was gaining on him, but his feet kept sinking into the soft and boggy ground, hampering his progress, and in his panic to get away he slipped, stumbled and fell. When he tried to get up again his foot was stuck, sucked under by thick mud. His pursuer was getting closer. With a gargantuan effort Mariner yanked his foot free. There was a loud squeal followed by a thump, and he woke up to morning brightness in an unfamiliar room and an oversized tabby blinking accusingly at him from the floor, its back aggressively arched. There was a gurgling from behind him, like water going down a plughole and Mariner turned to see the gentle rise and fall of a lumpy outline beneath the duvet, blonde bob fanned out on the pillow. Stephanie; was that her name? Christ, he couldn't even be sure of that.

He looked at his watch, the only thing he was still wearing; nearly quarter to eight. Simultaneously he remembered where he was, on the wrong side of the city, in yesterday's clothes with no shaving kit, and a nine o'clock appointment at Lloyd House. Scrambling out of bed, Mariner gathered his clothes and pulled them on. Stephanie didn't even stir. Should he be a gent and make her a drink before he left? He decided not. She was dead to the world, so it would be a waste of time he didn't have. He ripped a page out of his pocketbook and began scribbling an apologetic note. He paused, pen poised; leave a number, or don't leave a number? Only a split second to choose the latter, he left the note by the bed and hurried down the stairs and into his car, no doubt breaking all the codes of etiquette as he went.

As Mariner nosed his car into the traffic oozing on to the Aston Expressway towards Birmingham city centre, the usual creeping sense of shame came over him. Although it wasn't exactly the first time, this wasn't something he made a habit of, and now the guilt kicked in; guilt for taking what was on offer without making much effort with the pleasantries, guilt for sneaking out afterwards without even saying goodbye or thanks, and for feeling relieved to do it, so avoiding the usual pointless small talk. He couldn't imagine that he and Stephanie would have had anything much to discuss over the Fair Trade. Their only genuine shared interest twelve hours ago had been the mutual, and on Mariner's part fairly urgent, desire to get laid.

After a day-long meeting in the north of the city, she'd waited on him in the pub restaurant where he'd had dinner, and her easy smile had been an antidote to the tedium of the day. He must have been giving off signals because she'd flirted outrageously with him and he'd played along, not sure how far it would go, until she'd told him she finished at half-ten, if he could wait that long. Knowing that Millie was staying with Kat overnight, Mariner had, for once, been tempted and had waited, nursing a coke in the bar. She was all over him in the car, before suggesting they go back to her place. On the three-mile drive her hand stayed in his lap, and she'd taken him straight up to the bedroom of her neat semi. Once there she'd slowed the pace. It had been good. Just thinking about it tugged pleasantly at his groin.

And finally, even after all this time, Mariner was plagued by the dual and entirely irrational guilt brought on by perceived disloyalty and infidelity. These last two were groundless, deep down he knew that, but somehow it was masochistically comforting to continue believing in their existence. He allowed his thoughts to wander as far as what Anna might be doing now. Waking up in bed beside her new partner, she may even be getting a little early-morning action of her own, he thought miserably, and the dull ache that had for so many weeks been resident just under his diaphragm returned. Last night's diversion was exactly like the last time – great while it lasted but afterwards it felt like shit.

Letting himself back into his small canalside home, Mariner was greeted by the warm smell of frying bacon. Kat was in the kitchen, prodding at the pan on the cooker. 'Hello,' she greeted him brightly, with not a hint of reproach. Had she put two and two together? 'You like some breakfast?'

'No time,' Mariner called from halfway up the stairs, wanting to avoid that conversation until he was ready for it. 'I'll get something at the station.'

Ten minutes later he was back down again, showered and changed, and Kat was at the table poised to tuck into the full English. It made Mariner feel slightly queasy. It was a mystery how she got away with it, although at twenty she did, of course, have age on her side. She'd been staying with him for six months now, and had succumbed to all the worst of the British junk-food habits. Her diet was far removed from the one she'd been used to in her native Albania, yet she remained as skinny as a rake. 'You have a good meeting yesterday?' she asked.

'Oh, it was the usual thing,' Mariner said.

'It finish late.' She was all innocent observation. 'You find a woman?' She could be disarmingly direct.

Mariner's face flamed. 'It wasn't–' Like that? But that's exactly how it was. He gave up.

'Is a good thing,' she said brightly. 'You should meet a nice woman.' When Mariner didn't respond her hand shot guiltily to her mouth. 'I'm sorry. Is not my business.'

'That's OK. I know what you meant. Where's Millie?' Mariner thought his DC, who had quickly also become Kat's friend and chaperone, would have appeared by now, but perhaps she'd already gone.

Kat shrugged. 'She can't come. I think her family...' She trailed off vaguely.

'So you were here on your own all night?' Mariner was mortified.

'Is OK. I watch TV and go to bed.' *No big deal,* she was saying.

Mariner studied her expression for the brave face she must be faking, but slightly to his disappointment she looked genuinely unfazed. 'I'll get home early tonight,' he said. 'Get in a couple of films.'

She shrugged again. 'OK.'

'OK.' Now Mariner was the one disconcerted. She'd come a long way from the terrified young woman he'd first encountered cowering in a filthy room during a raid on a brothel.

Mariner had been well aware of the raised eyebrows when he'd offered to accommodate Kat, and he knew that the common consensus was that sharing his house with the stunningly attractive twenty-year-old would only lead to one inevitable conclusion, especially when he and Anna had so recently split up. It was only meant to be a temporary arrangement, a few days at most, and with DC Millie Khatoon in close attendance. But, as the days had stretched to weeks, Millie had succumbed to family demands and the station gossips had also been proven wrong. One day Kat might feel strong enough to make contact again with her natural parents back home in Albania but, until then, it seemed to Mariner that morally the only role open to him was to protect her.

Waking a little later, her eyes sticky and head muzzy, after the couple of hours of fitful dozing that these days passed as sleep, Lucy had come to a decision. She couldn't go on like this; she had to do something about it. The pounding water of the shower cleared her head and strengthened her resolve. Now was the time to do it. If she waited until Will came back he'd talk her out of it by telling her it was probably her imagination. Walking back into the bedroom, she glanced at the photo on her bedside table, the classic wedding picture, the happy couple arm in arm. She was glad she'd held out for formal dress, it had made the day all the more special, and Will hadn't resisted. He looked so stunningly handsome in his morning suit that it brought a lump to her throat; his dark skin, that Cherokee blood that he was so fond of talking about, offset by the pale grey of the suit.

'Whatever makes you happy,' he had said. That was a phrase she hadn't heard much lately.

By nine forty-five on Tuesday morning, Mariner was buttoning his shirt for the third time, this time in the clinical conditions of a consulting room, at the close of his annual routine medical; height, weight, blood pressure and the usual questions about diet and exercise which Mariner could, as always, answer truthfully with impunity. He'd just about made it on time.

'Getting much exercise?' Saunders asked.

Mariner side-stepped the obvious. 'Let me think... Last Sunday I climbed the Wrekin, the week before that walked fifteen miles of the North Worcestershire Way, and the week before that: the Malverns, end to end.' It had taken courage, that last one, standing at British Camp and looking out south-west towards the Black Mountains, knowing she was out there somewhere, but he'd made himself do it; all part of the healing process.

33

'That sounds a bit excessive to me,' commented Saunders. 'You running away from something?'

'I didn't know you'd qualified in psychology too.'

'It's an obvious question.'

Mariner remembered his dream. 'No, I'm not running away.' Staying away perhaps. After what Kat had been through, the last thing Mariner wanted to do was parade his own love life in front of her, which is why, he told himself, until last night he hadn't really had one.

'And how's the sex life?' Saunders asked, with uncanny insight.

The man was a mind reader, too. Mariner felt heat rise from his throat. 'What's that got to do with anything?'

'Nothing at all.' Saunders grinned. 'But it gives me and the wife something to talk about over dinner. You'd be amazed at how many people happily spill everything.'

'So what's the verdict?' Mariner asked, fully dressed.

'Bastards like you give the police a bad name. You're obscenely fit and healthy; at six one and eleven and a half stone your BMI is a bit on the low side if anything. How many of us would love to be able to say that?' Saunders himself was a squat ex-rugby player, who, since giving up the sport, had developed a significant paunch. 'You're eating properly?'

Mariner shrugged at the question. 'I eat when I need to eat.' Food wasn't something that interested him greatly and he could never understand the excitement it generated.

'Christ, you're not even losing your hair,' Saunders said irritably, running a hand over his own thinning pate. 'Well, you might want to consider upping your alcohol units or dipping into recreational drugs now and then. Oh, and get yourself a woman. Seriously, married men live longer.'

Christ, not someone else, too. 'Thanks.'

The eye test was a different matter. Stephanie had been right in her assessment and Mariner needed glasses, for reading anyway.

'Your age,' the optician told him. 'Most people in their late forties succumb in the end.'

Mariner took the prescription to the nearest of the force-approved opticians where the choice of frames was overwhelming.

'You might want to bring your wife in,' suggested the dispensing optician, presenting him with yet another set almost identical to the previous three he'd tried.

In the end Mariner settled on a mid-range pair, lightweight and flexible, that seemed to him to look OK.

Mariner had parked his car next to the

Mailbox, and from the opticians walked back through the busy shopping centre, down Corporation Street and across New Street. Despite the current economic crisis, people still seemed to have enough money to spend and he had to dodge the shoppers on the pavements. Suddenly among the bobbing heads in front of him, familiarity captured his attention; close-cropped reddish-brown hair, a slight figure with a spring in her step. Mariner launched himself forward through the crowd and grasped her arm, a little more enthusiastically than he'd intended. 'Anna?'

The woman spun round, alarm on her pale face, her features giving away immediately that the hair colour wasn't natural for her age. Mariner backed off as if he'd suddenly realised that she was carrying a contagious disease. 'I'm sorry. My mistake,' he stuttered. 'I thought you were–' Now he felt foolish, and it wasn't the first time in the last few weeks that he'd made that same error of judgement. How many times had he thought he'd seen her? He should keep a tally. Just as well he'd had his eyes tested. Mariner was aware that he spent more time than was healthy wondering what Anna might be doing, but couldn't help himself. All very well for Saunders, advising him to get himself a woman; he'd had one once but let her go.

Driving south out of the city towards Granville Lane, the traffic all seemed to be going the other way, the roads pretty clear until Mariner hit the usual bottle-neck at Selly Oak. As he sat idling he became aware of a faint buzzing in the background, like a bluebottle trapped behind a window, and suddenly realised that it must be his personal mobile. Since Anna had left, he'd hardly used it, everyone else called him on his work phone, so the sound was unfamiliar. Checking that the traffic ahead was stationary, Mariner applied the handbrake and fished the phone out of his jacket pocket. Someone had sent him a text. The only other person who had this number was Kat, for emergencies, though since her first uncertain weeks she'd never used it. So what could have happened in this short time? But when he looked, the text wasn't from Kat.

Thanx 4 a gr8 nite, it read, *look 4ward to next time, S xxx.*

S? Who the hell was...? Oh, Stephanie, of course. How had she got his number? She must have looked at his phone while he was asleep. Mariner didn't much like the idea of that. Nice message, though, especially the '*gr8*'. Hmm, he was fit, healthy and *gr8* in bed. What more could a man want? 'Shame there won't be a next time, though, Steph,' he murmured, and closed the phone without replying.

Arriving in CID, Mariner expected to find

everyone hard at work, but there appeared to be a party in progress.

'What's going on?' he asked, taking the paper cup proffered by his Detective Sergeant, Tony Knox. 'It's a bit early, isn't it?'

'Don't worry, Tom, there's no alcohol involved.' DCI Davina Sharp grinned from within the huddle. Tall and elegant and wearing a beige trouser suit that complemented her caramel skin, she looked radiant. 'You can blame this distraction on me.'

'What are we celebrating?' Mariner asked. She couldn't be pregnant, surely?

'Andrea and I are tying the knot,' Sharp said. 'I proposed to her last night.'

Mariner raised his cup towards her. 'Congratulations, ma'am. I hope you'll be very happy.' Mariner meant it. Though they'd only worked together a short time, his respect for the gaffer grew daily. One of few female DCIs in the city, and mixed race and openly gay at that, he knew that she had taken her fair share of flak, albeit covertly, from certain other senior officers. Mariner had felt proud from the start that none of his team had considered either her gender or her sexuality to be an issue and it was typical that she'd wanted to share her good news with them.

'Thanks.'

'So what happens about a ring?' Tony Knox asked. A working-class scouser with traditional views, even he'd been grudgingly accepting. 'Do you share it, or fight over who gets to wear it?' His years in Birmingham had done nothing to diminish his accent.

'That's the beauty of a gay engagement,' said Sharp. 'We get one each.'

'Well, make sure you get a good'n, boss, then when it all goes pear shaped–'

'Yes, thanks, Tony.' Sharp cut him off amid protests from some of the others. 'I'll bear that in mind. Now all we need to do is get you two clowns fixed up.' She looked pointedly towards Mariner and Knox.

'Yes, but who'd have them?' DC Jamilla Khatoon pulled a face.

'I've tried it once,' Knox reminded them, rubbing a hand over his shaven head. 'That was enough for me. It's him you need to work on.' He gestured towards Mariner.

'Too late,' said Mariner, holding up his hands in defence. 'I'm a lost cause.'

'You can say that again,' Sharp agreed. A phone rang on one of the desks, and the celebration began to break up. 'Anyway, thanks for all your good wishes, ladies and gents, but there's work to be done.'

Millie had answered the call. 'Don't make yourselves too comfortable, boss,' she said, seeing Mariner heading towards his office. 'We're wanted down in interview suite three.'

'What's down there?' Mariner stopped in his tracks.

'Brian Mann,' Sharp said. 'He's talking to a woman who's getting some funny phone calls.'

CHAPTER THREE

'Christ, not another one,' Mariner said, as he and Millie descended the stairs. The face of Jemima Murdoch had only just left the front pages of the national papers. Around a year ago she had complained to an OCU in the north of the city that she was being followed and her life was being threatened. Faced with flimsy evidence, the officers on the case had labelled her a neurotic and refused to take her complaints too seriously. They'd paid the price only a matter of weeks ago, with two fatalities; Murdoch's stalker, her ex-boyfriend, stabbing to death his prey before cutting his own wrists in the full public glare of a busy local shopping centre. It had made a whole lot of the top brass determined that it wouldn't happen again.

'Tenner says it's a duff,' said Millie. Her apparent flippancy was born of frustration. Since the killing, any reported incidents had to be followed up, and the policy played into the hands of every attention-seeker on the patch. While the number of harassments had risen significantly, the vast majority turned out to be false alarms.

'Any detail on this one?' Mariner asked, as he and Millie descended to the ground floor. Some of Sharp's dress sense was rubbing off on her, Mariner noticed. Not long out of uniform, Millie could dress more flatteringly for her fuller figure now and wore a fitted jacket and trousers that the DCI might have worn, her long hair tied back.

Millie shook her head. 'Only that Mann thinks it's worth our time.'

They descended the second flight. 'I understand you couldn't get across last night?'

Millie turned in surprise. 'Oh, I could have but Kat called and asked me not to come. She said that I didn't need to; that the two of you were doing something.'

'But I was out,' Mariner said. 'She told me you cancelled.'

'Not strictly true. What time did you get back?'

'This morning,' said Mariner.

Millie raised an eyebrow. 'And how did she seem?'

'Fine.'

'So maybe this is good,' was Millie's conclusion. 'It could mean that she's ready for some independence again.'

Suite three was one of the station interview rooms that had a softer touch, designed like an ordinary domestic lounge; a domestic lounge with recording equipment and CCTV that is. As Mariner knocked and pushed open the door, Lucy Jarrett looked up from where she was sitting. Dressed in baggy and shapeless clothes over a slim frame, she had an English rose face, with pale-blue eyes and a high colour in her cheeks. Her brown hair hung loose to her shoulders. She glanced uncertainly back at PC Mann, trying to figure out what was going on.

'This is Detective Inspector Mariner and Detective Constable Khatoon,' Mann explained. 'I'd like you to tell them what you've told me.'

'Inspector?' Lucy eyed them apprehensively. 'Isn't that quite senior? I'm not sure that this justifies–' Her voice was clear and devoid of an accent. As she spoke, she flicked her fringe back off her face. A nervous habit, Mariner thought.

Mariner pulled up a chair across the low table from her, Khatoon beside him.

'That's for us to decide,' he said. 'We just want to hear what you have to say. We take these kinds of incidents very seriously.' *Now.*

'Well.' Lucy flicked her hair again. 'As I told this officer, I've been getting some nuisance phone calls. I mean, I know they shouldn't bother me, but they're quite scary really.' The casual phrase wasn't fooling anyone, it was at odds with her posture; shoulders hunched and hands jammed down between her knees.

'Does the caller say anything?' Mariner asked.

'Only the first time.' She swallowed hard. 'He said, "You bitch, I'm going to make you suffer".'

'That's all? No hint about why or how?'

'No, and he hasn't spoken since. There's just a creepy silence at the other end, or this awful raspy breathing.' She was visibly reliving the experience. 'I tried blowing a whistle loudly down the phone but it hasn't deterred him.'

'You're certain it's a man?' Mariner queried.

The shadow of a doubt crossed her features. She had been, but now he'd asked her she wasn't so sure. 'Well, I assumed – I suppose the voice must have made me think that, but I couldn't be certain. I suppose I thought it was more likely.'

'You're right, it is, but, unless you're sure, we need to remain open to the idea that it might not be,' Mariner said. 'How many of these calls do you get each day?'

'I was getting about half a dozen; always at home in the evening. They usually stop at about eleven. Now, unless I'm expecting someone to call, I unplug the phone. And before you ask, yes, the number's always withheld.'

'And how long has this been going on?'

'About a month, I suppose. The phone rings the minute I get in the door.'

'Always?' Mariner checked.

'I'm sure he must be watching me. He knows exactly when I get home.'

'Unless he just rings frequently until you answer.'

Lucy looked up at him. She hadn't thought of that.

'Have you noticed if there's a pattern?' Mariner went on. 'Is it every night?'

She frowned. 'It never happens while my husband is at home.'

'Is he away often?'

'He travels a lot with his job.'

'And you never get these calls while he's there,' Mariner clarified.

'That's right.'

'What does your husband do?'

Her hands were in her lap now and she was twisting the ring on her left hand. 'He's a musician.'

'What kind of musician?'

'Folk-rock mostly. He plays the guitar and the mandolin.'

'Would we have heard of him?'

Lucy forced a smile. 'Probably not, but he plays in Leigh Hawkins' band.'

'Ah, him I know.' Mariner returned the smile. 'Is there anything else?' he prompted gently.

'This is going to sound silly,' Lucy said apologetically, 'but last week I've had an impression of being followed, in my car.'

Maybe this was going to be easier, Mariner thought. 'Did you get the make of car, any of the numbers on the registration?'

'No, it's been at night, after dark, on my way home from work. He gets too close.'

'Lots of people drive too close, in a hurry to get somewhere,' Mariner pointed out. 'How do you know it's the same car?'

'I just do. It always gets behind me at the same place, with the headlights full on. It feels as if he's trying to run me off the road.'

'And it's happened every night last week?'

Lucy thought for a moment, then shook her head. 'No, two, maybe three times. It happened again last night, I'm sure.'

In Mariner's experience, when a comment was qualified with 'I'm sure', it generally meant the opposite. He leaned forward on his seat, resting his elbows on his knees. 'Mrs Jarrett, let me tell you a little bit about what we know of stalkers. These days it's generally accepted that there are different types, and we need to consider what type this person might be. The most common type is what we call the "intimate partner" stalker. He or she is a partner or more usually an ex-partner who finds it difficult to accept that a relationship has come to an end. They can't move on. Most people are stalked by some-

45

one they know. Can you think of anyone who'd want to do this, to frighten you?'

'No, nobody.' She was adamant on that.

'Any ex-boyfriends who didn't want to let go?'

'No, I know what you're thinking. I read about Jemima Murdoch and her boyfriend in the papers, but there's no one around who's like that. Will and I have been together for just over a year, and before that I was single for a while. It's what I don't understand. There's no one I can think of who would want to do this to me.'

'What about your husband? Could he have any ex-girlfriends who might be jealous of you?' Mariner thought he saw something in her face then, but it was only fleeting.

'Not that I know of,' she said less certainly. 'I mean, we have talked about exes, but probably not all of them. Most of my husband's previous girlfriends aren't even in this country. He's American. He hasn't lived over here for that long; about six years.'

'You said that he's away working? When will he be back?'

'Later today, why?'

'We'll need to talk to him.'

'Is that necessary?'

Mariner thought he sensed a reluctance, but he left it for now. 'There still remains the possibility that this has something to do with him,' he said. 'We need to rule that out.'

'But Will doesn't know anything about it, really.' Her anxiety levels seemed to be rising.

'We will need to talk to him anyway.'

'OK.' But she didn't sound too sure.

'What line of work are you in, Mrs Jarrett?' Mariner asked.

'I'm a health visitor.'

'And you're working today?'

She glanced at her watch. 'Yes, I should have been in first thing, but I cancelled this morning's appointments'

'What I'd like to do is come with you and check over your house and make sure it's secure. It's just a precaution. Would that be all right?'

'Yes.'

'And then we'll take it from there.'

'Thank you.' Her relief seemed palpable.

While Mann escorted Lucy out to her car, Millie and Mariner collected their coats from CID. The wind had dropped today but the air remained chill.

'What do you think?' Mariner asked as he and Millie retraced their steps.

'She's not very relaxed, is she?' Millie said, understating the case somewhat. 'Something must be–' She broke off, interrupted by the thrumming of Mariner's personal mobile.

This time he automatically lifted it to his ear.

'Hi, it's Stef,' said a woman's voice.

'Stef?'

'Stephanie.' The voice cooled slightly. 'You woke up in my bed this morning.'

'Oh, of course.' *Shit.* 'Look, I'm sorry I had to rush off like that–' Mariner was suddenly acutely aware of Millie beside him.

'That's fine. You must be busy. You didn't tell me you were a policeman.'

No. 'Didn't I?'

'I hope you don't mind, I sneaked a look in your pockets while you were asleep.' *And went through my phone.* 'Don't worry, I wouldn't have read anything personal.' *Oh really?* 'A policeman, eh? That's a real turn-on.'

'Is it?'

'Oh, yes. Anyway, I was wondering, when can I see you again?'

They had come to the external doors. 'Look, Stephanie, I'm in the middle of something right now,' Mariner said. 'Can I call you back?'

'All right.' She sounded deflated. 'But make it soon, eh?'

'Soon, yes.' Mariner ended the call and for some reason felt compelled to explain. 'The woman I saw last night,' he said, with an apologetic glance at Millie.

'She's keen.'

'Mm, a bit too keen,' Mariner said absently.

They met Lucy back down in the car park and Millie travelled with her, in a Mercedes convertible that was under a year old, while Mariner followed in another car back to her house. They didn't have far to drive. Lucy's house was of the sort that was becoming commonplace on a newly created mixed estate of luxury apartments and houses, constructed on the former Cadbury family home, a short way off the main Bristol Road. Although extensive, there was only one road leading into and out of the complex, which was going to make life easier, and it was the kind of area where anyone loitering would be noticed. Number nineteen was a tall three-storey townhouse with, Millie guessed, at least four bedrooms, in a substantial garden and identical to those on either side. The women got out of the car as Mariner pulled on to the drive and he and Millie hung back while Lucy unlocked her front door.

'There's a bit of money here,' Mariner murmured, taking in the house and car.

Lucy opened the door onto a pile of post, mostly plastic-wrapped catalogues, and, as they stepped in behind her, Millie stooped to retrieve some of them.

'You're popular,' she said. 'All we ever get are brown envelopes.'

'We seem to be getting more and more,' said Lucy, scooping up the rest.

Millie noticed a catalogue for a nursery-design company, and another for maternity clothing. 'You're planning a big family?' she

49

asked, handing it to the young woman.

Lucy took it. 'No.' She studied it, bewildered. 'No, we're not planning a family at all.'

'It's just, it's a big house.' Millie glanced around her.

'I know. Seemed like a good idea at the time,' Lucy said. 'Come on through.'

Turning left, they followed her into a large kitchen that like many in the newly designed houses was at the front, overlooking the street. It gleamed with granite and polished steel.

'You moved in when you got married?' asked Millie.

'No, I was already here when I met Will. My dad died a couple of years ago so I came into some money. I decided I wanted a bit more space, and to move to somewhere greener. Plus it seemed like a good investment.' She picked up the kettle and took it over to the sink. 'Would you like coffee?'

'Yes, thanks,' Millie said. 'White, no sugar for me.'

'Not for me thanks,' said Mariner. 'I'll leave you to it and take a look around. OK?'

'Of course.'

The house was all mod cons. The coffee made, Lucy took Millie into the lounge, where a huge plasma screen TV and home cinema system took up one wall, and, when they sat, Millie sank so deeply into the expansive cream leather sofa that she thought she'd never get up again. 'It's a lovely house,' she said encouragingly, thinking of the modest home that she shared with her husband Suliman.

Lucy took the recliner that backed into the bay window. 'Thanks, yes, I do like it here. Well, I did. It freaks me out a bit at night.' She sat hunched in the chair, coffee mug cradled in her hands.

'What are your neighbours like?'

'Fine, I mean, I don't know them well, just say hello in passing, that kind of thing.' She was concentrating on the mug, and so avoiding Millie's gaze. 'The houses are new so none of us has been here very long.'

'So you haven't fallen out with anyone, no garden-boundary disputes or anything like that?'

'No, nothing like that.'

Millie leaned forward to place her coffee mug on the occasional table beside a wedding photograph. Only on a second glance did Millie realise it was Lucy, so different was the bride in the picture to the woman who sat before her. 'You look fabulous,' she said truthfully. The Lucy in the portrait glowed with good health. 'And that's a beautiful dress,' she said, picking up the picture.

'It should be.' Lucy smiled. 'It cost an arm and a leg.'

'Where? Do you mind me asking?'

Lucy gave a brief shake of the head. 'Brackleys. They were terrific, did the whole package for us.'

Somehow Millie wasn't surprised. People came from far and wide to the exclusive department store in Birmingham's city centre. It lent further weight to Mariner's comment.

'The food was a particular nightmare,' Lucy was saying. 'Will's lactose intolerant, but they were so creative with the menus.'

'How long have you been married?' Millie asked.

'Six months.'

Wow, Millie thought, a lot could change in six months. The radiant bride in the photograph was a far cry from the pale, gaunt figure curled into the armchair across from her, although the right make-up could do wonders. 'I got married just over a year ago,' she said, pleased to find some common ground.

Lucy's face brightened too, sharing in the coincidence. 'It's great, isn't it?' she said, though, to Millie's ears, the enthusiasm seemed a little forced.

'He's a good-looking bloke, your husband,' Millie said, replacing the picture and stating only what was an obvious truth.

'I know, I still can't believe it really. I'm so lucky.' She didn't sound lucky. 'Do you want to see the other pictures?' She was out of her seat and retrieving a big white album from the shelf before Millie had time to reply. But, in addition to satisfying Millie's natural curiosity, it would also help her to get some idea of Lucy's friends.

Lucy came over and sat beside Millie on the sofa. Judging by the number of guests and their dress, the wedding had clearly been a big occasion.

'Where did you have it?' Millie asked.

'The Wolverton,' said Lucy. 'Do you know it?'

Millie didn't, but she could see that it was quite a place. They got to the group photos. 'So who are all these?' As Lucy went through the names it was clear that the majority were her friends and family. 'Not many from Will's side,' Millie commented lightly.

'No, but he didn't seem to mind. His mum and dad, that's them there–' she pointed to a couple beside her in the picture '–and the guys in the band of course. But he was cool with that. It was a long way for his folks to come, and after years of being on the road he isn't that close to them any more. His friends and family these days are the band.'

'And you,' Millie added.

'Yes, of course. And me.'

'How did you and Will meet?'

'He turned up at the aerobics class I used to go to with Julie-Ann. I assumed he would be interested in her, she's much prettier than me. See, this is her, next to Tamsin.'

Lucy indicated one of the bridesmaids. 'I couldn't believe it when Will asked me out.'

'Lucky you.'

'Well, it wasn't so much "out" as to a gig, where he was working,' Lucy admitted. 'But he took care of me and apart from when he was on stage it was like a date. I broke my first rule that night; never have sex on the–' She broke off, glancing apologetically at Millie. 'Sorry, you probably don't want to know that.' Millie brushed away the apology. 'Antiquated rule anyway,' Lucy went on. 'How many people stick to that these days? Actually, I couldn't help myself. It turned me on just to be sitting next to him, and he knew it. I've never felt that way with any man I've been out with before. I usually go for quiet intellectual types. Oh, God, listen to me, prattling on.'

'And you're enjoying married life,' Millie reiterated, wanting to give Lucy the opportunity to disclose anything that wasn't so good.

'It was great, until all this started.' But she still couldn't muster much enthusiasm.

'What does Will think?'

'Between you and me? I'm not sure if he believes me.' She drifted off for a moment. 'Was your marriage...?'

'Arranged?' Millie offered.

'I'm sorry, I shouldn't make assumptions.'

'No, it's fine. I always swore I'd never go

down that route, but then my parents introduced me to Suliman and I really liked him. We ended up having the full traditional Asian wedding, but it was brilliant.' Millie turned back to the wedding photos. 'You said Julie-Ann is your best friend?'

'Yes, we do a lot together – or at least we used to before I got married.' As she spoke Lucy gazed down at the rings on her left hand, stretching out her fingers to straighten them.

There was some deep reflection going on there, but good or bad Millie couldn't tell. She wondered how Julie-Ann felt about the marriage. 'I'll need her details,' Millie said.

'Why?' It startled Lucy out of her thoughts.

'It's just routine,' Millie said casually. 'We talk to friends and acquaintances. In fact, is there anyone else you can think of who might be able to help?'

There were not many. Apart from her mother and work colleagues, Lucy didn't appear to have a rampant social life. It was a stark contrast with Millie. Since she'd married she'd never been out so much. But maybe Lucy and Will got all they needed from each other. Millie knew plenty of other couples who were like that.

Suddenly, Lucy turned to her. 'Listen, I don't know if this is allowed, but I'd love to see your wedding photos sometime.'

Millie smiled. 'I'm sure we can manage that.'

Mariner came back into the lounge, his survey of the property complete. 'Have you ever thought about having a burglar alarm?' he asked Lucy.

She shook her head. 'It crossed my mind, but I'd be concerned about it going off all the time and disturbing the neighbours.'

It was the reaction of many people these days and Mariner was, if anything, inclined to agree. 'Well, a couple of security lights front and back wouldn't hurt, but, otherwise, as you'd expect with a building this new, you're pretty secure. As long as you remember to lock the door behind you and keep the ground-floor windows closed, you'll be quite safe in here. There's nothing to worry about.'

'Thank you.' She seemed to genuinely take comfort from the simple reassurance.

Mariner's phone rang. It was Tony Knox. 'We need to get back,' he said.

Millie stood up and Lucy took the drained coffee cup from her. She saw them out into the hall.

'I'll keep in touch,' Millie said. 'There's a good chance that once whoever is doing this learns that we are involved it will be enough to make them stop, but if you get any further incidents it's important that you log them; date, time and exactly what happened, so that if we eventually get to court we have some specific evidence.'

'What about tapping my phone?'

Millie grimaced. 'It's not actually as easy as it looks on TV,' she said. 'And we don't have that level of resourcing at this stage.'

'It's not serious enough,' Lucy said. Stated so blandly, it sounded mean.

'But we are taking this seriously,' Millie added quickly. 'The two things are not the same.'

'No, you're right. I'm sorry. I guess I was just hoping you'd wave a magic wand.'

Millie pulled a face. 'Sorry, they're not part of the kit!'

'Thanks for your time, anyway.'

'Sure,' said Millie. 'We'll keep in touch.'

Reversing out of the drive, Mariner had to manoeuvre carefully to avoid a silver Honda, parked on the road, opposite Lucy's drive. With substantial parking bays, there seemed no need to park it there, but perhaps it was a visitor.

'How did you get on?' Mariner asked, as they drove back up the main road towards Granville Lane. Back at the station he'd have to complete a risk assessment, and was beginning to try to weigh up how serious this was.

'I'm not sure,' Millie said. 'Lucy's certainly anxious about something. She's a pale shadow of what she was on her wedding day, and something must be causing it. The phone calls are clearly real.'

'You handled the phone tapping pretty deftly, well done,' Mariner said.

'Thanks.'

'It's a tough one, because she's right, of course, a phone tap would soon clear it up. But if we offered that service to everyone who's made this kind of complaint in the last couple of months we'd have spent the annual budget.'

'This is most likely someone who knows her, isn't it?' said Millie.

'It usually is,' Mariner agreed. 'It would help to think about people Lucy has come into contact with at and away from work. Anyone she talked about?'

'Away from work it doesn't sound as if she sees anyone much, so that should be easy,' said Millie. 'Her husband is interesting. They've only been married six months and his background is a bit hazy.' They drove in silence for a few minutes. 'Is it me, boss, or is stalking on the increase?'

'That and road rage. Thanks to people like Jemima Murdoch, it's definitely reported more in the media, but it probably is on the increase too, because these days, with mobile phones and the Internet, it's so easy to do. We're all being stalked to some degree by the thousands of CCTV cameras around. And at the same time we're moving towards a blame and revenge culture, which provides the right person with the motive and the justification.'

Signalling, Mariner pulled into the Granville Lane compound. 'You seem to have established a good rapport with Lucy Jarrett,' he said. 'How would you feel about taking the lead on this?'

It would be the first time he'd given her this responsibility, and out of the corner of his eye he saw her visibly grow into it. 'I'd really like that, sir,' she said, beaming.

'You need to keep me and the rest of the team informed though, and if at *any point*–' Mariner placed a deliberate stress on those two words '–you feel out of your depth, you involve me, do you understand?'

'Yes, sir.'

'I mean it; no heroics. So, are you clear on what strategy you're going to adopt?'

'There are a couple of other leads to follow up; friends I can go and talk to. Also I'd like to find out more about the husband. Lucy said herself that she never gets the calls when he's at home. They haven't been married long and it seems to me that Lucy has made some compromises for him. She also more or less said that he chose her over her friend, Julie-Ann. According to Lucy, Julie-Ann is prettier, though it wasn't the case on the wedding day and I doubt it's true – her self-esteem is at rock bottom.'

'I wonder what Julie-Ann's financial status is?' Mariner mused. 'Lucy's clearly loaded.'

'Yeah, it did make me wonder what hubby brought to the union.'

'So, money and sex – our old favourites bob to the surface again.'

'Can't get enough of them,' said Millie. 'I'll go and talk to the mother and the best friend first, and see what they have to say.'

Mariner nodded agreement. 'Then maybe I'll come with you to talk to the husband when he gets home.'

Millie was still grinning from ear to ear when they got out of the car. Mariner's mobile pinged again, the arrival of a text; Stephanie once more, disappointed that he hadn't called yet.

'Another text from your admirer?' joked Millie. 'Maybe you're getting a stalker of your own, sir.'

'She's got a night off and wants to meet up,' Mariner said absently.

'Do you want me to go round and keep Kat company?'

'No, it's fine. I don't want to go anyway. She was all right in bed but she wasn't scintillating company.' Mariner caught Millie's expression and blushed hotly. That was rather more detail than he'd intended sharing with his detective constable. 'Sorry, I didn't mean to–'

''S all right sir.' Millie was struggling to

keep a straight face. 'Our little secret.'

Mariner did wonder for a fleeting second what it said about him; that he would rather spend his evening with his twenty-year-old charge than a woman his own age, but, if Millie thought it odd, she kept it to herself.

She'd made great strides, Millie, since she'd first joined the team. Only recently promoted to CID, so far she'd proven to be a thoroughly reliable officer, who could be trusted absolutely. Lucy Jarrett'd be in safe hands.

CHAPTER FOUR

Just as well really, because DS Tony Knox was waiting for Mariner at the top of the stairs, dressed as always in casual civvies, the detective's unofficial uniform of chinos and leather jacket.

'What's the excitement?' Mariner asked.

Knox shrugged. 'Dunno,' he said. 'Sharp wants you and me in her office.' He did a double-take. 'Don't look at me, boss. I've done nothing.'

In deference to her status, DCI Sharp's office was one of the bigger ones, but was pretty crowded by the time Knox and Mariner had squeezed in. The DCI had been joined by a couple of officers from uniform, one of whom was a giant. Mariner recognised and nodded a greeting to Sergeant Gordon Powell, but, to his knowledge, he'd not met the young black PC who dwarfed Powell. They were standing beside Sharp's desk with hands clasped and heads bowed, as if waiting for a prayer meeting to begin.

'What's up?' Mariner asked.

'You know Sergeant Powell? And this is PC Ralph Solomon,' Sharp said. 'We want you to have a look at these.' As she spoke, Powell spread out some 10x8 crime-scene photographs on the desk.

Over the years Mariner had naturally seen his share of shocking and gruesome deaths, and this was another to add to the list. But while those that he'd witnessed to date involved copious amounts of blood, and/or body parts arranged in a way that had never been intended, this one was different. The victim, a woman, had met with a violent and obscene death. That much could be seen in the paroxysm of pain and fear that had contorted her features even after the life had ebbed away. Her mouth, shaped in a crooked 'o', was an unnaturally dark crimson and her hands were at her throat. Radiating out from the beautifully manicured fingertips and up towards her chin were angry red, vertical lacerations. The frayed ends of a fine thread were grasped between the fingers of her left hand, and there was a scattering of what looked like small pellets around her head, spread out like a halo. In fact, the whole tableau had the look of a religious painting.

The unusual feature was that, while the death had clearly been a violent one, there was not a drop of blood to be seen, and from what could be ascertained from the dozen or so multi-angled photographs, aside from the scratches on her neck, her body was unmarked. Mariner's first thought was heart attack; severe pains in the chest, the inability to breathe and fear that she was going to suffocate to death. He stood transfixed by one particular full-face shot. It was the eyes, always the eyes. He glanced up. The other three were waiting for him and Knox to process what they saw.

'Nina Silvero,' Powell offered, although that wasn't the information Mariner needed right then. The name sounded vaguely familiar, but then it was pretty exotic. 'A sixty-one-year-old widow, lived alone, taught dance classes, although she was due to retire soon.'

'Heart attack?' ventured Knox, though as he said it Mariner knew that it was wrong.

'Sulphuric acid,' said the sergeant calmly. 'She drank it. According to the pathologist, it would have burned through the lining in her throat first of all, then, on the descent into her body, the heat would have radiated out and slowly cooked her internal organs.'

Mariner gulped back the bile that had suddenly heaved up into his own throat.

'Fucking hell,' murmured Knox, beside him.

'Croghan said she would have died in agony.'

'That much I can see,' said Mariner.

'It was the smell.' For the first time the young constable spoke up, though his comment wasn't directed at anyone in particular. He was thinking aloud, reliving his horrific discovery.

'What was?' his sergeant asked.

'It was what I noticed first when I went into the house – it was like the smell of burning meat,' Solomon said.

This time they all visibly balked.

'Our first thought was suicide,' the sergeant added.

Mariner looked up at him. 'But you've changed your mind.' He had a sudden unwelcome flashback to several years before, a suburban house and an apparent suicide that had changed his life for ever.

'The stepdaughter tells us she wasn't suicidal.'

'Families always say they're not suicidal,' said Knox reasonably.

The sergeant placed another photograph on the desk. This time it was a still life of a collection of items on a table-top; a bunch of flowers, wrapped and awaiting a vase; a grey plastic bottle of the kind that might contain detergent; a Chardonnay bottle and a single wine glass. He pointed to the detergent bottle. 'This is what killed her. It's industrial-strength drain fluid, according to the label.'

'And this stuff would be easy to get hold of?' Mariner asked.

'Looks as if it's the kind of thing you can pick up at any number of DIY stores locally. As you can see, though, only one wine glass, and the wine bottle is empty,' he said. 'The stepdaughter also tells us that Mrs Silvero wasn't a drinker. She wouldn't drink alone, and she certainly wouldn't drink a whole bottle herself.'

'Unless she was plucking up the courage to switch to the other bottle,' Mariner said, feeling as though he was stating the obvious. 'People do deviate from their habits–'

'–and kids don't always know what their parents get up to,' added Knox. He spoke from bitter experience. Estranged from his wife for three years now, Mariner knew it grieved his sergeant that he hardly ever saw either of his grown-up children.

'We also found this.' With a flourish that suggested he'd saved the best till last, Powell handed Mariner a poly pocket that contained a document. It was a letter headed with the crest of Buckingham Palace, informing Nina Silvero that she had recently been a recipient of the MBE. The date suggested that it had arrived only a few weeks previously. 'It seemed to me like a weird way to celebrate,' Powell observed.

'Not necessarily,' Mariner began. 'It could be that–'

But Sharp cut him off. 'I know it's not conclusive,' she admitted. 'And poisoning's rare these days, now that we've come up with rather more imaginative and convenient ways of killing each other. But I think there's enough here to keep our minds open until we know more. And until that point is reached I'd like you and DS Knox to take this one on.'

There was something the DCI was keeping to herself here, thought Mariner, studying her face. As he did so the familiar ring of the name crystallised into something more. 'You said that Mrs Silvero was a widow?'

'That's right.'

'Would that be as in "the widow of a former chief inspector"?'

Sharp had the grace to look uncomfortable, and Mariner wondered at what point she had been going to tell them. 'She was the widow of Chief Inspector Ronnie Silvero, yes.'

Mariner and Knox exchanged a lengthy glance.

'I see,' said Mariner.

'It genuinely isn't certain,' Sharp continued, in self-defence. 'If it was, believe me, I wouldn't be prolonging this.'

On balance, Mariner thought that was probably true. One of the first things he'd learned about Sharp was that she wasn't a bullshitter. The likelihood was that pressure was being applied on her from above. Now, in front of the others, wasn't the time to broach that one, but he'd raise it with her at some point.

'And for what it's worth,' she added, clinching it for Mariner, 'Stuart Croghan has serious doubts too.' The pathologist was an experienced one and had worked with Mariner on numerous cases before. If he was questioning it, then it was good enough for Mariner.

'You say you've spoken to the daughter?' Mariner asked Powell.

'Stepdaughter,' Powell corrected him, 'and only by proxy. She lives away, so Somerset police broke the news to her and reported back on her initial reaction. She's driving over with her husband now. They're going straight to the morgue for the identification. Should be there at any time, so you'll be able to talk to her.'

'This Ronnie Silvero, is he the one who...?' Knox began.

'Conveniently died? Yes, if that's at all possible,' Mariner said. 'Just as he was about to be prosecuted for manslaughter.'

The city mortuary was never a favourite

place among police officers, and wasn't a visit to look forward to. Knowing they wouldn't have much appetite afterwards, Mariner and Knox stopped on the way to get something to eat. Despite Mariner's efforts to broaden his DS's culinary outlook since his arrival in Birmingham several years ago, Knox still resolutely refused anything that had been near garlic for his lunch. 'A curry after a few pints, like, is fine,' he was fond of saying. 'But not in the daytime.' So today they had detoured via a Greek deli for soup and cheese rolls. While they sat in a lay-by and ate, Mariner filled Knox in on what little he knew about the late Ronnie Silvero.

'What was the manslaughter for?' Knox wanted to know.

'Death of a prisoner in custody,' Mariner said, through a mouthful. 'The inquest verdict was unlawful killing, and Silvero as the senior officer was deemed responsible. The CPS had just made the decision to go ahead with the prosecution and were assembling the case, when Silvero keeled over with a heart attack.'

'So what happened to the case?'

'Big, fat nothing. Silvero obviously couldn't stand trial and lesser charges against the other officers were dropped through "insufficient evidence".'

Mariner's mobile buzzed again. 'Christ, what now?' he muttered, retrieving it. There was another message from Stephanie, asking if she could see him tonight.

Knox was waiting expectantly. 'Everything all right, boss?' he asked, when no explanation was forthcoming.

'Fine,' said Mariner shortly. 'I met this woman last night. It was just a casual thing, you know – or at least I thought it was.'

'You must have made an impression,' said Knox. 'Either that or she's desperate.'

'Thanks.'

'You think there was a cover-up because Silvero died?' Knox asked, as if the interruption had never occurred.

'That's what the victim's family alleged, of course, and who knows?' Mariner said. 'They certainly thought he'd got away with murder.'

'Tough on the grieving widow,' Knox observed.

'Yes, but from what I remember, Nina Silvero didn't fold. I seem to remember some statement when she complained that her husband had been persecuted.'

Finishing his roll, Mariner crumpled the paper bag into a ball and, disposing of the rubbish in the nearest bin, he and Knox made for the city mortuary.

Mariner parked in one of the reserved bays at the end of Newton Street, alongside a modest-sized people carrier with a child seat in it and a sticker in the rear window extolling the virtues of Cheddar Gorge. Nina Silvero's stepdaughter had already arrived. Mariner and Knox went directly to Croghan's office, where it was also lunchtime, and they found the pathologist tucking into half a roast-beef baguette. The other half sat on the plate, the rare-meat filling pink and glistening. Mariner didn't know how he could stomach it. Though he must have been approaching forty, Croghan still looked boyishly young, with keen, dark eyes and his dark hair always fashionably tousled. He had Nina Silvero's spanking new file open in front of him.

'What do you think?' Mariner asked.

Croghan swallowed a mouthful of sandwich. 'I've never seen anything like this, not first hand anyway. I've only read about it in the history books.'

'This has happened before?' Knox, like Mariner, was surprised.

'Not recently, and usually only accidentally,' Croghan said. 'Years ago before the advent of safety caps, and when people used noxious ingredients more indiscriminately, you'd occasionally get a child helping themselves to the brightly coloured bottles under mum's sink. There were some terrible cases, but, like I said, not for years.'

'And you go along with the theory that this was murder?' Mariner asked.

'If Nina Silvero wanted to kill herself,

there are much quicker and less painful ways of doing it,' Croghan pointed out.

'Would she have realised what she was letting herself in for, though?'

'Unless you're pretty sure of your chemistry, drinking noxious substances is always a huge gamble,' Croghan said. 'You never quite know what they'll do. Did Nina Silvero have that kind of background?'

'Not that we know of.'

'Well, what killed her in this little cocktail was the sulphuric acid; it's the most active ingredient among other things. I guess most people would know a little bit about it, but at the same time would be able to roughly predict the kind of effects it might have. Acid burns – most of us know that. Armed with that knowledge I think there are not many folk who would choose to inflict that kind of damage on themselves, not unless they had some kind of weird penitence thing going on.'

'And that's why you think this wasn't suicide?' It didn't seem much, Mariner thought.

'It's one of the reasons,' Croghan corrected him. 'The other thing was the crime scene. It was all a bit too neat, don't you think?'

'How do you mean?'

'I saw the body *in situ,* got to look at the scene and presumably you saw the snaps? The wine glass she apparently used was sitting there neatly on the table beside the

71

bottles, which doesn't add up. When she drank this stuff it would have hit immediately and she would have fallen where she stood. It's pretty unlikely that Nina Silvero would have had the time or the presence of mind to replace her wine glass tidily back on the table.'

'She'd have dropped it,' Mariner said. 'Or someone took it from her. How much did she swallow?'

'A couple of mouthfuls would have been enough. Barely any made it as far as her stomach; it would have been absorbed on the way down. Rest of the stomach contents were a pasta-based meal consumed earlier in the evening, but interestingly no trace of the Chardonnay she was meant to have drunk. I hope you're having that bottle tested.'

'As we speak,' said Mariner. 'At least it looks as if we're dealing with an amateur here.'

'Either that or someone in a tearing hurry,' Croghan said. 'On the surface it's designed to look like a straightforward suicide, but it hasn't really been thought through.'

'So, if we're saying this is murder, this is also someone who wanted to make her suffer,' Mariner said.

'If they knew what they were doing, yes. I understand it happened not long after she got the call from the palace. Maybe she's got some jealous friends,' said Croghan.

'What about the time of death?' Mariner wanted to know.

'It would have been late on Sunday evening.' Croghan wobbled his head from side to side. 'Somewhere between eight and midnight.'

A knock on the door interrupted them and one of Croghan's assistants put her head in. 'The family are ready,' she said.

'Thanks, Kirsty.' Wiping his mouth on a paper napkin, Croghan got to his feet. 'Now, if you'll excuse me I need to get Mrs Silvero ready for her close-up.'

At roughly the same time, DC Jamilla Khatoon was sitting in the lobby of Wood Green School. It was a typical inner-city Victorian primary, not dissimilar to the one Millie herself had attended, though, unlike this one, most of her classmates had, like her, been from the Asian sub-continent.

Eventually the school secretary reappeared with Julie-Ann Shore, Lucy Jarrett's best friend, at her elbow. Julie-Ann was as pretty as her bridesmaid photo; petite, blonde and tanned as a catwalk model, although Millie was surprised that as a teacher she could get away with the low-cut T-shirt and tight trousers she was wearing. One way of encouraging fathers to attend parents evening, she thought. Julie-Ann smiled a white toothy smile and offered Millie a limp handshake.

'Let's go down to the classroom,' she said. 'I've got a few minutes before the little horrors come in from the playground.'

It was a while since Millie had been inside a primary school, and her first impression walking into the classroom was that everything seemed to have shrunk.

'Do you mind if I carry on with my preparation, only I need to sort out these work sheets?' Julie-Ann went over to a pile arranged on top of a low cupboard.

'No, that's fine,' said Millie, perching on one of the tables, where she couldn't resist letting her legs swing. 'I just wondered what you could tell me about Lucy Jarrett. We're following up on some malicious phone calls she's been getting.'

'She's still getting those?' Julie-Ann said. 'What do you need to know?'

'Anything. First off, can you think of anyone who might want to make her life a misery?'

Julie-Ann looked up. 'I really can't, Lucy's lovely; sweet and caring.'

'She told you about these calls?'

'She did mention it, but I didn't realise what a big deal it was. It was a bit of a joke when she told me – I've got a heavy breather, she said. In fact, we laughed about it.'

'When was this?'

'About three weeks ago.'

'And since then?' Millie asked.

'I haven't seen her.'

'How long have you known Lucy?'

'Oh, since the year dot,' Julie-Ann began. 'No, that's not quite accurate. We met at secondary school.'

'Which one?'

'St Felix.'

'Is that local?' Millie didn't know it.

'Yes, but it's a private school and it's pretty small. It's the one your parents send you to if they want the kudos of an independent, but can't quite stretch to Edgbaston Girls.'

'And you made friends with Lucy there. You and Tamsin too?'

Julie-Ann looked up at her.

'Lucy showed me her wedding photos.'

'That's right. The fabulous three.'

'It sounds like you guys were close,' Millie said. 'But when I talked to Lucy yesterday she seemed quite in need of friends.'

'To be honest, I haven't seen much of Luce since the wedding,' Julie-Ann admitted. 'Newlyweds have better things to do than hang out with their mates, don't they?' She raised a suggestive eyebrow at Millie. 'Babies to make and all that.'

'It's possible to do both, surely,' said Millie, slightly affronted, though she knew Julie-Ann wasn't being personal.

'Oh, I think Will likes to have Lucy all to himself. I can imagine what's on his mind most of the time. Did she tell you about how we all first met?'

'She said it was at your aerobics class,' Millie recalled.

'That's right, he made quite an entrance.' Julie-Ann's eyes had gone dreamy. 'He came in late while we were still warming up. I mean most people coming into a group of strangers for the first time would just sneak in quietly, wouldn't they? Especially if he's a man and the class is mostly women. But not Will; he was so full of himself – he just flashed that gleaming smile at everyone, then he calmly walked over to the benches and stripped down to his underwear, you know, like Nick Kamen did in those Levi ads, and put on his sweats.'

'That took some nerve,' said Millie.

'That's Will. Sexy and knows it. I remember when I managed to tear my gaze away, I caught Lucy's eye. We just went "wow"–' Julie-Ann mouthed the word in exaggerated fashion '–and it was all we could do not to giggle. After the session he came over to talk to us, and a couple of weeks later he asked her out.'

'Was that a surprise, that he asked her and not you?'

'Actually he did ask me.'

'Oh?'

'He asked us both out to the gig with him that first time, but I withdrew gracefully. I don't do shared dates.'

Millie wondered if there was a hint of regret in her voice. 'What do you think about the way it's worked out?' she asked tentatively.

'I think it's great.' Julie-Ann bent forward, suddenly intent on sorting her papers, but not before Millie had noticed the rush of colour to her face. 'I mean, Will didn't on the face of it seem like Lucy's type, but I'm really glad that she's found someone.' She lifted her face, composed once more. 'I hope they'll be very happy together.'

To Millie's ears, it sounded a bit forced. 'When did you last see Lucy?' she asked.

Julie-Ann grimaced. 'Now you've got me. It was a while ago, I guess.'

Some best friend, thought Millie.

The distant clanging of a hand-bell was followed by a growing crescendo of voices, and small children in regulation navy sweat-shirts began trickling into the classroom. Seeing Millie, their chatter faded away, but their presence signalled the end of the interview.

'Thanks for your help,' Millie said, getting up from her perch. 'I'll find my way out.'

Millie's next task was a pleasant drive out to Fairfield, a village tucked into the green fields of the commuter belt between Birmingham and Bromsgrove. It was a beautiful spring day; the sun bobbing in and out of white fluffy clouds and giving off an unseasonable warmth. Millie had to stop and consult her map a couple of times to locate the cottage where Lucy's mother lived, before finally coming to wooden gates opening on to a lengthy gravel drive that intersected several acres of immaculately tended gardens.

Grace Copeland was out in her garden watering a number of large plant pots on a rear terrace, but straightened up, watching the approach of the car with interest, waiting to greet Millie as she got out. Tall, like her daughter, she had a healthy out-doors glow to her cheeks and was dressed in jeans, polo neck and gilet that looked to be her customary garb, her shoulder-length greying hair loosely tied back.

At the sight of Millie's warrant card she was instantly alarmed. 'Is everything all right?'

'Yes,' Millie reassured her. 'Your daughter has reported some nuisance calls and I just need to ask you a few questions.'

'Oh, of course.' She seemed relieved. 'It's about time for a cup of tea,' she decided. 'Would you like one?'

The brew made, Grace Copeland brought it out to where Millie sat in the sunshine, on an ancient wooden bench under a spreading cherry tree. 'I know Lucy has been getting these calls, and she told me she thought she'd been followed in her car.'

'I'm just trying to establish a bit of background,' said Millie, taking a mug from her. 'We've had a look at the house too, checked that it's secure.'

Grace sat down beside her. 'Paul, her father, died two years ago. He'd had a good job and invested shrewdly, so he left her a substantial amount of money. It seemed a good idea for her to invest in a bigger house, but I don't think she's been happy there.'

'How do you get on with your new son-in-law?'

'Will?' Grace pondered for a moment. 'Well, he's very handsome and charming. But I wish he had a more traditional job, I suppose. Lucy seems to be left on her own an awful lot. I've suggested that she come and stay here, but she has her own life to get on with.'

'It looked a lovely wedding,' Millie said.

'Oh it was.' Grace smiled, remembering. 'Brackleys did us proud. It all came as a bit of a surprise. Lucy hadn't to my knowledge had a boyfriend for some time, then all of a sudden there was Will and they were talking of getting married. I'm thrilled for her. It's what she wanted so much. And to tell you the truth I was beginning to give up on the idea of grandchildren altogether.'

So, as well as her best friend, Lucy's mother didn't know about the change of plans either. Millie decided it was not her role to disillusion the woman. 'Do you have any reason to think that Lucy might be unhappy with Will?'

Grace Copeland was taken aback by the question. 'No. Why ever would she be? Though I must confess I haven't seen much of her since the wedding. We talk on the phone regularly, of course, but, since she started getting these calls, it has become more difficult. It's so expensive to call her on her mobile.'

'Is there anyone you can think of who might want to upset Lucy now? Any old boyfriends you remember, who might have got too attached?'

But Grace couldn't think of anyone. Millie had finished her tea and was mindful of the twenty-minute journey ahead of her. 'Do you mind if I use your bathroom before I go?' she asked. 'It's a bit of a drive back into the city.'

'No, of course, I'll show you where it is.'

Grace took Millie into the house, directing her to an upstairs bathroom. Without seeming obvious, Millie took the opportunity to have a quick glance around. It was a typical middle-class home, Millie thought, though the photographs on the wall alongside the stairs were interesting; mostly corporate shots at formal functions. Paul Copeland, Millie presumed, had been photographed with various dignitaries, including, she noticed, the current assistant chief commissioner. Grace Copeland caught up with her at the bottom of the stairs.

'Your husband knew some important people,' Millie commented.

'I suppose he did,' Grace said proudly. 'He was a prosecutor with the CPS. I think at one time he'd hoped that Lucy would go into law too; she was bright enough, but Lucy was determined to do a job that was more obviously helping people, and she loves being around small children. She didn't think much of the people Paul used to mix with.'

'Like the ACC?' Millie suggested.

Grace smiled. 'Hm. Paul belonged to the Masons. It wasn't something I liked or particularly approved of, and neither did Lucy, but Paul felt that it was good for his career, so we tolerated it.'

Through the door into the lounge Millie could see a cabinet full of trophies. 'Lucy's?' she asked, and on cue Grace Copeland walked her through to look at them.

'She was a cheerleader of all things,' she said. 'Paul hated it. It was all so American and – tacky. I think the girls mostly liked it because of the glamour and the costumes. Girls of that age love dressing up, don't they? But to their credit they worked hard and they were very good.'

'So I see,' Millie said. The array of first-place awards was impressive.

'And it kept them out of trouble.'

'What would Lucy's father have thought of Will?' Millie wondered.

'Oh, I'm sure he would have got along with him.'

They walked out again into the sunshine. 'Well, thank you for your time, Mrs Copeland,' Millie said, getting into her car. And, after checking her route back to Granville Lane once more, she left Grace Copeland to her garden.

CHAPTER FIVE

Mariner saved his questions for Rachel Hordern until after she had made a positive identification of her stepmother. Until then he simply introduced himself and waited quietly in the background. Stuart Croghan and his staff had managed somehow to make Nina Silvero serene in death, and Rachel tearfully confirmed that it was her stepmother. A member of the morgue staff sat with the Horderns' energetic two-year-old, while the ritual took place, and, though Rachel remained remarkably composed throughout, it was seeing her child again that brought emotion to the surface. Mariner allowed her some time alone with her husband, Adam, before going into the visitors' lounge with Knox.

'Did she suffer?' was Rachel's first question to him, her eyes eager for reassurance. A heavily built woman, her face was covered in pale freckles and fine, strawberry-blonde hair touched her shoulders. They sat round on low chairs and Rachel clung so tightly to her son that he was squirming, trying to wriggle free.

'It was over quickly,' Mariner replied tactfully. 'I'm very sorry. Were you close to her?'

'Yes, I was. I'd stopped thinking about her as a stepmother long ago.'

'How long had she been–?'

'–my mother? Since I was six. I think I was hideous to her for the first couple of years, but Mum – Nina – did all the right things. We've been closer than ever since Dad died.' She paused to wipe her eyes.

'What happened to your natural mother?' Mariner asked.

'She and Dad split up years ago, before Nina came along. She ran off with a Swede.' She broke into an unexpected giggle, which in seconds turned into a sob. 'Sorry, it's just for some reason my friends and I used to find that hilarious.'

'Where's your mother now?'

'Still in Stockholm with Lars, as far as I know. I haven't seen her in a long time.' She blew her nose, then looked up at Mariner. 'Mum wouldn't have committed suicide, you know,' she said emphatically. 'She had no reason to. She'd got her first grandchild, she loved being with Harry, and she'd just been given the MBE, for God's sake.'

Mariner knew that, given the right state of mind, those two factors didn't necessarily make a difference, but she'd been through enough today, so he went along with it for now. 'What did she get the award for?' he asked.

'Services to dance; she runs a local ballet school – she's been doing it for years.'

Mariner hesitated. 'This is a difficult question to ask, but is there any chance that the MBE could have uncovered some kind of skeleton in the closet, something she might have been ashamed to have made public?'

'Like what?'

'I don't know,' Mariner admitted. 'Some kind of impropriety?'

'Absolutely not!' Rachel was beginning to get impatient now. 'My stepmother did not kill herself.'

Harry began to grizzle loudly, making further conversation impossible. Knox stood up. 'Why don't we take Harry to look at the boats on the canal?' he suggested to Adam, who responded immediately. 'Yes, of course. Come on, soldier.' He held open his arms and Rachel gave her son a final squeeze before letting him break free and go to his dad.

'Be careful by the water,' she called after them.

When they had gone, Mariner asked, 'Who knew about the award?'

Rachel was calm again. 'Lots of people,' she said. 'We placed an announcement in the local paper. There were people she'd lost touch with over the years, and it was good publicity for the school.'

'Is there anyone you can think of who might have resented the MBE, or felt that your stepmother didn't deserve it?' Mariner asked. Seeing her blank expression, he added, 'Was there any rivalry? Any other dance schools that might not have liked the attention she was getting?'

'Enough to kill her? That's ridiculous.'

'It probably is,' Mariner agreed. 'But I do need to ask these things. When was the last time you saw your stepmother?'

'A couple of weeks ago, we came up for the weekend, Harry and me.'

'And how did she seem?'

'She was fine, looking forward to finally retiring. I mean, she hasn't had a very good year healthwise, so it seemed the right thing to do.'

'She'd been ill?' Mariner queried.

'Just silly, niggling things,' Rachel said, shrugging it off. 'Mostly tiredness and lethargy, and she'd had a couple of tummy bugs lately. It wasn't like Mum to be ill. She's always been so active what with the dancing and everything. We put it down to the number of hours she was working, so she had cut those down. I suggested she get some help around the house; it's a big place to look after all on her own, but she wouldn't even consider it. And we were talking about the possibility of her moving down to be nearer to us, except that she didn't really want to leave the friends she has here.'

'She had close friends?' Mariner asked.

'Two in particular that she sees on a regular basis; the Golden Girls they called themselves. Some throwback to years ago.'

'Estelle Waters, was she one of this group?' Mariner recalled the name of the woman who raised the alarm.

'Yes, Estelle's probably Mum's closest friend.'

'And neither of them would be jealous about what your stepmother has achieved?'

'I suppose it's possible that anyone could be envious, but enough to do this to her? No, I'm certain. They're good friends to Mum and were very supportive.' Rachel, like most people, was inclined to believe in the essential goodness of people, though Mariner knew differently.

'Was your stepmother anxious about anything, or had anything changed in her behaviour recently?' he probed.

'Not recently. She went through a bad

time when Dad died. But then, you'll know all about that.' She looked up at Mariner, a hint of challenge in her eyes, he thought.

'I know a little, yes,' he said evenly. 'But it was before my time.' He needed to distance himself from it, to encourage her to talk.

'It was terrible. He didn't deserve to go that way. If he hadn't been persecuted the way he was–'

'I'm not sure that–' Mariner began gently, but she wasn't listening.

'Dad was made a scapegoat. And afterwards that man's family were horrible to Mum. She got these hate letters saying that they were glad that Dad was dead, and we had bricks through the windows and everything.' She stopped suddenly. 'Do you think this could be related to what happened with Dad?'

'It's a possibility we'll have to consider,' Mariner admitted.

'But why now?' she demanded.

'That's what we'd need to find out. How had your stepmother been since then?'

'Of course she missed Dad, but she'd got her life back together. She always was an independent woman and with all that was happening lately... It's why this just doesn't make any sense.'

'So, a couple of weeks ago, was that the last contact you had with your stepmother?' Mariner checked.

'No, we spoke every couple of days; the last time was the day before yesterday, in the evening. Oh, God, it would have been later that night that she...' As she tailed off, Mariner could see her visualising the sequence of events till emotion overtook her and she broke down into gentle sobs, fumbling in her handbag for a tissue.

Mariner passed her the clean handkerchief he always carried for just such occasions.

'Would you like another drink?' he asked.

'No, I'm fine, thank you.'

When she seemed ready to resume, he asked, 'What time would it have been when you called her?'

'It was after we'd eaten, at about seven thirty, I suppose, maybe quarter to eight. Harry was in bed.'

'And how long did you speak for?'

'Not for long as it happened. Someone came to the door, her door.'

'Did she say who it was?'

'No. I don't think she could see. She hung up the phone before opening the door. She just said, "Got to go, darling, I've got a visitor, I'll speak to you soon," and rang off. And it was fine because I just thought, yes, I'd speak to her later, or the next day, and now...' She wiped her nose again.

If that timing was right, Mariner realised, then that visitor could also be Nina Silvero's killer. 'And you're certain she didn't give any indication about who this person might be?'

'Absolutely, she gave no hint, though I didn't get the impression she was expecting anyone.'

'Did your stepmother have any close male friends?' Mariner asked.

'You mean boyfriends?' Rachel was taken aback. 'No, she didn't go in for that kind of thing.'

'Do you think she would have told you if she did?'

'Of course.' She was affronted. 'We used to talk about everything. In fact, from time to time after Dad died I used to tell her she should find someone, but she always said no, she was quite content as she was. Maybe if there had been a man around–' She broke off as the door opened and Harry came running in, flinging himself at her, Adam and Knox following. It was a good enough time to end the interview.

'Where will you be staying?' Mariner asked, as he and Knox prepared to leave.

'I've booked us into the Norfolk Hotel, on the Hagley Road,' Adam said.

Mariner took out a card and passed it to him. 'If you have any questions, those are my numbers,' he said. 'And we will need to talk to you again.'

'What about the funeral?' Rachel asked. 'When can we...?'

'We'll release her body as soon as possible; probably in the next couple of days.'

'And the house?'

'Is still a crime scene,' Mariner pointed out. 'I'm afraid we can't let you in there for the moment. But if there's anything specific you need, as long as we don't consider it relevant to the inquiry, one of my officers will retrieve it for you.'

Rachel shook her head vaguely. 'No, there's nothing special.'

'So it's looking pretty definitely like murder, boss,' Knox remarked as they picked their way through the afternoon traffic.

Mariner was in agreement. 'Croghan seemed sure. And, if that timing's right, it ties neatly in with our mystery caller. We need to find out who that was. We'll put out an appeal as part of the next press release. How did Adam Hordern seem?'

Out of the corner of his eye, Mariner saw Knox shrug. 'He seemed pretty fond of his mother-in-law. He particularly appreciated her generosity; she'd pretty much paid for their wedding, he said.'

'What does he do for a living?'

'He's an entrepreneur.'

On Tuesday evening, Lucy was leaving the office on time, her stomach churning with conflicting feelings; she was eager to get home to Will, who was due home tonight, but at the same time she felt sick with trepidation, anticipating the journey home. However, she had decided to stop being such a wimp; she was going to confront her tormentor. In her handbag, in preparation, she had her phone, a panic alarm and a notebook, determined that, if she was followed home tonight, she would make sure to get the vehicle registration at least. Climbing into her car, the adrenalin began coursing through her, making her mouth dry and her heart thump. Tonight she would take control of this and end it once and for all.

Last night, despite the build-up, nothing had happened. Maybe this was all in her imagination. Tonight she would take her normal, quicker route home and all would be well. As always she had a choice; she could take the route that followed the main road until she was almost home, or she could take the little-used short cut that threaded through the back roads, ending with a quarter-mile stretch through the Holloway, little more than a deep tree-lined lane, designated one way only. Since developing the suspicion that she was being followed, she had avoided it completely. It was time to try it again.

The first part of the journey went smoothly, though Lucy was occupied so much with looking in her rear-view mirror it was a miracle she didn't collide with something. It was rush hour so the major roads were busy. Each time headlights fell in behind, her heartbeat quickened, but then just as suddenly the headlights vanished again. Then, as she turned into the Holloway, there he was, up close and headlights on full beam. Her palms, grasping the steering wheel, were suddenly sticky. Off the main road he kept close, crowding her as always, but instead of increasing her speed, as she had before, Lucy slowed down until she realised she had ground to a complete halt. The lane was dark, street lights widely spaced, and for several seconds they sat there, one behind the other. Her foot hovering on the accelerator, Lucy waited to see what he would do. Nothing happened. There was just enough space for him to squeeze by, but the car remained stationary behind her, silent and menacing.

Clutching her panic alarm in one trembling hand and her phone in the other, Lucy got out of her car and approached the vehicle cautiously, giving it a wide berth. The driver had stayed where he was, but as Lucy reached the driver's door, the window slid smoothly down. With a shock, Lucy saw an elderly man, frail and white haired and with a face as petrified as her own. 'What do you want?' he pleaded, voice quaking. 'I haven't got any money, you know.' White-knuckled hands gripped the steering wheel.

Suddenly Lucy realised that, in the dusk, her hair tied back, and wearing trousers and a bulky jacket and as tall as she was, she must have cut an intimidating figure. She almost wept with relief. 'I'm sorry,' she said. 'I thought you were following me. You were driving so close.'

'Following you?' the old man was baffled. 'But I couldn't help it. You slowed down.'

It was true, she had.

'I'm sorry,' she said again. 'I made a mistake.'

After the high tension of the encounter, Lucy's mood was almost euphoric when she saw Will's transit parked on the drive, and she pulled in behind it. Suddenly, it seemed ridiculous that she had gone to the police at all. What if this *was* all in her head? She'd convinced herself that the car had been following her but really it was a harmless old man. Whatever had she been thinking about? She took her mobile out of her handbag on the seat beside her, and dialled DC Jamilla Khatoon. Millie answered right away.

'Thanks for all your help,' Lucy said. 'But I don't want you to take it any further. I'm sure Will is right. It's just a few silly phone calls and the rest is just me imagining things.'

'Lucy, I'm not sure that you're the kind of person who imagines things,' Millie said. 'Has something happened?'

'No, nothing. I've just changed my mind.'

'It seems to me that there's enough for us to look into,' Millie persisted.

'No, I really don't want you to.'

'I'd prefer it if we could come and talk to Will, too.'

'No, it's fine, really, I'd rather you didn't.' And Lucy ended the call.

She went into the house feeling relieved. It had been a moment of madness, but, thank God, no harm had been done. Climbing the stairs to the bedroom, she was instantly comforted by the sight of Will's things lying around, his holdall dumped on the floor and spilling out dirty washing. 'Will?' she called out.

'In here.' His voice echoed back at her from the bathroom. 'Why don't you come and join me?'

As soon as she saw him naked in the bath, any remaining doubts evaporated. His lean body was one of the things that had attracted her to him. He was as toned as she was. His dark eyes focused on her as she undressed slowly before climbing into the sunken roman-style bath facing him. Her toes explored him. 'Well,' she remarked. 'You seem pleased to see me.'

'Oh, I sure am.' Will leaned forward and kissed her.

Mariner was on his way out of the office at

the end of the day, when he noticed Millie sitting at her desk, holding the telephone receiver a little way from her ear and looking slightly dazed.

'You OK?' he asked.

'I think so,' she said uncertainly. 'Lucy Jarrett has asked us to drop the case.'

'Really?'

'Yes, she says she thinks it was all in her imagination, just as her husband has been telling her.'

'That's a sudden turnaround,' Mariner said. 'What do you think?'

'Well, to be honest, I haven't got very far. The calls have been made from an un-registered mobile, so we can't trace them. Apart from the initial one, it could just be someone making a mistake. I think she's lonely, too. I've talked to her mum and her best friend. Neither of them seems that enamoured with her new husband and he does sound like a tit.'

'Not much we can do about that,' Mariner observed.

'No. It's just that, when you talk to Lucy, she's the one who seems to do all the compromising in the relationship, and I'm sure she's called me off because she's concerned about how he would react to us being involved.'

'Have you managed to find anything out about him?' asked Mariner.

'There's this.' Millie clicked the mouse a few times and came up with the website for the Leigh Hawkins Band. It gave the dates of future gigs that were coming up and there were biographical paragraphs on each of the band members, including Will Jarrett. His blog described him as a guitar and mandolin player who hailed from Asheville, North Carolina. The closing sentence announced that he had recently married.

'His name comes up on one or two older sites as well,' Millie added, 'bands that he's been in previously, though they only mention his name. I was just thinking it might be worth a call to the Asheville police department, when Lucy phoned to call it all off. Should I make the call or do you think I'm wasting my time now?'

'On what grounds would you be doing it?' Mariner asked.

'Well, I've never met the man, but I've got a feeling about him.'

'A gut reaction?'

'Yes, I guess that's all it is,' she admitted.

'Well, go with it,' said Mariner. 'Nothing wrong with following your instincts. Just don't take too much time over it. Maybe just make the call to Asheville, and see what that throws up. If Lucy doesn't want to pursue it there's nothing much else we can do. She seemed sure about that?'

'She was pretty adamant,' Millie said.

Mariner could sense her disappointment. 'Don't worry,' he reassured her. 'There will be plenty more where that came from, and other opportunities for you to take the lead. Meanwhile, we can certainly use your skills on the Nina Silvero case.'

Millie shuddered. 'I heard about that. It sounds pretty nasty.'

'I have to agree with the DCI that it's pretty conclusively suspicious, but we've got no sense of who could be behind it yet,' Mariner said. 'We have a mystery visitor on the evening that she died, so he or she will be our priority.'

Millie slowly shook her head. 'Why do people do these terrible things to each other?'

'If we knew the answer to that our lives would be a hell of a lot easier,' Mariner said. 'And don't sit here all evening fretting about that. You've got a husband to go home to.'

'Right, see you in the morning, boss.'

On his way home that evening Mariner stopped off at what he still referred to as the 'video shop' even though the shelves had long been taken over by computer games and DVDs. He spent a while perusing the shelves, deciding what would hit the mark just at the moment. Watching DVDs was something he and Kat had done a lot of. She had settled well into a different life at his house, but evenings were always tricky, followed as they were by the point at which she would be going up to bed.

The Rainbow project, managed by refuge counsellor Lorelei, had housed Kat for a few days after her rescue but had been too much in demand to keep her, which is why Mariner had stepped in. But Lorelei specialised in helping traumatised young women and had continued to advise and support. With help from Millie and Lorelei, Mariner had tried to make Kat's bedroom look as far removed as possible from the one in which she'd been incarcerated, when she'd been brought to Birmingham and forced into prostitution. But it had still taken months until she was relaxed enough in the evening to climb the stairs. Until then Kat had stayed up very late, often falling asleep on the sofa, where Millie at first, and then Mariner, would cover her with a duvet and leave her. DVDs had been a good way of passing the long evening hours without putting too much pressure on Kat, and they had helped to improve what was already pretty good English, helping her to secure a job as a freelance translator based at a city-centre language school.

Mariner had been careful in his choice of films and in the early days they had been pure escapism, anything to get her away from the horrors that Kat and her friends had endured. She had quickly developed a taste for the Ealing comedies, because, Mariner supposed, they were quaint and ridiculous and so very English. It was during those that he'd first heard her laugh. Since then they had progressed to meatier drama and contemporary thrillers, but he was careful to try to judge her mood and usually offered at least one alternative. It had encouraged him to broaden his horizons too, encapsulating costume dramas – a genre he normally went out of his way to avoid. And Kat's tendency of late veered towards the light romantic comedy, which was far removed from Mariner's taste, but he went along with it to indulge her. After the life she'd had she deserved some indulgence.

It was a good time to observe her, too. Often when she lost herself in the films that they were watching Mariner could tell her true state of mind. He'd talked at length about it to Lorelei, who had advised him to keep a close eye on her body language at this time. It had been a revelation. In the first few weeks Kat had positioned herself as far away from Mariner as she could, curled up tight and seemingly squeezing herself into the corner of the sofa. Gradually, over the weeks, through Alastair Sim and Margaret Rutherford, Jack Lemmon and Marilyn Monroe, Gene Kelly and Debbie Reynolds, like a flower, Mariner had watched her unfold. More recently she would often choose to sit beside him, her long legs stretched out before her while she chuckled along. Sometimes, usually in response to some sarcastic comment about a costume drama, she would playfully punch him, and, if the tension was high, she would grab his arm and squeeze tight. It occurred to him once that this was what it might have been like if he'd had a teenage daughter.

Now Kat was beginning to make her own choices too, films that she had talked about with her work colleagues and wanted to see. He tried to remember which film it was she'd mentioned at the weekend. Then he saw it: *Girl with a Pearl Earring*. Mariner scanned the case. He didn't hold out much hope: Colin Firth and Vermeer; it would be about as exciting as watching a Dutch Old Master dry. Still, if that was what she wanted. He picked up a couple of cartons of Häagen-Dazs as well and went to pay.

Mariner was pleasantly surprised by the selection. Notwithstanding the leisurely pace, the film was absorbing and beautifully photographed, but tonight it was Kat who was edgy and distracted from the plot, and a couple of times he had to remind her of what was going on. Every few minutes she would jump up to get something from the kitchen, take off her jumper, put it back on. Mariner began to wonder if she was having a relapse. Up until recently her mobile phone had been rarely used, but this evening it was like an extension of her hand as she continually texted her friends throughout the film. Mariner tried to assess her mood, but this wasn't one of his strengths, especially where women were concerned. On the other hand, Kat didn't seem unhappy. And for once, as soon as the film ended, she went up early to bed.

During the night, Mariner woke with a jolt. Something had disturbed him. For a moment, and not for the first time, he was disorientated, thinking he was in Anna's bed at her old house in Harborne. Disappointment swept over him as his mind adjusted. He got up for a pee and walking back from the bathroom he heard the noise that had woken him, a terrible animal wailing. It was coming from Kat's room. The door was ajar, as she always left it. After more than a year of imprisonment, she couldn't bear the door to be closed. Mariner gently pushed it wider and went in. By now the sound had diminished to a whimpering, but he couldn't judge whether she was awake or asleep.

'Kat? Kat?' Mariner said softly. She didn't respond and her breathing was becoming even now. Mariner perched for a moment on the chair by the bed, uncertain about what he should do; he could never remember the best strategy for nightmares. Should you wake someone or leave them? If he did wake her and she was distressed how could he help? He wasn't a stranger any more but a man in her bedroom at night was the last thing she needed. Also the sight and smell of her was doing things to him that he wished they weren't. The curtains were open and in the moonlight he could see her bare shoulder and the strap of her vest, the curve of her breast. Suddenly instead of Kat he saw Anna's head on the pillow. Kat murmured and stirred a little and, shocked by the power of his own imagination, Mariner stole out again.

Lucy and Will surfaced hours later to order a takeaway curry and were lying comfortably together on the sofa watching TV. But as they talked Lucy could barely stay awake. It was, she realised, the most relaxed she had felt for weeks.

'I'm so glad you're home,' she said.

Will smiled lasciviously. 'Mm, me too.'

For some reason the woman's voice on the phone came back to her. 'Really?'

'Sure, I get to spend some time with my wife.' He slid a hand under her robe.

'You could spend even more time with her.'

'Oh, yeah, how?'

'Don't go away again.'

Will withdrew his hand. 'What?'

'Joke!' Lucy grinned, hoping he couldn't

tell that was only half-true. 'It's just that this is so nice.'

'Maybe it's this nice because I do go away.'

'Hmm, could be,' Lucy conceded. 'Who were you out with last night anyway?' she asked carefully.

'Uh? Oh, just the guys in the band.'

'Oh, I thought I heard women's voices.'

'We were in a bar. I guess there were probably some women in there.'

A note of tension had crept into his voice, but she couldn't stop herself. 'Who?'

'I don't know; just some women. What is this? Come on, honey, you promised you would never do this to me.'

'Do what?' Lucy was all innocence.

'Interrogate me about where I've been, what I've been doing.'

'I'm not interrogating you.'

'Really? It's how it feels. How do I know that you're not hanging out with some guy while I'm not around?'

'Don't be ridiculous,' Lucy protested. She tried to snuggle up to Will, but the atmosphere was broken and he got up. 'Do you want a coffee?'

Lucy had no choice but to go along with it. 'Yes, thanks, that would be nice.'

She heard him clattering around in the kitchen, but, quite abruptly, the sounds stopped. Did she hear him swear? Something he couldn't find. Smiling to herself, she got off the sofa and walked through to the kitchen.

Will looked up as she came to the doorway. 'Is there something you need to tell me?' His voice seemed unnaturally calm; a stillness in the air before the storm broke.

Lucy's stomach turned to lead when she heard his tone of voice.

'What do you mean?' she asked. Then she realised a drawer was open and several plastic-wrapped catalogues lay on the countertop. He was holding something in his hand, turning the small cardboard box over and over, while they both stared at it.

'What's this meant to be?' He threw it down on the counter and it skidded towards her. It took Lucy a few seconds to work out what it was, but as her eyes came into focus she made out the words 'Clear Blue'. Oh shit. She had meant to throw it away.

'A pregnancy test?' He was incredulous.

Despite herself, she blushed. 'It came in the post, a couple of days ago. I meant to throw it away. It just arrived.'

'What do you mean, "it just arrived"?' He picked up the padded envelope it had fallen out of. 'It has your name and address on it.'

'Which they've got from some list somewhere. That doesn't mean anything. It's been happening all the time. It's probably tied up with the phone calls.'

Will spread his hands, exasperated. 'What

phone calls?' He was right. There hadn't been any all evening.

Lucy moved across to pick up the offending item, and at the same time Will took a step towards her and, grabbing her arm, twisted it up towards him. Lucy gasped. 'You're hurting me.'

He leaned over her, staring into her eyes. 'I don't understand why you're doing this, Lucy. We talked about this. We both knew where we stood, and now you've hooked me you think you can change your mind?'

'Hooked you? What's that supposed to mean? I still feel the same way as I did before we married. I'm fine about not having kids. Yes, I might have once wanted them, but now I'd rather have you. I told you that at the time and it's still the truth.'

'Which is why we have this in the house, is it?' There was something in his eyes. He didn't believe her. With his free hand he sorted through the catalogues. 'Maternity clothes; nursery furniture? All addressed to you.' Pushing her away from him, he scooped up the pregnancy test and threw the packet on the floor, before striding out of the kitchen. 'I wish you wouldn't lie to me, Lucy.'

Lucy dropped down to retrieve the packet as a wave of nausea hit her, and she had to crouch there for a moment while it passed. She daren't tell Will about that; she knew just what he'd think. Getting slowly to her feet, she threw the Clear Blue into the bin in disgust, something she should have done the moment she received it.

She went back into the lounge but Will wasn't there; she could hear him moving about upstairs. Following him up, she found him putting clean clothes back into his overnight bag. 'What are you doing?' she asked stupidly. 'You can't just walk away from this. We need to sort it out.'

'We had an agreement,' Will said coldly. 'You need to give some thought to whether you want to stick with that.' He hurried down the stairs and moments later the front door slammed.

Trembling with fear, Lucy heard Will's van start up and pull out of the drive. As soon as it did, the phone rang and she cried out involuntarily, wrenching the line out of the wall socket to silence it.

CHAPTER SIX

The 999 call came into the West Midlands call control centre at eleven forty pm, the caller claiming to have seen a couple arguing what looked like violently, and concerned that the woman involved might be in danger.

'I've just seen someone being attacked,' he said.

'Where are you, sir?'

'The address is nineteen, Hill Crest. You need to get someone over there right away.'

'Is that your address, sir?' the telephonist asked.

'No, it's where the attack is taking place.'

'Could you give me your name, sir?'

The caller ignored the question. 'I saw him attack her, she fell on the floor, and now he's gone out and she's not answering her phone.'

'Are you a friend or neighbour, sir?' But the phone had gone dead.

Ten minutes later Lucy Jarrett's doorbell rang. She peered out into the darkness. There were two emergency vehicles parked on the road, their lights flashing, and a group of people was gathered at her front door. What was going on? When the doorbell rang again, she opened the door cautiously. It was quite a party: two young policemen and a man and woman in the green paramedics uniforms, one carrying a bulky holdall.

'Good evening, madam.' The taller of the police officers spoke; he looked barely old enough to have started shaving, Lucy thought. 'We're just checking that everything's all right. We received a phone call to say that a woman at this address was being attacked.'

'What?' Lucy was aghast. 'They're mistaken. My husband and I had a disagreement, that's all. I'm fine.'

The officer peered behind her and into the hall. 'Is your husband at home?' he asked.

'No, he went out. I think he's gone to stay with a ... a friend.' Lucy realised how strange it must have sounded, but it was after all the truth. 'I'm absolutely fine.'

'You're sure?' the police officer asked again.

The paramedics exchanged a word or two, and were beginning to back away.

'Really,' said Lucy. 'Who did you say phoned you?'

'It was an anonymous call.'

'Oh, God,' Lucy blurted out.

'Are you sure you're all right?' The officer was reluctant to go. 'We could come in and check.'

'No really, thank you,' Lucy heard herself insist. 'There's no need. Goodnight.'

She watched as the two policemen reluctantly retraced their steps down the drive and back to their car, one of them speaking into his radio. Then she closed and securely bolted the door. After climbing the stairs again, she went to draw the curtains in the bedroom and saw a light upstairs in the house across the road. He wouldn't, would he? Lucy didn't think she could possibly sleep tonight, but after the wine she'd drunk she suddenly felt so tired.

'Did you sleep well?' Mariner asked Kat on Wednesday morning.

'Sure.' She seemed surprised by the question. Today she had scrambled some eggs and was eating them runny, the way she liked them.

Mariner had stepped into the kitchen to deposit his empty coffee mug. 'You called out,' he said. 'In your sleep. Did you have a bad dream?'

But she shrugged. She didn't remember.

Mariner was one of the first in the car park that morning. But, as he got out of his car and began to cross the compound, a woman called out to him. At first he didn't recognise her.

'What are you doing here?' he said, when the penny had dropped. Stephanie looked older than he remembered and had clearly made an effort with her make-up, but in daylight she looked somehow different; not his usual type at all.

'I brought you this.' She handed him a plastic lunch box. 'You need fattening up. I thought you were probably the kind of man who wouldn't have time to prepare anything, and you need to eat.'

Mariner was both embarrassed and irritated by the presumption, but she'd clearly gone to some effort so he gave in gracefully. 'Right, er, thanks.' He took the plastic box from her. 'How did you know where to find me?'

She touched the side of her heavily powdered nose. 'Oh, I have ways. When do you finish?'

'I don't know,' said Mariner truthfully. He'd just seen Tony Knox pulling into the compound. 'It's pretty busy just at the moment.' He began moving towards where Knox was reversing into a space.

'Well, don't forget to call,' Stephanie called after him. 'Actually I was wondering if you were free tonight?'

'I'm not sure, er...' Mariner picked up his stride. 'I'll let you know.'

'Only we seemed to hit it off so well, didn't we?' Stephanie persisted.

Did we? 'I'll need to check my diary,' Mariner stalled, quickening his pace. 'Excuse me, I need to have a word with my sergeant.'

'Well, keep in touch, won't you?' she called after him.

Waving a vague acknowledgement, Mariner walked over to where Knox had come to a halt, opened his passenger door and got in.

Knox visibly jumped. 'Christ, where did you spring from?'

'Don't bother getting out of the car,' Mariner said. 'We've got work to do.' He put the lunch box in the foot well.

'What's the rush?' Knox asked, putting on his seat belt again and re-starting the car. 'I was looking forward to a cuppa.' Nevertheless, Knox manoeuvred back out of the parking bay and towards the entrance, driving past Stephanie who still stood watching them go, waving frantically to Mariner.

'She's the rush,' said Mariner, returning a reluctant acknowledgement. 'I'm trying to get away from her. Just make it look as if we're discussing something important.'

Knox smirked. 'Oh, is that your admirer?'

'Don't laugh,' snapped Mariner. 'We're talking about something serious.'

'Course we are, boss,' Knox said, stifling his amusement.

'What's she doing?' Mariner asked as traffic out on the road brought them to a halt at the car-park entrance.

Knox glanced in his rear-view mirror. 'She's getting in her car, but she's still watching you, to make sure you're safely on your way.'

'How the hell did she find me here?'

'She'll have googled you,' said Knox, pulling on to the main road.

'Oh, she did that all right, and the rest,' Mariner began, events of a couple of nights ago, fresh once again in his mind.

'Perhaps you'll have to put in for a transfer,' Knox said mischievously.

Mariner winced, though Knox couldn't have known why. If he'd done that a year ago he might not have lost Anna.

'So where are we going?' Knox asked now that they were out on the road.

'Nina Silvero's house,' said Mariner.

A little later that morning, as Millie ascended the stairs to CID, she heard heavy breathing from behind and Brian Mann caught up with her. 'Thought you should know,' he gasped, falling into step with her. 'Two of our lads got called to Lucy Jarrett's house last night. We had a 999 to say that she was being attacked.'

'What?'

'It's OK,' Mann wheezed. 'Turned out to be a false alarm. Apparently she and her old man had a bit of a barney, but he'd gone by the time we got there. She said it was nothing, so they came away again.'

'Do we know who made the call?'

'Pretty sure it was a man, but he wouldn't give his name.'

'Did he have any kind of accent?' Millie wanted to know.

'Not that I remember,' said Mann.

'Thanks, I'll go and talk to her. You know she wanted us to drop the investigation?' Millie told him.

Mann nodded. 'Our guys thought she was pretty wound up, especially when they told her it was an anonymous call. She might change her mind now.'

On a Wednesday morning, Lucy should have been at work, but, when Millie got to the health centre, she wasn't there. In fact, the only person in the broad, open plan office was an older woman with a mane of wild greying hair. Her clothes were garish and flowing, and she wore the heavy narrow-framed glasses that were currently in vogue. She came over to Millie. 'Can I help you?'

Millie took out her warrant card and asked for Lucy.

'Lucy's out on visits this morning, but I work on her team. Paula Kirkwood.' She held out a hand for Millie to shake. 'She should be back fairly soon and you're welcome to wait here. Is there anything I can help with?' She led Millie over to her work station in the corner of the room, adjacent to the small kitchen area, and invited her to sit. Paula's desk was piled high with stacks of files that competed with the collection of small soft toys banked up against the wall. 'Would you like a drink?' Paula asked. She was already filling the kettle as Millie accepted. 'I've got the prime spot here,' she went on. 'Though it does mean that I've developed a caffeine addiction. Tea?'

'Yes, thanks.' Millie's attention was snagged by a number of striking photographs on the wall of young African children.

Paula saw her looking. 'Beautiful, aren't they?' she said. 'They're from Ghana. I did some volunteer work out there for a number of years. In fact it was a bit of a culture shock when I came back a couple of years ago, but Lucy was great; the whole team was. They really helped me to settle in. Do you take milk?' The kettle had boiled.

'Please,' said Millie.

The drinks made, Paula came and joined Millie beside her desk.

'You know that Lucy's been getting unwelcome phone calls?' Millie said.

'She had mentioned it,' Paula said curiously. 'I didn't realise it was bad enough to involve you.'

'Well, that's the thing,' said Millie. 'I'm not sure if we are involved. Lucy came in yesterday morning to talk to us, but as of yesterday afternoon she asked us to drop the investigation. Then late last night we had an emergency call from someone who was concerned for her safety. Basically I just wanted to check that she's OK. Have you seen her this morning?'

Paula shook her head. 'She must have come in early and gone straight out again, but that isn't unusual. There's a lot to pack into a day. How serious is this?'

'Well, we don't know yet, but after Jemima Murdoch–'

'Oh, yes, I heard about that. We get the same thing from time to time; the one incident that makes it imperative to follow up anything similar.'

'Exactly,' said Millie. 'I only met Lucy yesterday. What's she like?'

Paula didn't hesitate. 'She's a highly experienced health visitor, great at her job.'

'Popular?'

'Oh yes.' Paula smiled. 'Lots of families become very attached to Lucy. She's a very warm person and takes the time to get to know them. And I've seen her in action; she's lovely with the children.'

'How well do you get to know your families?' Millie asked, well aware from her time as a family liaison officer that lines could sometimes become blurred.

'What do you...?' The penny dropped, and Paula shook her head emphatically. 'Oh no, Lucy isn't like that. She knows the professional boundaries and stays well within them.'

'But you said it yourself, she's a nice woman. Things can get misconstrued. Is there anyone who might have misread the nature of her role?' Millie wondered.

'I doubt it.' Paula was firm. 'We work primarily with new mothers. Most of them are far too tired and busy to be thinking beyond their families.'

'Any tensions here in the office?' Millie asked, taking a different tack. 'Difficult relationships with colleagues?'

'Well, we work pretty well as a team,' Paula said. 'There are disagreements sometimes about working practices, especially as the government seems to want things changed every few months, but we thrash things out in team meetings. Everyone gets their say.'

'Do you socialise much?'

'Occasionally, you know, birthdays, that kind of thing.'

'So you've met Lucy's husband?'

'Partners don't always come along, and of course Will is away such a lot.' Paula thought for a moment. 'He hasn't really been to anything that I can remember. Apart from seeing him at the wedding, the only times I've met him are on the odd occasions when he's picked Lucy up from work. I wouldn't say that I've had much opportunity to get to know him. No one has.'

It was a loaded remark. 'How do you mean?' Millie asked.

'It just all happened rather suddenly,' Paula said carefully. 'It seemed that Lucy had hardly started to mention Will's name before he was moving in with her and they were making wedding plans, or at least Lucy was. I feel disloyal saying this because she's... I was going to say "in thrall" to him

116

but perhaps that's too strong. "Besotted" with him might be more accurate. But as an outsider it seemed to me that he had everything to gain and nothing to lose from the liaison. He moved into Lucy's house and as far as I'm aware he's brought nothing material to the relationship.' Paula stopped suddenly. 'God, listen to me, I'm sounding like a real bitch, aren't I?'

'You're being honest,' Millie said diplomatically.

'It's just that so much of the relationship seems to be on Will's terms. Still he didn't get it all his own way.'

'Oh?'

'I'm sure it would have been Will's style to have a low-key, registry office wedding, but Lucy insisted on the works, morning suits, the lot, and she can afford it so she got her way in the end.' Paula was suddenly pensive. 'Although they would have got some decent gifts out of it so maybe that's how she sold the idea to Will.'

'He's mercenary?' Millie asked.

'Let's just say that what Lucy tells us about him doesn't quite add up,' Paula replied. 'She's always saying what a free spirit he is, non-materialistic and all of that but she always seems to be buying him presents and he likes his gadgets. He didn't turn down the offer of a brand-new custom-liveried tour van when Lucy offered it to him. Sorry, this must sound as if I'm being a real cow, but no one likes to see a friend get taken advantage of.'

'And that's what you think is happening here?' Millie asked.

'Well, obviously I don't know exactly what goes on between them, but–' She left the sentence hanging, her views clear.

'Has Lucy changed much since she got married?' Millie wondered.

'She changed when she first met Will. We all noticed it. Before that she had always been quite conservative with her clothes. She made the most of herself but dressed stylishly. When Will came on the scene Lucy started wearing quite outrageous things.' Paula laughed, holding out her berobed arms. 'Says me, who dresses exclusively from Oxfam. But this was different; some of Lucy's outfits were quite revealing. To be brutally frank, I got the distinct impression that she was dressing to please Will, as if she was slightly awkward in these clothes. I know our line manager had a word with her about it. We have to be careful to dress appropriately to go into people's homes. And Will has tattoos, so soon after they met Lucy was sporting one as well, though I think she mainly keeps it covered up now.'

More compromises, thought Millie. 'What about since the wedding?' she asked.

'If anything, Lucy's reverted more to type

118

really, quietened down again, as if she took the manager's comments on board.'

Lucy came back into the office just as Millie was finishing her tea. 'Hi, how are you?' she asked, thinking that Lucy looked tired and preoccupied.

'Hi, I'm fine, at least–'

'What is it?'

'Something else has happened.' Scrunched in her hand was a scrap of paper. She passed it to Millie. 'I've just called in at the super-market to get a sandwich, and when I came out this was on my car.'

Millie opened out a crumpled, slightly grimy square of paper on which a note had been scrawled: *Sorry, scraped your car when I backed out,* followed by what looked like a mobile phone number.

'Well, let's call the number.' Millie was mystified about what the problem was.

'I've already tried,' Lucy said. 'It's not recognised.'

'Well, that's really not so remarkable,' said Millie. 'People are not as honest as we'd like to think. Is there much damage to your car?'

'No, that's the point,' Lucy said im-patiently, as if Millie was being dense. 'I've been over it practically with a magnifying glass and can't find anything. I was only gone about ten minutes, tops, and as far as I remember the cars parked on either side of me were the same ones that had been there.

The back of my car, which was the only bit exposed, is untouched. You can see for yourself.'

'Sure, let's go and have a look.' Handing her empty mug to Paula, Millie followed Lucy back out to the car park.

Close examination verified what Lucy was saying; the car was pristine with not even the slightest scratch that Millie could see.

'There may still be a rational explanation,' Millie reassured her, as they walked back to the office. 'Perhaps whoever left the note was mistaken and had hit one of the cars adjacent to yours. Or perhaps they did clip your car but not hard enough to do any damage, but felt guilty about it so left the note.'

'In that case, why leave a false phone number?' Lucy demanded. 'It doesn't make any sense. I can't stand this! Who's doing it to me?'

By the time they got back to Lucy's desk, she was shaking. Paula was on hand with more tea. She had her coat on. 'I've got to pop out so I'll leave you to it,' she said. 'Nice to have met you, DC Khatoon.'

Millie smiled her thanks and pulled up a chair beside Lucy. 'I understand some of my colleagues came out to your house last night,' she ventured.

'I wish they hadn't,' Lucy said sulkily. 'I don't know who would have called them. It was nothing.' She looked up at Millie. 'Is that why you're here?'

'The caller said he thought you were being attacked,' Millie said.

'Well, he was wrong.' Her defiance lacked conviction. 'It was a disagreement, that's all. Whoever it was had no business involving you. As I said yesterday, I want to drop this whole ridiculous nonsense.' Her hands, clasped around the mug, were trembling slightly and Millie could see the effort it was taking for her to keep things together.

'So you're saying nothing happened?' she confirmed. 'The caller said he saw you fall to the floor as if you'd been struck.'

Lucy's brow creased to a frown. 'There was nothing like that. Will didn't touch me.' Her voice wavered. 'I might have bent down to pick it up from the floor but–'

'Pick up what?' Millie asked.

Finally, Lucy broke down, and placing the mug shakily on her desk she fumbled for a tissue as the tears began to come. 'Will found a pregnancy test,' she sobbed. 'It was one of the things that came in the post, along with the other stuff.'

'What other stuff?'

'More catalogues like the ones you saw; dozens of them, all related to kids and parenthood. They're all addressed to me so Will thinks that's what I'm thinking about.'

Millie was genuinely puzzled now. 'But

121

why is that a problem, Lucy? You're newly married. It's natural that–'

'I told you,' she cut in. 'We're not having children; not ever. Will doesn't want them. The kind of lifestyle he has, it's not conducive to raising a family. And that's fine with me.'

'Is it?' Millie challenged her.

'Yes.' Lucy met her gaze. 'I mean at one time I might have thought about it, but it's not that important to me. And now we are married and Will found a pregnancy test and it makes it look as if I've changed my mind.' She began to weep again.

'But you haven't?'

'No! Of course not.'

'But Will didn't believe you and he got angry.'

'He's got a bit of a temper,' Lucy admitted. 'Haven't lots of men? But he's all noise, that's all. All couples argue sometimes, don't they? Don't you and your husband?'

Millie didn't even have to think about that one. Suli had never even raised his voice to her. But saying that wasn't going to help. Instead she asked, 'Does Will ever frighten you, Lucy?'

'That's ludicrous.'

But there was something in her voice that didn't entirely convince Millie. 'Who else have you told about this decision not to have kids?' she asked.

'I don't know; lots of people.'

'Lots of people?' Millie queried. 'Julie-Ann doesn't seem to know, nor your mum.' She could have added Paula to that list but it was probably enough.

'I haven't seen Julie-Ann lately. And I haven't yet plucked up the courage to tell Mum. She's so looking forward to her first grandchild. I know she is. But I've mentioned it to other people I've seen. It's kind of an expectation, isn't it? I've just got married in my thirties and people are very fond of telling me about how my biological clock is running out, so I've sort of felt compelled to make it known that we're not planning a family.'

'Have there been any more phone calls?' Millie asked.

'Yes. No. I don't know. They stopped while Will was at home but the phone rang just after he went out. I unplugged it.'

'How long after Will went out?'

'Straight away, pretty much. That's why I didn't even answer it.'

'If we're going to help you, we do need to talk to Will,' Millie reminded Lucy.

'He's away again.' She seemed relieved to say it. 'The band has got a couple of gigs this week. I'm not sure when he'll be back.' She was sounding vague and unable to meet Millie's eye. Finally she did look up. 'Will thinks I'm imagining things.'

'What do you think?'

Her eyes were glistening. 'Honestly? Just lately I sometimes think I must be going mad.'

Millie was aware that her next question was a sensitive one. 'The people I've spoken to,' she said carefully. 'They seem to think that you and Will getting married was quite sudden.'

Lucy was instantly defensive. 'Well, maybe that's just jealousy speaking.'

'Julie-Ann maybe. But your mum? They're all worried about you.' Millie was experienced enough to know that it was a subject they'd have to come back to later. There was nothing to be gained by turning Lucy against her. 'I'd like to see all the stuff you've been getting in the post,' she said. 'Can we go back to the house now?'

'Sure, I'll just let my manager know that I'm taking an hour out.'

CHAPTER SEVEN

The houses on Nina Silvero's street were spaced apart and in mature gardens, each uniquely designed; a mock-Tudor rubbing shoulders with Rennie Mackintosh and post-modern concrete and glass. This was an afflu-

124

ent district; half a million apiece at least, Mariner thought, and the kind of residents who would be unsettled by the blue-and-white striped tape and the police officer at the gates of number fifty-two. House-to-house enquiries were being conducted, though Mariner could see no evidence of activity this morning and, as far as he was aware, nothing significant had yet been uncovered. It was common in neighbourhoods such as these, and a phenomenon that Mariner had encountered before. Walking up the drive he had a powerful sense of *déjà vu* that took him back to a night in February about five years before, but, even so, he was astonished when Knox said, 'Reminds yer of Eddie Barham, this one, doesn't it, boss?'

The murder had been a significant one for Mariner, for all kind of reasons: it had been the first case he and Knox had worked together, when Knox was still in uniform, and during the course of the investigation Mariner had come to know the deceased's autistic brother, Jamie, and, more importantly, his sister, Anna. It had begun their rocky three-year relationship, which had only ended, Mariner was beginning to acknowledge, because of his own stupidity.

'Have you heard how she's getting on?' Knox asked carefully.

'I'm sure she's just fine,' said Mariner tightly, and he continued on to the house, subject closed.

The Silvero residence was a nondescript red brick. The tarmac drive smelled strongly in the afternoon sun and was tacky underfoot, and Mariner was careful to wipe his feet thoroughly on the doormat when they got inside. Closing the solid front door behind them, Tony Knox paused. 'Look at that little lot,' he said, referring to the hardware on the inner door. There were sturdy bolts top and bottom and a heavy chain. 'They look new.'

Mariner thought about Lucy Jarret. 'Perhaps Nina Silvero was nervous about something, too.'

In the kitchen the back door had been boarded up, the window pane broken when PC Solomon had forced his way in. Mariner had brought along the SOCO photographs so that they could reconstruct the scene found by Solomon when he first arrived. The wine rack was well stocked, though mostly with red Burgundys, Mariner noticed, and he retrieved a bottle of household cleaner from under the sink to represent the drain fluid.

'That's interesting,' he said, squatting by the open door of the cupboard under the sink. He began removing the bottles one by one, arranging them on the floor beside him.

'That Nina Silvero was an obsessive compulsive?' Knox offered watching the collection accumulate.

'Not that,' Mariner said. 'Look at the labels.'

Knox picked up a couple of bottles at random and examined them, but couldn't spot what Mariner had seen.

'Croghan said it would only have taken a couple of mouthfuls of the drain fluid to kill her, yet, according to the crime-scene report, the bottle of drain fluid was nearly empty,' Mariner said. 'I assumed that it was because Nina Silvero had already used some of it for cleaning her drains. But look at all this lot–' he craned his neck to peer over the sink '–and the washing-up liquid.'

Knox did, but his expression remained blank.

'Ecover,' said Mariner. 'And if you look at these others, they're all the same. All her cleaning stuff is environmentally friendly. Nina Silvero didn't keep any of the noxious substances in her house.'

'So the killer brought the materials along,' said Knox.

'Exactly.' Mariner indicated one of the photographs. 'And despite the fact that there was a wine bottle and glass on the kitchen table, there was no wine in Nina Silvero's stomach.'

'Because the wine in the bottle had been replaced with drain-cleaning fluid,' Knox took up his train of thought.

'There's only one wine glass on the table, to make us think that she'd have been drinking alone.'

'So the killer choreographed the scene afterwards.'

'Yes,' Mariner was inclined to agree. 'The bottle of drain fluid wouldn't have been produced until after Nina Silvero was dead. The wine glass the killer used would also have been washed and replaced, or they might have even taken it with them.'

Knox reached up and opened the cupboard that contained glassware; only one space where a wine glass had been.

'We'll get the rest of these tested for drain fluid. I'll bet that there are traces in one, and if the killer hasn't been careful enough we may even get a print or some DNA.'

'So, if this is someone who Nina Silvero was comfortable about having a drink with, it was someone she already knows,' Knox concluded. 'She's on the phone to her daughter when the doorbell goes. She ends the call and answers the door. It's someone on the doorstep with a bottle of wine, inviting themselves in to help her celebrate.'

'Or does the killer simply hand over the bottle as a gift and hope that the invitation follows?' Mariner wondered.

'Nah, too much of a risk,' Knox said. 'They need to see Nina drink it. Otherwise, she might not bother; she might just pass it on to someone else, or share it with someone else. We already know that Nina Silvero wasn't in the habit of drinking alone.' What he said made sense.

'So they both come into the kitchen and one of them pours the so-called wine,' Mariner continued. 'That suggests a level of informality.'

'Croghan said that Nina Silvero fell where she stood, and if we look at these scene photos it doesn't look as if the chairs were pulled out, so that could mean that it's someone Nina doesn't want to hang around,' Knox pointed out.

'Or it could just be that she intended them to move into the lounge,' Mariner countered. 'Or that the killer's in a hurry. *Just a quick glass then I'll have to go.*'

'What about the cork? If the bottle's already been opened wouldn't Nina have noticed that?'

'We'll check with forensics.' Mariner peered at one of the photos. 'Hard to tell if this was a screwtop; that would have been easier, but Nina would still have noticed. All the more reason for the killer to be in control of the situation. Perhaps he or she even offered to do it.' Mariner role-played the gesture. '*"Let me do that,"* while Nina gets the glasses. They make a toast, probably to Nina's MBE success, then the killer stands back and watches while Nina Silvero takes a couple of mouthfuls of the wine and dies an agonising death.'

'Christ.'

They paused for a moment, imagining the scene.

'Then the killer calmly tips the rest down the sink, rinses and replaces the extra glass, puts the half-empty bottle of drain cleaner on the table beside the empty wine bottle and leaves us to believe that Nina Silvero has taken her own life,' Mariner speculated. 'But the sixty-four-thousand-dollar question is: why?'

'The rest of the house is undisturbed, so it wasn't about robbery,' said Knox.

'Which gives us a pretty nasty motive,' Mariner said. 'Someone wanted to inflict pain on Nina Silvero and watch her suffer. She can't have been as popular as her daughter thinks she was.'

'Christ, what kind of person would do this to another human being, though?' Knox shook his head in disbelief.

'Someone who's pretty sick themselves.'

'Sick or angry.'

'Or both,' Mariner said. 'We need to find out what forensics have come up with on the wine bottle. If what we're saying is correct, that's our murder weapon. Let's have a look at the rest of the house.'

Nina Silvero kept a neat and orderly home.

The only untidiness was on the table in the dining room, where, it appeared, she'd been interrupted mid-task. A photograph frame lay face down, its back opened up and beside it, ready to be displayed, a colour photograph of Rachel and Adam Hordern on their wedding day, the backdrop a country house hotel of some kind.

'Not what you mess about with if you're about to top yourself either,' observed Knox.

An antique bureau in one corner of the room seemed to contain current correspondence and bills. In this too, Nina Silvero had been systematic, though there was enough material to fill several evidence bags. In a drawer below, Knox found two keys on a ring and held them up for Mariner to see. 'A safe?' he wondered.

They went around the room lifting up pictures and, behind a Sisley print, found a small safe. Inside it were several boxes of jewellery, some share certificates and a copy of the deeds to the house. 'But no will,' Mariner noted. 'That must be with her solicitor.'

The answer machine revealed a number of hang-ups, but it was an older-generation machine and not sophisticated enough to give them the dates and times; they would trace back phone records to find out if the calls had come before or after Nina Silvero's death. The ground floor completed, Mariner took the stairs two at a time to look

131

around the bedrooms. But the only item of any interest, in the small bedroom, was a PC not long out of its box; the packaging carefully preserved and stored beside the desk it stood on. As was routine these days, Mariner disconnected the tower and carried it down the stairs to be taken with them as evidence. 'We might as well take it, though, if it's that new, there won't be much on it,' he said to Knox.

There was nothing more to be done here. After securing the door again, Mariner stopped for a quick word with the bored constable on duty and they headed back to Granville Lane with their booty.

As Knox was driving, Mariner took the opportunity to clear up a couple of things with Rachel Hordern. There was no reply from their room at the Norfolk Hotel, but Rachel had also given Mariner her mobile number. When she answered his call, the background noise was an interesting mix of squawking and whistling.

'We're at the Botanical Gardens, by the aviaries,' Rachel explained apologetically. 'We needed to get out with Harry. Hold on a minute, we'll find somewhere quieter.' There was a pause and some scuffling, and Mariner heard her talking to her husband and son. Finally she spoke again to him. 'OK, go ahead.'

'We were at your stepmother's house, and

132

we noticed that she had upgraded her security,' Mariner said. 'Was there any special reason for that?'

Rachel thought about that for a moment. 'Yeah, a while back she had some strange phone calls – someone ringing and just hanging up on her – you know, like people do. I think it bothered her a bit.'

She broke off as someone in the background spoke, her husband presumably. 'Oh, God, yes, I'd forgotten about that. Sorry,' she said to Mariner, 'but Adam's just reminded me. At about the same time someone sent her some flowers. That was what frightened her.'

'Flowers frightened her?' Mariner didn't understand.

'Sorry, I'm not making myself clear. They were dead flowers – beautifully wrapped and in a presentation box, but, when she opened it up, they were all dead.'

'Could they just have been left too long in the box?'

'No, there was a note with them, something about "these flowers are dead and soon you will be too".' Mariner scribbled it down as she spoke. 'I think there was mention of an anniversary, except that it wasn't the anniversary of anything. I remember Mum was quite scared by it. It happened ages ago, though, and I'd completely forgotten about it.'There was sudden silence as the implication hit home. 'Do you think it could have been Mum's killer?'

'Can you remember exactly when this happened?' Mariner asked, side-stepping her question. 'It may be really important.'

'Adam might, hold on a moment.' Rachel turned away from the phone and in the background Mariner heard a discussion ensue, as she and her husband tried to pinpoint the occasion. Mariner waited patiently, giving them as much time as they needed. This could be crucial.

Eventually, Rachel returned to the phone. 'We can't be a hundred per cent, but we think it was around this time last year; March or April. In fact, it must have been early March. It was just before our wedding.'

'Would your stepmother have told anyone else about this?' Mariner asked.

'She might have. I don't really know.'

'Did she report it to the police?'

'I don't think so, because after that the phone calls and everything dried up, so I think she just thought whoever it was had lost interest, or maybe even had made a mistake and sent the flowers to the wrong person.'

'Have you any idea if she kept them, or the note?' Even as he asked, Mariner knew that the chances were slim and that either way Rachel was unlikely to know.

'I can't imagine that she did. I think she

couldn't wait to get rid of them.'

With the customary undertaking to keep in touch, Mariner ended the call.

'Something for you to look out for,' Mariner said to Knox. He recounted the episode with the flowers, as Rachel had told it to him.

'Sounds charming,' said Knox.

Knox drove them back to Granville Lane, and Mariner went to pick up his own car. Thankfully there was no sign of Stephanie.

'Don't forget this,' Knox called as he got out. Reaching down, he picked up the lunch box and tossed it to Mariner, who deftly caught it.

'Thanks,' he said. 'Get the computer across to Max and make a start on going through the paperwork from Nina Silvero's. Meet me at the dance school at three.'

'Where are you going, boss?' Knox asked.

'To see her best friend.'

It was a day of sunshine and showers; a squall had blown up as Millie arrived with Lucy at her house, and they had to make a dash from their cars. Late morning the estate was quiet, most people out at work, but the postman had already delivered and Lucy opened the front door on to a deluge of plastic-sheathed catalogues, from, among others, an outfit called Yummy Mummy Maternity clothes and baby products for the

135

mother-to-be, as well as others on nursery furniture and design.

'It's getting worse,' Lucy cried, starting to gather it all up. 'There are more today than ever. How can I stop Will from seeing them?'

'I'll take them with me,' said Millie, picking up what Lucy couldn't manage. 'I'll follow up with the companies and see if there's any chance of tracing who ordered them.' Though she knew it was unlikely.

Between them they took everything through to the kitchen and dumped it on the counter, where Lucy ripped open one of the more legitimate-looking envelopes. 'I mean, look at this!' She waved a letter in front of Millie's face. It was to thank Lucy, in person, for her enquiry into nursery design. *We will be happy to come and see you as arranged on Thursday, 27 April…* 'I haven't booked this appointment. What if they turn up when Will's here?' Lucy cried. 'He'll go ballistic.' Suddenly her face paled and, clamping a hand over her mouth, she ran out of the room.

Seconds later Millie heard the sound of retching. After pouring a glass of water, Millie took it down the hall to the cloakroom. By the time she got there Lucy was wiping her mouth.

'Are you OK?' Millie asked, squeezing her arm.

'Must be something I ate.' Lucy took the

glass gratefully.

Back in the kitchen Millie steered Lucy to a breakfast-bar stool. 'Don't worry, I'll phone and cancel and explain what has happened.' She picked up the letter. 'Come on, you need to try to calm down a bit. Let's sit and go through these systematically.'

Moments later Millie held up a card, the kind the postman leaves when there's no one home. 'Are you expecting a parcel?' she asked.

Lucy shook her head.

'It's been left at number sixteen.'

'That's Martin's house across the road.'

'OK, I'll go and get it.' Millie got up and retrieved her car keys. 'If it's more of the same I can put it straight in my car, OK?'

Lucy nodded miserably. 'I've been getting lots of junk on the computer too. You should probably see that. I'll go and switch it on.'

'Good idea.'

Outside, the rain had stopped and the sun was shining again. Millie crossed the road to number sixteen, though it took her a couple of minutes to be sure she had the right house, the numbers were so obscure. No car on the drive, but perhaps it was in the garage. She rang the doorbell, which she could hardly hear above the constant droning of what sounded like a distant lawn-mower. Minutes later she was still waiting. She rang again and walked across to the window and peered in. No sign of life inside. She looked at the time on the card – it had been filled in a couple of hours ago. Whoever had taken in the parcel must have subsequently gone out. Coming back down the drive, she noticed for the first time the silver Honda parked a little way down the street, half on the pavement. She was sure it was the car that had been there yesterday. It looked empty and walking a bit nearer confirmed it. She looked around; it could have belonged to someone visiting any of the adjacent houses, but she noted down the description and number anyway.

Millie went back to Lucy's house and found her upstairs staring at the computer screen. Her in-box was stuffed with junk emails, mostly with a similar parental theme, along with the acknowledgements for registering with several Internet dating sites.

'I keep getting these replies from some new mothers' forum.' She pointed at the screen. 'But I haven't joined those sites, why on earth would I?'

'This person is trying to unnerve you, Lucy, that's the intention. Try not to let it get to you.' But even as she said it Millie knew what a tall order that was.

'I feel so foolish.' Lucy dragged her fingers through her hair. 'I'm meant to be an intelligent and confident woman, yet I feel like a wreck, and all because of a bit of stupid post.'

As if to underline the point, the phone rang and Lucy jumped out of her skin. 'It's him! It's happening again! How does he know I'm here?'

'He might not,' said Millie calmly. 'And I'm here now anyway. Let me.' She picked up the ringing phone. 'Hello?'

A woman's voice responded uncertainly: 'Hi, is that Lucy?'

'No,' said Millie. 'Can I ask who's calling?'

'Sure, it's Tess Maguire. I was actually hoping to catch Will before he leaves. Is he there?' With the hint of an Irish accent, this woman sounded bright and relaxed. Millie was sure this wasn't their nuisance caller. 'Just a moment,' she said. Covering the mouthpiece, she said, 'It's someone called Tess, for Will?'

Lucy had recovered enough to roll her eyes in response. 'Tell her I'll ask him to call her back when he gets in, or to try his mobile. At least it means he hasn't gone running to her.'

'Did you think he might have?'

'No, not really.'

Millie did as she was bidden and ended the call. 'Who is she?' she asked Lucy.

'She sings with the band,' Lucy said, making it sound as if that was a bad thing. 'She calls him quite a lot.'

'Are they close?' Millie asked.

Again the defences came up. 'Look, I

don't know what you're trying to imply, but Will and Tess go back a long time, they're old friends, and that's it.'

'I'm not implying anything, Lucy,' Millie said calmly. 'I just want to find out what's going on.'

'Yes, of course. I'm sorry.'

'What's bothering you, Lucy?'

Lucy sighed heavily. 'The other night, when I called Will, there was a woman nearby. As I ended the call I heard her say, "Kiss me, baby"' It was like she said it when she thought he'd switched off his phone.'

'You sure she was talking to Will?'

'I can't be sure, of course, but it was very close.'

'Was it Tess?'

'I don't think so, but I couldn't be sure.'

'Where do you think Will went last night?' Millie asked.

'I don't know. To Leigh's probably. I guess he'll go straight to the gig from there.'

Millie glanced down at the computer. 'We could really do with taking this in to the station, so that our technicians can do a thorough search of the hard drive. That way we may be able to trace back to where some of these emails have come from.'

If it were possible, Lucy looked even more stricken. 'I don't think Will would like that. He uses it a lot when he's at home, dealing with correspondence for the band, setting

140

up gigs and all that.'

And the rest, thought Millie. 'Whose computer is it?'

'Well, it was mine before Will moved in, obviously, but–'

'Well, then, with respect, it's your decision, Lucy. Can I take it now? The quicker we do it, the quicker I can get it back to you. Will may never even need to know.' Millie was more than aware that she was taking advantage of Lucy's vulnerability, bulldozing her like this, but there were several reasons why she wanted their technicians to examine Will Jarrett's online habits. 'It won't take long, I promise.'

What else could Lucy do but cave in? She shut down the computer and between them they disconnected it so that Millie could take it away.

As Millie turned to leave the room, something glinted out on the street and caught her eye, but, when she peered more closely out of the window, she couldn't determine what it was that she'd seen.

Having stowed the computer safely in her boot, along with all the junk mail, Millie waited while Lucy locked up the house, and watched her drive away and back to work. She was just starting up her own car, when, in her rearview mirror she noticed some activity around the silver Honda. A woman was standing behind the open boot, heaving in a wet and dry vacuum cleaner and what looked like a couple of baskets of multi-coloured dusters. She wore a green tabard, and Millie realised that this must be the estate's 'little treasure'. Millie wondered if she regularly serviced houses in the area. If she did, she was the kind of person who just might notice what went on. Weighing up the pros and cons of disclosure, Millie decided that the advantages were more. She got back out of her car, warrant card at the ready, and retraced her steps along the road. She suddenly wondered what Suli would think about the idea of them having a cleaner. The parents would disapprove, of course, but he'd probably be OK and it would make her life a whole lot easier.

As Millie got close to the car a gust of wind snatched a couple of dusters out of the woman's basket and blew them down the pavement towards her. Millie deftly caught them and passed them back to the woman.

'Thanks.' The woman smiled. 'It's really blowing one today, isn't it?' Though not especially tall, she was a large woman and still slightly breathless from the exertion of loading the vacuum. Her hair was tied back behind a headscarf making it difficult to ascertain her age, though Millie would have said in her sixties.

'No problem,' Millie said. 'You do cleaning round here?'

'Yes, and I know what you're going to ask.' The woman gave an apologetic smile. 'I'm sorry, but I don't have any vacancies at the moment. I clean for people elsewhere as well as on this estate.'

'Sounds like you're in demand,' Millie said.

'It's one of those things that people never have enough time for these days, and people know I'm reliable and trustworthy. If I had a pound for everyone who's asked me to do for them...' She shook her head. 'Everyone thinks I can just squeeze in one more, but I really can't; not and do a proper job of it.'

'Who do you clean for in this street?' Millie asked.

'Mr and Mrs Harrison at number thirty-one and Mr Coyle at number eight, and I have a few other clients on the estate, on Woodcroft Road, and Larch Crescent.' She gestured with her head further into the estate. 'As far as I know they have no plans to change that arrangement in the near future.'

'So you must spend some time around here.'

'Yes, I'm here three days.' She was wondering where the conversation was going now.

Millie lifted her warrant card so that the woman could see. 'I'm not actually looking for a cleaner,' she admitted. 'Or at least I wasn't. We're investigating some unwanted phone calls that the person at number nineteen is getting. It's possible that she may be being followed too. Have you noticed anyone suspicious hanging around at all just lately?' Millie asked. 'Or any cars that you wouldn't normally expect to see?'

The woman shook her head. 'No. It's generally very quiet here during the day. Most people are out at work. And I'd notice anyone different hanging about – they'd really stand out.'

'It's what I thought,' said Millie, turning to go, 'thanks, anyway.'

At the last minute she turned back again. 'Out of interest,' she asked, 'if you did have any vacancies, would you go out as far as Hall Green?'

The woman laughed. 'I would, but I'm not kidding. I'm completely full at the moment, couldn't fit another client in.' She sighed and gave a wry smile. 'But if you want to give me your contact details just in case–'

Millie took out a business card. 'Thanks, and, if you should happen to think of anything, give me a call on that number anyway, will you?'

'Yes, of course.'

Estelle Waters lived in a private flat behind electronic gates, with a security guard who gave Mariner a thorough visual going over before he went in, directing him to the correct one of the three huge blocks. No question here of the lifts not working, and he was elevated smoothly to the fifth floor. Waiting for a response to the doorbell, Mariner could hear the yapping of a small hound, and, as Ms Waters opened the door, a bundle of fur came hurtling out at him, did a couple of circuits of his feet, then bolted back into the flat, where it vanished.

'You've got a good guard dog there,' Mariner remarked, showing his warrant card.

'He wouldn't last five minutes with a burglar.' Estelle smiled. 'All bark and no bite. Please, come in, Inspector.'

The apartment smelled of furniture polish and some kind of strong floral scent that Mariner couldn't identify, and heavy dark-wood furniture and dull soft furnishings rendered it dark and gloomy, but for the impressive views from a wide window over leafy Edgbaston, towards the county cricket ground. Estelle Waters was at odds with her surroundings, dressed as she was in light-grey slacks and a pale-yellow sweater and a pair of flat, trainer-type shoes, as if she was just about to go out and play golf. Her naturally greying hair was cut stylishly short, and her lined face had a light, healthy tan. There was a certain gentility and, when she offered him tea, Mariner just knew that it would be Earl Grey served on a tray, with a teapot and bone china cups. Throughout the interview she clutched a crushed tissue in her fist, releasing it every so often to dab at her eyes and nose.

'I still can't believe it,' she said, when they had settled, Mariner in a hard, overstuffed armchair and she on the sofa opposite.

'It was you who raised the alarm, I understand,' Mariner said.

'Yes, that's right. Nina and I were supposed to have met for afternoon tea on the Monday, but she didn't come. She would never miss one of our get-togethers without letting me know why. Then when I rang her house there was no reply, so I knew that something must be badly wrong. I rang around a few people, but no one seemed to have seen or heard from her for a few days. I could have gone round perhaps, but I don't drive and, whilst it's not far, it's not at all a direct journey on public transport. I thought long and hard about contacting your service, Inspector; I'm well aware of the time-wasters you must get, but I felt I was justified.' She turned her gaze to Mariner, her pale-blue eyes misted with tears. 'I thought at worst that perhaps she had fallen or something, I had no idea it would turn out to be so awful.' She brought the tissue to her face to stem the tears.

'It's a good thing you were so vigilant,' Mariner said gently. He sipped his tea before saying, 'You and Nina were obviously close friends.'

She nodded wordlessly.

'Were you aware of anything that was bothering her?'

'I don't know about *bothering* her,' said Estelle. 'She'd suffered a bit of ill health recently, and I think the school was getting her down a bit.'

'Why do you think that was?' Mariner asked.

'It was hard work, and I think was less successful than it had been, but then, getting her MBE, she was thrilled to bits about that. It had given her a real lift. All of us in fact.' She smiled.

'All of you?'

'Three of us meet up regularly; Nina, me and Madge Llewellyn. It's a bit of silliness really, we call ourselves the "Golden Girls" and we all go out together regularly, dinner and the theatre, that kind of thing. Madge will be devastated when she gets back. I haven't been able to reach her yet.'

'She's away?'

'Yes, on holiday for a month. She and Donald are doing one of those tours of the United States. Madge was diagnosed with breast cancer last year, but just before Christmas she was given the all-clear, so they're celebrating.'

'How did you all meet?' asked Mariner.

'Through our husbands; we were thrown together at the same business functions years ago and we just seemed to gel.'

'So you've known each other a long time,' Mariner observed.

She nodded in agreement. 'Must be thirty years or more, through thick and thin; my divorce, Madge's illness. We've all supported each other, come what may.'

'Nina must have been glad of that, eighteen years ago, when her husband died.'

'Of course, you must have known Ronnie.'

It was, Mariner supposed, a reasonable assumption, from her point of view. 'I knew of him,' he said, 'though we never met. That must have been a difficult time for Nina.'

'It was awful; those allegations being made at the same time too, and completely unfounded.'

'You sound very sure of that,' Mariner said.

'I knew Ronnie,' Estelle Waters said simply and Mariner could only admire her blind loyalty.

'So you must also know Rachel.'

Estelle smiled. 'Yes, all our kids grew up together really. We used to spend time together as families.'

'Was Rachel close to her stepmother, would you say?'

'Oh yes. Nina didn't have it easy at first, but they grew very close. I think Rachel just regarded her as she would have her natural mother. After all, her own mother wasn't much of a role model.' She hesitated, choosing her words carefully. 'Rachel was quite an indulged child, not surprisingly I suppose, being an 'only'. We did witness some spectacular tantrums when she was little, if for any reason she couldn't get her own way. And it was Ronnie who was the indulgent one, perhaps because of what had happened with her mum. Nina was always quite firm and felt that Rachel should stand on her own two feet, whereas Ronnie would have given her anything.'

'And you can't think of anyone who would want to hurt Nina like this, for any reason?' Mariner asked.

'To be honest, Inspector, I'd be quite horrified to think that anyone I know could be capable of such a dreadful thing,' Estelle said, her emotions getting the better of her again.

Mariner had one more sensitive area to explore. 'Nina's husband had been dead a long time and she was an attractive woman.' He replaced his empty cup on the tray. 'Are you aware that she had any male friends?'

Estelle flushed. 'Not that I knew of, though I suppose it's possible. She had her admirers, of course, and there was–'

'What?'

'It was probably nothing. I ran into her once, some time ago, in town and she was with a man then. She said he was her cousin, but there was something odd about the way she introduced him. She paused for a moment, thoughtful. 'She didn't tell me his name. I remember thinking at the time that it was peculiar. Normally when you introduce someone you say, "This is my cousin Fred," don't you? But she just said, "This is my cousin. He's staying for a few days." And I got a definite impression that she couldn't wait to get away from me.'

'And you didn't know who this man might be?' Mariner asked.

'No.'

'What did he look like?'

'Middle aged; about our age, I suppose.' Mariner hoped by 'our' she meant herself and Nina. 'He was quite tall and thickset, and his hair was dark, but going thin on top. He was well dressed, in a suit I think. In fact, I remember thinking that he looked as if he should be at work, a solicitor perhaps.'

'And how long ago would this have been?' Mariner asked.

'Oh, it was some time. It must have been soon after Ronnie's death but I can't be sure. The time goes so fast when you get to our age.'

Mariner stood up to go. 'Thank you, Estelle, you've been very helpful.'

'You will catch the man who did this, won't you?' she asked, seeing him out.

'I hope so,' said Mariner. It was the best he could do.

CHAPTER EIGHT

Driving over to his rendezvous with Tony Knox, Mariner felt frustrated by the lack of progress. Nina Silvero's body lying undiscovered for twenty-four hours, and the initial suicide theory had lost them valuable time, and now, coming up to three days on from the murder, they seemed to have gained little ground.

The dance school was held in one of the many Quaker meeting houses in the south Birmingham area, set back behind a row of houses within an acre of impressively tended gardens. Mariner had hoped to catch Susan Brady before the class began, and was pleased to see that the only other vehicle in the car park was Knox's pool car.

Walking across to the building, Mariner updated Knox with the little he had learned from Estelle Waters. 'How's it going with the paperwork?' he asked.

'Well, I haven't found the signed confession from the killer yet, if that's what you mean, boss,' said Knox. 'The finances all seem to be in order and the bank have talked me through her statements, which seem pretty straightforward. She'd paid off her mortgage and had a reasonable income from her state pension along with the salary she was drawing from the dancing school. Quite a few investments too. The estate will be worth a tidy sum.'

Mariner's phone pinged.

'That your admirer again?' asked Knox. He took Mariner's lack of response as confirmation. 'If you don't want to see her again you should let her know.'

Mariner looked up in disbelief. 'Relationship advice? From you?'

They had to ring the bell to be admitted, and were met by Susan Brady; small and slight, in a white T-shirt and black leggings, her hair piled up on her head and held in place with a clip, a few stray frizzy strands escaping. She brought with her the scent of vanilla. She seemed young to have such responsibility, Mariner thought, though recognised that he'd reached the age where it wasn't just the coppers who seemed just out of kindergarten.

Introductions made, she took them through a small entrance lobby and into the main hall, with high windows that flooded the room with late-afternoon sunshine. At the far end of the hall an elderly woman pounding on an upright piano nodded an acknowledgement to them and continued with her playing.

'Sorry to have kept you,' Susan apologised. 'But it's coming up to audition time and I'm going to have to break it to some of the parents this evening that their daughters aren't being entered, and explain why. I need to be prepared.' She was softly spoken with a slight lisp.

'Auditions for what?' Mariner wanted to know.

'Some of the girls try out with the Birmingham Ballet or the Royal College in London. It's crunch time because what we're saying is whether or not some of the girls have a future in dancing. It can shatter a few illusions.'

'Do many of the girls go through?' Mariner asked.

'To be honest, they're in the minority. Most girls are just not built for the long haul, or don't have the discipline. They start off well while they're little but then they grow, and in reality very few girls have, or can maintain, the right physique to be successful ballet dancers.'

'And who makes that decision, whether or not to audition?'

'The final call is down to us,' said Susan. 'Some of it is about cost – we have to pay to enter girls – and we do get parents who want to pay themselves, but the main thing we have to consider is the standing of the school. If we enter too many girls who are really not up to scratch, simply on the off-chance that they might get in, we'd soon start to develop the wrong kind of reputation. Sometimes that means making harsh choices.'

'Do you meet much resistance?' Mariner asked.

'Most of the girls usually know themselves. It's most difficult with the pushy parents, who have been convinced all along that their offspring is going to be the next Darcy Bussell, regardless of ability. They don't have a realistic view of what the standards are like.' She flashed a wry smile. 'It's one of the many times I'm going to miss Nina. She was a great believer in honesty, and never one to mince her words if she felt any of the girls weren't going to make it.'

'That must have upset some people,' Mariner said.

'Oh no, she was always tactful about it. I'm just a wuss. I hate having to break that kind of news.' Her face clouded. 'I'm sorry, wittering on. It's Nina you came to talk about, isn't it? It's terrible what happened to her; I can't believe it. The parents are upset and it's been really difficult knowing what to tell the girls. They're so young, some of them. It's too much for them to take in, but of course a lot of them have seen it on the news and recognised her name.'

Mariner wondered if she was always this garrulous or whether nerves were playing a part. 'How long had you worked with Nina?'

he asked.

'For the last fifteen years; I was a pupil of hers when I was a kid and, though I gave up when I left school, I never really went away. We're – we were a team; Nina, me and Mrs Parker.'

'Mrs Parker?'

'Our pianist.' Susan gestured across the room.

'She looks as if she could run the class,' Mariner observed.

'Oh no, she's a formidable woman, Mrs Parker, and she plays the piano beautifully, but she'd be the first to admit that Nina was the one with the magic touch.'

'How old is she?' Mariner asked, thinking that the old dear looked about to keel over.

'About a hundred and twenty I think.' Susan smiled. 'She's been doing this for ever.'

'And being paid for it?'

'Of course.'

'How is the business doing?' Mariner asked.

'We get by, though I'd be lying if I said that it's thriving,' Susan admitted. 'Ballet for little girls isn't as popular as it once was. Far too much competition from other activities.'

'Was it doing well enough to provide two incomes?'

She smiled wryly. 'Well, I'll never be a millionaire, but that's not what I'm in it for. And I think, for Nina, she had her husband's pension and all that, so she didn't go short.'

'But I understand Nina was about to retire anyway.'

This time Susan laughed out loud. 'Nina has been going to retire ever since I've been here. I don't think she ever would have, she loved it too much.'

'How did you feel about that?'

She was thoughtful for a moment. 'I'd have to be honest and say it could be frustrating at times. Nina wanted to run things as she always had, teaching only the purist stuff. I think it would have been good to diversify a little and offer some modern dance. With traditional ballet there's a lot of hard work before it even starts to look like anything impressive.'

'What will happen to the business now?'

She shrugged. 'I really don't know. We talked hypothetically about me buying Nina out if she ever did give it up, but I haven't any idea whether she ever did anything about it.'

'And, if she did, you'd introduce modern dance?' Mariner queried.

Susan wasn't stupid, she could see how it looked. But she was honest. 'Yes, I probably would,' she said, a touch discomfited.

As they were talking, the room had been steadily filling up, parents arriving with their diminutive offspring in pink leotards and cardigans, some of them impossibly small. It was a paedophile's wet dream, Mariner's twisted copper's mind told him. Both children and adults regarded Mariner and Knox with suspicion, though the adults at least may have been able to guess who they were. As if suddenly noticing all the activity, Susan checked her watch.

'We won't keep you much longer,' Mariner said. He lowered his voice. 'The girls who don't get chosen to audition – do any of the parents take it personally?'

'They're disappointed naturally,' Susan replied. 'We're always aware of the keen ones, and sometimes they've invested a lot–' She broke off. 'You mean enough to harm Nina? Absolutely not. Ballet's competitive, like anything else, but no one I know would take it to that extreme.'

'Even so, we'll need the details of all your pupils and their parents, past and present.'

'Is that really necessary?'

'We need to check anyone who might have been in contact with Nina in the last few weeks.'

'Oh yes, of course. I haven't got a full list here, but there's one at home on my computer. I'll send it to you.'

'That would be helpful,' Mariner said. 'Some of the girls must have been coming here for years. Nina will have built up strong relationships.'

Susan nodded. 'Some better than others, yes.'

'Would she ever have invited any of the parents round to her house?' Mariner asked.

'I doubt it.' She pulled a face. 'Nina was very professional. Though she loved it, the dance school was her job.'

'And how about you? Did you and Nina socialise at all?'

'No, we got on well and we had a laugh, but it was strictly business.'

'So you wouldn't know if she had any men friends.'

'Nina was quite a private person in that sense, and I'm so much younger than her. I don't think she would have told me about things like that. Although once, ages ago, a man picked her up after the session,' she confided. 'When I came out they were just driving off. He had quite a big car, a saloon like a Jaguar or something. But after that I never saw him again and she never mentioned him. Could have been anyone I suppose.' *Like a cousin.* The crowd at the other end of the room was getting restless and she cast anxious eyes towards them. Mariner terminated the conversation.

'Our Siobhan used to do ballet,' Knox said of his now grown-up daughter, as he and Mariner walked back out to their cars. 'I suppose most girls go through that phase, don't they?'

'Do they?' It was beyond Mariner's experience. 'Was she any good?' He'd never met

158

Siobhan, but, if she'd inherited her dad's powerful, wiry physique, then she might have been.

'I don't know. She gave it all up when she was about ten; wouldn't be seen dead in a tutu. Theresa was gutted.'

Mariner didn't know why he'd agreed to meet Stephanie Rieger on Wednesday evening. Following Knox's dubious advice, he'd intended to finish it over the phone, but somehow he couldn't bring himself to do that. Instead he had committed to meeting her face to face so that he could let her down gently. Not that 'it' had ever started; only in her head. Did one shag constitute a relationship? He remembered the old joke about one swallow not making the grade, but then that took his thoughts off in completely the wrong direction. He'd arranged to meet Stephanie in a city-centre bar, off Colmore Row; neutral territory and with public transport for her to get home, so avoiding any last-minute temptation.

Driving into the city, Mariner caught the local news bulletin on BRMB, which included a thirty-second slot for Nina Silvero, during which the announcer said that police were appealing for a key witness to come forward. They'd got in just in time. The MBE had raised the profile enough for some media coverage, but another twenty-four hours and

Nina Silvero would be old news, replaced by the regular stabbings and shootings that seemed an almost daily occurrence in the city these days. Already the top slot had been taken by a twenty-three-year-old attacked by a gang on the Birchfield Road, who weren't keen on his overtaking strategy.

Mariner arrived at the agreed rendezvous first, ordered himself a beer and was beginning to think optimistically that Stephanie might not show up, when there she was, tottering in on incredibly high heels and planting a heavily perfumed kiss on his cheek. 'Hi, sorry I'm late, darling.' *Did she just call him darling?* 'Had to wait ages for a bus and then it took for ever. I hate buses – they're such nasty, smelly things.'

She seemed to Mariner to be way over-dressed for a bus ride and a quick drink, in a tight dress with a neckline that finished some way down her cleavage, magnetically drawing his gaze.

'What would you like to drink?' he asked, seeing a temporary escape route at the bar.

'Oh, my usual please, dry white spritzer.'

Bringing it back to the table, Mariner was keen to get the business over with then and there, but as she'd only just arrived it seemed a little unreasonable. And he didn't really get the chance.

'You look tired,' Stephanie said proprietorially, as he sat down. 'Had a hard day?'

160

'We're working on a difficult case, yes,' Mariner admitted, reluctant to get into a discussion about it.

'I heard about it, it's that murder, isn't it?' Her eyes gleamed and Mariner wondered if she was getting some kind of thrill from being linked, however tenuously, with the drama. 'I said to my friend, "I bet Tom's working on that one." I was so excited to find out that you're a policeman,' she went on, confirming his fears. 'I've never been out with a policeman before.'

'Yes, did I actually tell you that?' Mariner said, feigning memory loss.

'You must have done, how else would I have known? Cheers!' Raising her glass, she sipped delicately at it.

'I didn't give you my phone number,' Mariner pointed out.

'Oh, I know, that was a bit naughty of me but, when I picked up your jacket to hang it up, your mobile fell out of the pocket, so I thought I may as well make a note of your number then, and save you the bother later.'

It was said so smoothly that Mariner was sure she'd convinced herself that it was really what happened. He needed to put a stop to this now. 'The truth is, Steph, this is what we need to talk about,' he began. 'Don't get me wrong, I mean, I like you, but I'm not ready to get into another relationship. I've only recently finished–'

'I know, with Anna,' she cut in. 'But that was over a year ago, wasn't it? And she's moved on. Got to dip your toe back in the water sometime, Tom.'

'I told you that?' Mariner was reeling now. He had absolutely no memory of having any discussion with her about Anna. He never talked to anyone about Anna. But how else could she know?

She leaned over and put her hand over his. 'It's all right. I can understand that you're afraid of committing yourself after you've been so badly hurt, but we can take things slowly.'

Christ, was this what she called slowly?

'Look, you really don't understand,' Mariner said, pulling his hand away. 'The other night was very nice, but it was a one-off, that's all. We were attracted to each other, we slept together, end of story. I thought we were both grown up enough to understand that.'

Mariner knew instantly that he'd made a mistake. Her eyes, behind spidery mascara, hardened. 'Oh, I see. I was just a quick screw, was I, while you wait for something better to come along?' Her voice was just a little too loud and one or two people at the adjacent tables turned in their direction.

Mariner lowered his voice, aware that this was morphing into a drama cliché. 'I thought it was the same for you,' he said.

162

'You were flirting with me. You made the offer.'

'I was being nice to you,' she retorted. 'Do you think I go that far with any man who comes into the restaurant?'

She was practically yelling now and Mariner had to resist an urge to crawl under the table to avoid the accusing stares that were coming his way. 'Of course I don't–'

'Bastard!' And she finished the tirade with a textbook finale, picking up his drink and throwing it in his face, except that he'd been there a while and the glass was practically empty, so, instead, a single, pathetic drop dribbled out and ran down her hand. It looked so comical that Mariner couldn't help himself. He laughed, a deep belly laugh. For a split second he thought the whole glass was coming his way, and prepared to duck, but, to his amazement, her expression crumbled and Stephanie laughed too. Mariner was itching to turn to the other customers and say 'show's over folks,' as they do in all the best movies, but instead he passed Stephanie a napkin to dry her hand. 'You realise you've ruined my reputation now, don't you?' he said lightly, glancing around to check that they were no longer the main attraction.

'Mine too, probably,' she said wryly.

'I really am sorry,' Mariner said. 'I got it wrong. I thought you wanted the same as me. One night, no strings.'

'You got it spectacularly wrong.' She fixed her gaze on him. 'I don't do that kind of thing. Yes, I flirt with the male customers, even the ugly ones, but I've never taken anyone back to my place before. It took me all evening to pluck up the courage to ask you, because you seemed nice and I really hoped it could be the start of something.'

Oh fuck, thought Mariner, now she's going to cry.

Instead, she said, 'And now I've made a real idiot of myself too.' She started to gather up her things. 'I should go. I'm sorry I've wasted your time.'

'You haven't,' said Mariner. 'Honestly, you cheered me up.' He stood up with her. 'I haven't had a laugh like that all day; all week. At least let me drive you home.'

Despite giving her a lift, Mariner had resisted a further offer from Stephanie, but they had parted on reasonable terms, at least good enough that he was confident that his suits would be safe.

When he got up on Thursday morning, Kat was in the kitchen. No cooked breakfast today, but she'd made fresh coffee, which was a welcome wake-up.

'I like to go out tonight,' she announced.

Mariner curbed momentary disappointment. 'Who with?'

'Is *with whom*,' she corrected him cheekily.

164

'I go with my friends from the English centre.'

'Where will you go?'

'We go to Angelo's on Broad Street.'

Mariner's disappointment was displaced by anxiety. 'Angelo's?'

'Is a club,' she told him.

'Yes, I know.' It frequently featured on the Intranet bulletins at work as the regular venue for late-night disturbances. Mariner didn't like the sound of it. 'I'm not sure that it's a good idea,' he said moderately, and watched her face fall. 'Some people get very drunk,' he followed up lamely. 'They might pester you.'

'Pester?'

'Come after you; bother you.'

'Is OK, Giles is take me,' Kat said brightly.

'Giles?' Mariner's ears pricked up. She hadn't mentioned that name before.

'He's my friend.'

'Oh. Where did you meet him?'

'At the centre.' She was being vague.

'What does he do?'

She looked blank.

'His job?'

'He's a businessman.'

'What kind of business?' Mariner knew she didn't deserve the interrogation, but at the back of his mind he was thinking that the two men who had lured Kat into prostitution would doubtless have described themselves

165

as businessmen.

She shrugged. 'I think he tell me, but I don't remember.'

'When is he picking you up?' Mariner asked, thinking that he'd be sure to be around then. But again he was foiled.

'He meet me from work,' said Kat.

So it was a *fait accompli*. Mariner wanted to say no, it's not safe for you to go out in the evening, that she belonged at home with him where he could keep an eye on her, but deep down he knew that it was not his place. 'Just be careful then,' he said.

Kat stopped chewing her toast and went distant.

'What?'

'Is what my dad say,' she told him. She turned to Mariner. 'I think that I like to see my mum and dad again one day.'

'Good,' said Mariner, hoping that it was an adequate response.

Tony Knox was already at his desk and had resumed his painstaking analysis of the paperwork taken from Nina Silvero's bureau.

'How'd it go with Stephanie? How did she take it?' he asked.

Mariner coloured a little. 'Fine,' he said simply but firmly closing off that conversation. 'Found anything useful?'

'I came across this.' Knox passed Mariner a white embossed booklet, the order of service for Rachel Hordern's wedding. 'Must have been a lavish affair and it looks as if Mum paid for it all. There are some pretty hefty sums going out of her bank account around that time to Brackleys.'

Mariner perused the booklet. 'No crime against that, if you've got the money, I suppose.'

Across the room, Millie also seemed to be preparing to spend Thursday morning engaged on a paper chase. Mariner couldn't help but notice the mound of catalogues on her desk. 'I hope you haven't brought your home-shopping habit in to work, DC Khatoon.'

'I went back to see Lucy Jarrett yesterday,' Millie said, with a shake of head.

'I thought she'd asked you to drop it? Something else has happened?'

Millie told him about the 999 call.

'And what did Lucy say about the attack?' Mariner asked.

'That it wasn't,' said Millie. 'According to her, she and Will had just had an argument.'

'Do you think he might be knocking her about?'

'I didn't see any physical damage, but she seemed happy for me to pick up the investigation again.'

'OK,' said Mariner. 'Did you get any joy from the Asheville police?'

'They were pretty responsive,' Millie said.

'Got back to me almost straight away. I spoke to a Lieutenant McCoy. They have no record on Will, but McCoy's going to make further enquiries. Meanwhile, I thought I'd get stuck into this little lot; this is just what came in yesterday's post.'

'Christ, the postman must love her,' said Mariner. 'What's the common theme?'

'Mostly that it's all stuff that would make Will angry,' Millie said. 'And he seems to be on a short fuse as it is. This is looking more and more like someone trying to drive a wedge between them.'

'Have you come across any likely candidates?'

'Well, no one seems that overjoyed about their marriage,' Millie told him. 'Apparently it all happened pretty quickly. Best friend clearly had her nose put out of joint because Will chose Lucy over her, mother thinks he's not good enough for her – except of course that all mothers think that. Her colleague at the health centre thinks he's only after her money.'

'All of which brings us to the possibility that it could be the man himself,' said Mariner.

'That's what I'd been thinking. And he's the one in a position to arrange it all; knows their postal address, obviously, has access to the computer, and knows when she's at home. Lucy said it herself, the phone calls never happen while he's there.'

'But what's the motive?' Mariner asked. 'Surely he knows which side his bread's buttered. He has a life of luxury from what you've said, plus he has the freedom to go off and do what he wants, while Lucy waits at home for him, the dutiful wife.'

'There's another woman around,' Millie said.

'Now why didn't I see that one coming? Lucy knows about her?'

'Yes. I don't mean "around" in that sense, at least I don't have any evidence of that yet, but she's the singer in the band. She called while I was there, wanting to speak to Will. According to Lucy there's a history, but now they're just good friends. The woman clearly isn't her bosom buddy, but she seems happy that it's all perfectly innocent.'

'We've heard that one often enough,' Mariner pointed out. 'It could be a scam set up by the two of them. Will meets Lucy, finds out that she's loaded, marries her after a whirlwind love affair, then Lucy starts to behave bizarrely, claiming that she's being followed and getting funny phone calls and he divorces her for unreasonable behaviour. It's like *Gaslight* all over again.'

'What?'

Mariner shook his head. 'Never mind; before your time. But, as a consequence of all this, Will would end up with his share of

Lucy's worldly goods, leaving him financially secure and free to go off with this other woman.'

'It could explain why he's so desperate that they don't have children too,' Millie added. 'Much harder to go through all that if there are kids involved.'

'Yes, it makes you wonder how well Lucy really knows her husband,' Mariner said.

'I'm hoping to get something from their computer,' said Millie. 'Max is looking at it for me now. Meanwhile, I'm contacting the companies that have sent all this stuff to see if we can trace any of it back.' She indicated the pile of catalogues.

'Anything yet?'

'Not so far.' She looked despondently at the stack. 'None of these companies keeps records of who contacts them for information. The assumption is that it's the person at the address where it was sent.'

'OK,' said Mariner. 'Well, keep at it and let me know if anything turns up. Actually, Lucy's not the only one getting nasty things in the post. Nina Silvero got sent some dead flowers with a nasty note.'

'This is a continuous campaign, though. Hardly the same thing, is it?'

'No, you're right.' Mariner turned to go, but hesitated.

'Everything all right, sir?'

'I'm a bit concerned about Kat.' Mariner

recounted the girl's lack of concentration on the film they'd watched. 'And now she's going out with some bloke. Do you think I should do something?'

'Maybe you should talk to Lorelei,' Millie suggested. 'She's got more experience with that kind of thing.'

Mariner had the number of the refuge counsellor written down somewhere. But it took him a good ten minutes to locate the scrap of paper it was scribbled on; he phoned Lorelei straight away. 'I'm not sure what's going on. What do you think?'

'How does she seem?' Lorelei asked.

'Happy enough, I suppose, but distracted.'

'It sounds as if Kat is at the point where she needs more independence. She's doing what any other twenty-year-old would be doing. You should be pleased. If she's feeling secure enough to do that, it means that you've done a great job. And, as for this guy, maybe you need to trust her on this.'

Mariner wasn't so sure about that, and was considering possible tactics, when there was a knock on his door and he looked up to see Millie. She handed him a printout.

'What's this?'

'Leigh Hawkins' itinerary, Max got it off Will's computer. It's a bit short notice, I know, but I see he's performing at the White Hart in Bilston tonight. Looks like the kind of poky little Black Country pub that's right up your street. I thought it might be worth going to see what he's like, without him noticing us. Fancy coming with me?'

'You asking me on a date, DC Khatoon, and you a married woman?'

'You need to get out more.'

'Kat might like to come,' Mariner said brightly.

Millie pulled a face. 'She's twenty years old. A folk club? I don't think so.'

No, and Kat had other arrangements for tonight of course. 'OK. I'll meet you there. Something I have to do first.' And he was saved from further explanation by Millie's phone ringing out in the bull pen.

CHAPTER NINE

Millie's caller was Lucy Jarrett. 'I went and collected the parcel from across the road,' she told Millie. 'It's a Pound Puppy.'

'What on earth's that?' Millie hadn't come across them before.

'It's like a kid's soft toy,' Lucy explained.

'So, continuing with the baby motif then,' said Millie.

'Sort of,' Lucy agreed. 'But it is strange because, although it's washed and quite

172

clean, I don't think it's new. It's quite worn in places. It looks sort of familiar, too.'

'Like one you had when you were little perhaps?' Millie hazarded.

'No, it's not that,' said Lucy. 'It's more that I feel I've seen it before somewhere.'

'Can you remember where?'

'That's the thing.' Lucy sounded exasperated. 'I've racked my brains, but I just can't place it.'

'OK,' Millie said. 'We'll have it in to get forensics to look at it. That might help us to establish where it's come from. Could you drop it in at the station, along with all the packaging?'

'Sure,' said Lucy. 'I'll bring it in at lunchtime.'

'How's everything else?' Millie asked.

'I'm OK,' said Lucy, but she didn't sound too sure.

Susan Brady had fulfilled her obligation and, when Mariner logged on to his computer, there was an emailed list of dance-school pupils, past and present, waiting in his in-box. Going back to 1981, it ran into dozens of names. With all the paperwork they'd brought back from Nina Silvero's house, they would have their work cut out for them, but Mariner was reluctant to hand it over to any junior officers and risk important connections being overlooked.

'This is just what I joined the police for,' muttered Knox, when Mariner took the list out to him.

'Me too,' piped up Millie, from behind her own paperwork. 'I'd love to see them make a two-hour drama special for the telly out of this.'

'Oh, yeah, and I found this earlier this morning, boss.' Knox passed Mariner a small florist's card, inscribed: *A flower that isn't nurtured withers and dies. I'm going to make sure it happens to you. Happy Anniversary.* 'Not sure how it helps though.'

It was the kind of card that florists included with flowers all the time, but, aside from the floral illustration, bore no other distinguishing features. 'Nor me,' admitted Mariner. 'It looks as if it could even be homemade. All it confirms is that this time last year Nina Silvero was getting threats. Doesn't help us find out where they were coming from.'

In actual fact, Knox didn't really mind his new task. Making a few phone calls would be a welcome change from trawling through the contents of Nina Silvero's bureau. At least this way he got to speak to someone. That was the theory anyway, but in practice it turned out to be less straightforward.

He began logically at the beginning of the list, and not surprisingly, in the twenty-odd years since their daughters had attended

174

ballet classes, many of the parents had moved on. After several wrong numbers and even more of the 'not-been-recognised' variety, he almost crowed with excitement when at last a woman picked up the phone and announced her name as the one he had in front of him. When Knox explained the reason for his call, she made the customary sympathetic noises; yes, she had seen the news and couldn't believe it. Nina was such a lovely person, whoever would want to do that etc. No, she couldn't think of anyone who might want to harm her. She herself hadn't seen Nina for years, since her daughter had left the school.

'Jonquil adored her,' she said.

'And is your daughter still dancing?' Knox asked finally, completely unnecessarily, but heady from the prospect of crossing off a name on the long list.

There was an ominous pause before the woman said, 'My daughter died five years ago, sergeant.'

'So I'm either completely wasting my time, or putting my size tens in it,' Knox grumbled to Mariner and Millie later, over lunch in the canteen. 'Most of the numbers don't exist, or the people don't live there any more, and the one result I do get, that happens. Imagine how that was. I'm there getting her to go over all these memories, and all along – I mean, talk about tactless.'

'Did she say how she died?' Mariner asked.

'No, and I didn't ask. I just wanted to get off the phone.' Knox stopped chewing his sausage and mash. 'You think it could have been a fatal *pas de deux*?'

Mariner cringed. 'You need to keep a rein on that so-called sense of humour of yours.' But even he could see that the exercise wasn't the most efficient use of his sergeant's time. 'Call Susan Brady back and go through the list with her to see if she remembers any parents who had any kind of issues, especially with their daughters not being auditioned, any who might have felt aggrieved. That should cut down the numbers.' Though he was inclined to agree with Brady, that murder, especially one so vile, seemed a disproportionate response to failing a dance audition. It was just that at the moment there seemed little else. 'Start with them and, if it's not going anywhere, we'll think again.'

Millie had hardly started her pasta bake when her pager went off. 'My Pound Puppy's arrived,' she told the two men. 'Don't ask.' Having arranged her knife and fork, she got up from the table.

'What about your dinner?' Knox was horrified that she would simply abandon it.

'I want to speak to Lucy, make sure she's OK,' Millie replied. 'I should have had a

176

salad anyway. Suli thinks I'm putting on weight.'

Both Knox and Mariner watched her go. 'Do you reckon her Suli needs his eyes testing?' Knox wondered aloud.

When Millie got down to reception, Lucy had been and gone. The toy was there waiting for her: a soft black and white dog with floppy ears. Nothing-overtly sinister about that.

Taking it back upstairs, she met Mariner and Knox returning from lunch. Seeing the toy, Knox was equally dismissive. 'I remember these,' he said. 'Our Siobhan had loads of them. In fact, one of these got me into trouble.'

'Oh, yes?'

'It was Siobhan's exam mascot. But she forgot to take it to school one morning, when she was doing her GCSEs. I'm out on patrol, and I get this panic phone call from Theresa, asking me to pick it up from the house and get it to school for her before the exam started.'

Mariner could see what was coming. 'And you used your blues and twos,' he said.

'How else was I gonna get through the rush-hour traffic?' Knox said indignantly. 'And I missed a briefing session too. I got a right bollocking over that.'

Millie was inclined to agree with Lucy that

this was a strange one. After bagging up the Pound Puppy, she passed it straight on to forensics.

The results from Nina Silvero's computer had come back, and were on Mariner's desk along with a forensics update, when he got back from lunch. The PC was a new one as they'd thought and consequently the hard drive was practically empty, though interestingly the history indicated Nina had been looking at some Internet dating sites for the more mature person, making Mariner wonder again about the man she'd been seen with. But there was no indication that she'd registered with any of these sites, and the only emails she'd sent, formal affairs, written in the style of letters, were to her stepdaughter.

The forensic report seemed only to support what Mariner and Knox had already worked out. The screwtop for the wine bottle on Nina Silvero's kitchen table had been found in the bin, and there were traces of acid in the sink's u-bend; in other words, nothing that contradicted the version of events that he and Knox had put together. There was also a note about the contents of the grey plastic bottle, which Mariner couldn't fully decipher, so he rang the lab.

'It was something unexpected,' Rick Fraser told him, 'though I'll leave you to work out the implications. We did a full chemical analysis on what was left in the plastic bottle. It wasn't the original content.'

'How do you mean?' Mariner asked, feeling dense.

'I mean the bottle was an old one, and the original contents must have been disposed of, because what was in there doesn't match with what the label says. It's close; the main ingredient is still sulphuric acid, but it's combined with anionic wetting agents.'

'Meaning?'

'What was in the drain-cleaner bottle wasn't drain cleaner, but paint stripper, more specifically, one designed to remove paint from rubber surfaces. The wetting agents reduce the surface tension of the paint, allowing it to be lifted off.' Good old Rick, always providing far more information than was needed.

'So who might use that?' Mariner asked, cutting to the chase.

'As far as I know it's not a domestically used product,' Rick said. 'But it would be used anywhere where industrial-scale painting goes on; anywhere that surfaces need to be cleaned afterwards, maybe a paint shop or something like that.'

'OK, thanks, Rick, that's been helpful.' Mariner was studying the report again and considering the implications of what Fraser had said, when a shadow fell across his desk and there was a tentative knock on the door. He looked up to see PC Solomon.

'Come in.' Mariner gestured to the chair opposite him. 'How are you doing?'

'I'm fine, sir, thanks,' Solomon said, lowering his considerable bulk.

'Not easy, making that kind of discovery,' Mariner said. 'Are you coping all right with it?'

'Yes, sir, I think so.' Solomon was clutching his notebook.

'What have you got for us?'

'I was assigned the house-to-house on Mrs Silvero's street,' Solomon said. 'I thought you might want to know this.' He consulted his notebook. 'The woman who lives next door to Nina Silvero, Audrey Patterson. There was no one at home when I first went round, so I had to go back this morning. It might be nothing but–'

'Go on,' Mariner prompted.

'She was out working in her back garden a couple of weeks back when she overheard what she called a "heated exchange" between Nina Silvero and her stepdaughter.'

Suddenly Mariner was interested.

'She said that basically it sounded like Rachel Hordern was asking for money, a loan so that she and her husband could start some kind of business enterprise.' Solomon read from the notes he'd taken. 'Nina Silvero refused, the two of them argued for a bit, and then Rachel left.' He looked up again at Mariner. 'I thought you might want to speak to her.'

'You thought exactly right,' said Mariner, lifting his jacket from the back of the chair. 'Well done, Ralph. You just got yourself another Brownie point.'

Audrey Patterson had been Nina Silvero's neighbour for thirty years, she told Mariner as they sat in a conservatory overlooking her garden, and, Mariner deduced, was probably about the same age. The shoulder-length hair would have long since ceased to be naturally ebony, but her face was smooth and unlined. She had agreed to see Mariner before her Thursday-afternoon yoga class and was dressed in preparation for it in a plum-coloured velour track suit.

Audrey had been devastated by what had happened to Nina. 'I feel terrible, because Ray and I always try to be good neighbours. We were out at a church function the night she died, but we were at home all day on that Monday, so we must have been going about our business here while she was lying in the kitchen–' She broke off, unable to say the word. 'I feel dreadful about it.'

'You weren't to know,' Mariner reassured her. 'We'd all like the gift of x-ray vision sometimes. But I understand you overheard an argument between Nina and her stepdaughter quite recently.'

'Yes, it was a couple of weeks ago. Rachel and the baby came to stay for the weekend.'

'Not Rachel's husband?' asked Mariner.

'No. Rachel visited her mother quite often – every couple of weeks or so – and I think it was more difficult for Adam to get away.'

'And you overheard a disagreement?' Mariner prompted.

'Yes, it was on the Sunday afternoon. I think little Harry must have been having a nap because I noticed that the back curtains were drawn. I wasn't eavesdropping, I couldn't help but hear.' She was keen to make that clear. 'I was doing some weeding in the flowerbed just down here–' she indicated an immaculate border just beyond the window '–and they were out on the patio, and speaking quite loudly.'

'So you heard exactly what was said?' Mariner checked.

'Oh, yes. Nina was saying, "I can't do it any more. I've given you what I can and I've got my own old age to think about." Then Rachel suggested that Nina could sell the house and get somewhere smaller, but Nina wasn't having any of it. She said, "This is my home," and I remember thinking, good for you. Rachel always was rather spoiled, especially by her father. Not long after that, I saw her and the baby leaving.'

'Do you think Rachel and Nina parted on

182

good terms?' Mariner asked.

'Oh I think so.' She seemed sure. 'I saw Nina a few days later and she said what a lovely weekend they'd had.'

'She didn't mention the argument?' Mariner asked.

'Oh, no. We've been neighbours a long time but we don't interfere with each other's business.'

Pity, thought Mariner. 'You must have been aware of who came and went at Nina's house, though,' he said.

'Sometimes, of course,' she said.

'Do you ever remember seeing any male visitors?'

'Not recently,' Audrey said. 'Just after Ronnie died, there was a man who came to the house now and again.'

'A workman?'

'No, he was too well dressed for that. I did wonder at the time what kind of relationship it was. None of my business, of course, but it did seem a bit soon to be taking up with someone else. But he stopped coming after a few months.'

'Do you remember what he looked like?' Mariner asked.

Audrey sighed. 'Not really. This was a long time ago.' A squirrel scampered across the lawn, distracting her momentarily. 'I think he was quite tall and well built, with dark hair, though balding a bit. He drove quite a big car; a Rover or something like that.'

Sitting in his car out on the street, Mariner made a phone call, and on his way back to Granville Lane he took a detour to the offices of Mercer, Brooke and Hanley, an old and well-established partnership that had offices in a Georgian villa on the Harborne side of Five Ways. Outwardly a traditional law firm, Nina's solicitor, Sarah Wagstaffe, clearly brought the glamour to the practice. She took Mariner into a refurbished modern office that overlooked the car park.

'Have you been Mrs Silvero's solicitor for long?' Mariner asked.

'About seven years. Nina was one of my first clients. I took her on from Mr Brooke, by mutual agreement of course.'

'And did you have much contact with Mrs Silvero?'

'We've met about half a dozen times. She has been very conscientious about keeping her will up to date, so I last saw her shortly after her grandson was born. A sensible woman.'

And lucrative client, Mariner thought, but he kept that to himself. She had copies of the will ready for Mariner to take, and on the way out they passed an older man in reception.

'Ah, this is Mr Brooke,' Sarah introduced them.

It occurred to Mariner as he shook Brooke's hand that he vaguely fitted the description of the man Estelle Waters and Audrey Patterson had seen. 'What sort of car do you drive, Mr Brooke?' he asked.

'A Range Rover,' said Brooke, understandably taken aback by the question. 'Always have done.'

Mariner took the will back to Granville Lane where he and Knox pored over copies, Knox glad of the respite. Nina Silvero, it transpired, had been generous in her donations to charity, including the police benevolent fund, so it didn't appear that she bore any grudges there. The ballet school, along with any profits or losses, was bequeathed to Susan Brady, and, apart from a sum to be put into trust for her grandson, the remaining estate, running into several hundred thousand even before the house had been sold, would go to Rachel Hordern.

'The ballet school is an interesting one,' Mariner remarked.

'In what way?' said Knox.

'*Along with profits and losses,*' Mariner quoted. 'Susan Brady admitted to us that it was beginning to struggle. Much better for her to take control of it while it's still viable and she has a chance of turning things around than wait until it's in real trouble.'

'Taking into account that argument,

wouldn't Rachel Hordern have been pretty anxious to get her hands on her cut sooner rather than later, too?' Knox speculated. 'You reckon there's any chance that these two women knew each other?'

'The stepdaughter and the business partner?' Mariner hadn't considered it before. 'They must be about the same age. I would say there's every chance.'

'Perhaps we should find out for sure.'

'Well, we should bump into them both tomorrow at the funeral,' said Mariner. 'Something to look forward to.'

CHAPTER TEN

On Thursday evening, Mariner really had no justification for being in the bar opposite the Brass House language centre other than spying. From where he sat idly turning the icy beer bottle in his fingertips, he had a perfect vantage point for seeing who emerged from the building. As it was he almost missed them because he didn't immediately recognise the glamorous young woman who emerged arm in arm with a tall, dark young man in a sharp suit. Kat had changed out of her formal work clothes and was wearing a short, clinging dress and high heels, a short jacket over the top. Mariner had never seen her dressed like that before. It made him feel uneasy.

Giles, if this was him, and Mariner was certain that it was, was speaking into a mobile. He wasn't what Mariner had expected or hoped for; for a start he was younger and better looking. There was clearly some playful banter going on between him and Kat as they came down the steps of the centre and turned to walk along Broad Street. Mariner abandoned his beer and started after them at what he hoped was a discreet distance. As he followed, he watched Giles take Kat's hand, raise it to his mouth and kiss it.

Mariner tailed them at a distance down a side street and into the entrance to a multi-storey car park. Once in the winding concrete stairwell he lost sight of them and had to monitor their ascent by the sound effects. A flight below, he fell into step with the rhythmic echoing footsteps, until they halted suddenly, and a few seconds of silence was punctuated by the clanging of a door. Mariner bolted up the remaining stairs and pushed open the next exit door on to what he hoped was the right level. Casting about the rows of parked cars, he was just in time to see Kat, fifty yards away, duck into a low-slung sports car. Giles had already vanished and, as Mariner watched, the car, that must have cost upward of thirty thousand, fired up, reversed slowly out of the parking bay and accelerated towards the exit ramp with a throaty roar, giving Mariner more than enough time to note down the registration. It would do for a start.

Leigh Hawkins was popular. There were no reserved seats in the first-floor room of the tiny Edwardian pub and, half an hour before the venue was due to open, the queue snaked down the stairs and into the street. Millie was having to stand and wait on her own as Mariner hadn't yet showed up. She wondered what was keeping him. Perhaps, despite what Knox had told her, he was seeing that Stephanie again. She hoped so. It would do him good. Having experienced the pleasures of married life first hand, Millie felt it her mission to secure the same happiness for everyone. It was a mystery to Millie, and always had been, why the boss hadn't been married, with his mandatory 2.4, years ago. OK, he was knocking on a bit now, but he was still an attractive bloke. Even the grey beginning to streak his hair suited him. And she happened to know from very limited personal experience that he was an all right shag. It was such a pity things hadn't worked out with Anna. It was still a source of some shame to Millie that she was the one who could potentially have jeopardised that relationship for him, but, no, in the end he had managed to screw it up all on his own.

At seven sharp the doors opened and the line began to shuffle forward up the stairs, giving Millie her first glimpse into the gig venue. Seeing how crowded it was becoming, she hoped there wouldn't be a problem with reserving two seats, though she had her warrant card to back her up should she need it. Most of the punters were middle aged or older, ageing hippies many of them, universally dressed in jeans, T-shirts and open-necked shirts. And all of them, from what Millie could see, were white. She'd long passed the stage where this could make her feel uncomfortable, and she certainly didn't feel under threat, but it was an interesting observation. Soon she was next in line at the ticket table, and at last Mariner arrived, squeezing his way breathlessly up the stairs past the tail-end of the queue. And, for God's sake, still wearing his work suit.

'You know how to blend in, sir, don't you?' Millie said, eyeing him up and down as she handed over the money for their tickets. 'I can see why they never ask you to go under cover.'

'What? Oh, no time to change,' Mariner said, distracted.

Tickets bought, they walked into the rapidly filling room and Millie chose a table about halfway back.

'What are you having?' Mariner asked. He took Millie's order and went up to the bar, leaving her to keep their seats.

'Been somewhere nice?' Millie fished, as he rejoined her with their drinks, his own already half-depleted.

'Nowhere interesting,' he said, with a minimal shake of the head. 'God, it's ages since I've been in here, I used to come in regularly. But the landlord still keeps a good pint, well half-pint, anyway.' He looked warily around at the audience. 'I hope this isn't going to be your finger-in-the-ear purist stuff.'

And from that, Millie surmised, the subject was closed.

When the band appeared Lucy Jarrett's husband was instantly recognisable from the wedding photos Millie had seen. 'Though he's better looking in the flesh,' she told Mariner. Lean and tanned in black jeans and T-shirt, with dark, spiky hair, he was every inch the rock musician, his arms branded with elaborate tattoos and a string of beads at his throat. The band was a five piece and, apart from Will, was as predominantly Irish as Leigh Hawkins himself. The eponymous front-man was tall and rangy, his long grey hair tied back in a ponytail, his beard almost white.

The bass player and drummer kept a pretty low profile but the front line was Leigh Hawkins himself, all gravelly voice and acoustic guitar, Will Jarrett on guitar, mandolin, banjo and occasional harmonies and a female singer whose crystal pure voice was a clean counterpoint to the gruff male vocals.

'That must be Tess Maguire,' Millie said.

'She's the other woman?'

'She phoned to speak to Will while I was there. Lucy wasn't impressed. Touch of the green-eyed monster, I think.'

Occasionally the two sang backing harmony to Leigh Hawkins, and when they did they shared the mic, standing close to one another, often Will's hand at the young woman's back, and as they moved back and forth across the stage, in and out of the songs, they exchanged frequent intimate glances.

'He's not behaving much like a newly married man, is he?' observed Millie.

The performance ended at close to eleven thirty and afterwards, while Mariner went to find the gents, Millie queued by the table at the back of the room to buy a CD. She purposely joined the line nearest to Will, but had to wait some time, as the woman ahead of her was clearly a long-time fan.

'Back again then, Sally.' Will turned his pearly smile on her.

'Of course,' the woman twittered. 'You were fabulous as always.' She picked up one of the CDs. 'Will you sign it for me. I've already got that one, but I can't go away empty handed.' Having paid for the CD, Sally produced a camera. 'One for the album?' Will dutifully posed, then she turned and handed Millie the camera. 'Would you mind?' Before Millie could respond, Sally was round to the other side of the table, her arm gripped tightly around Will, her face pressed close to his. Millie focused and snapped. To Will's credit, he seemed totally relaxed about it all, though the woman must have been too close to be comfortable.

'See you again soon, darling,' she said, holding Will's hand for much too long and squeezing it tight, until finally relinquishing it.

'You take care now.' Will smiled, turning to Millie, brows raised.

'You have a fan,' Millie observed.

'Yeah.' Will gave a wry smile. 'Thankfully just the one. Sally's pretty harmless though.'

Millie handed over the money for her chosen CD. 'Your wife is Lucy, right?'

He looked up in surprise, the smile in place. 'Yeah, you know her?'

'Kind of. I'm the police officer who's investigating the nuisance phone calls she's been getting.'

There was a definite reaction in those dark eyes, but Jarrett recovered quickly. 'I didn't know she'd got you guys involved,' he said casually. 'You really think there's something in them?'

'I think there's something bothering your wife, and I'd like to try to find out what it is,' Millie said pleasantly.

The smile had faded somewhat. 'That's very conscientious of you.'

'It's my job,' Millie said lightly.

Mariner caught up with Millie as she walked away.

'Do you think that was wise?'

'I wanted to make him squirm a bit.'

'What if he goes back and takes it out on Lucy?'

Millie stopped and turned. The thought clearly hadn't crossed her mind. 'He wouldn't, would he?'

'It wouldn't be very sensible, especially now that he knows we're watching him,' said Mariner. 'But it might complicate things.'

Sally, Will's fan, was hovering in the car park close to an ornately decorated transit van when they emerged from the pub. 'Waiting for another glimpse,' she confessed. 'Don't you think he's just gorgeous?'

'You know he's married,' Millie said gently.

'Ah, but for how long?' Sally grinned, a little manically Millie thought. 'I mean, she seems like a nice woman but she's bound to get fed up with the travelling, isn't she?'

'You've met his wife?'

'Not met exactly. Will introduced her at one of the gigs. The novelty must have worn off, though – she doesn't come along any more. A long way to come, I suppose.'

'Have you come far?' Mariner asked. 'Can we drop you somewhere?'

'Oh no, thank you. That's my little car there.' She pointed across the way to a light-coloured compact hatchback. They should have known it was hers. There were Leigh Hawkins stickers all over the rear window. 'And I don't live too far away. South Birmingham, in Kings Heath. Do you know it?'

'A little,' Mariner said.

'It's not far from where Will lives as a matter of fact.'

'You know where he lives?' Millie said.

'Oh, I've driven past a few times, and seen his van on the drive. I couldn't help myself.'

They left her standing outside in the freezing air.

'Christ, she's a bit scary,' said Mariner, under his breath, when they were on the other side of the car park.

'Will thinks she's harmless,' Millie said.

'I'd say she's got the motive and the opportunity.'

'And now I've got her registration number,' Millie said, snapping shut her notebook.

'Good. I'll see you in the morning.'

It was well after midnight when Mariner got home, but the house was dark and empty;

Kat was still out. This was a first and, combined with what he'd seen earlier, it bothered him. Where the hell was she? Was she still with Giles? What were they doing? He moved on from that one. It had been a long day, but, even though he was shattered, Mariner didn't want to go to bed. He paced around a bit then made himself a coffee, paced around some more, while it went cold, then tipped it down the sink.

'This is stupid,' he told himself. 'She's twenty years old, a grown woman.' He went upstairs and brushed his teeth and got undressed, then came down and paced around yet again. Eventually, fatigue forced him into bed, but he couldn't sleep and lay awake listening. Finally, at two fifteen am, he heard a car draw up outside, footsteps and voices, followed by the clunk of the front door closing. After that it went quiet, so at least Giles hadn't come in with her. Mariner padded down the stairs and found Kat in the hallway, standing precariously on one leg, trying none too successfully to take off her left shoe without falling over.

'Hello, Tom. You're awake.' She grinned widely, though she seemed to be having some difficulty focusing on him.

'And you appear to be drunk,' Mariner observed, stating only what was obvious.

'I jus' had a little drink.' Concentrating hard, she held up her finger and thumb, half an inch apart.

That wasn't all. The herby smell of weed wafted towards him along the hall. 'Good night?' he asked.

'It was great!' She straightened up, stumbling a little.

'You're late home.'

'After we go to club we go to a guy's house for party.'

'Where?'

'I don't know. An apartment. It's groovy I think, and wicked, very wicked.' She giggled again. Dumping her second shoe with a clonk, she wobbled towards him, but at the last minute missed her footing and fell against him, giggling. Her hand slid under his T-shirt, landing on his bare stomach. Mariner drew breath involuntarily.

'Oh.' Kat gazed drunkenly up at him. 'You like that? You like me to do something for you?'

'No!' Appalled, Mariner wriggled free and backed away from her. 'Go to bed, Kat.'

Lucy Jarrett couldn't sleep either. She had been sick again earlier in the evening; the anticipation of an evening alone enough to make her ill now. She'd spoken to her mother on the phone earlier, and the instant she'd replaced the receiver the phone had rung again; silence at the other end. She'd spent the rest of evening with the phones unplugged, but for the last couple of hours had been more jumpy than ever. Where was Will? Their gig tonight wasn't exactly on the doorstep, but it was near enough for him to come home if he wanted to, and it must have ended hours ago. It was a long time since she'd seen him play. When they'd first met he was keen that she should go along; she felt that he was showing off to her, but then after the time he'd caught her yawning during a set he'd actively discouraged her from going.

'You're bored, of course you are,' he'd told her. 'One gig is pretty much like another, and you've been working all day. You don't have to come along, really.' At the time it had seemed like genuine empathy, though now she doubted that. But she'd taken him at his word and, even when he was performing just a few miles away, she stayed at home and waited for him. And it did have its upsides. Often when he came home after playing he was on fire, pumped to the brim with adrenalin. It was when their lovemaking had been at its most passionate, and that was saying something. But not lately. Not since the calls had started. Was that down to him, or her? DC Khatoon had planted the seeds of doubt about Will, making Lucy realise how little she knew about him. When they first met she'd been mesmerised by him, even she could see that. But it had seemed mutual. They couldn't keep their hands off each other. When had that changed?

She was actually dozing off when the headlight beams swept across the lounge and she heard the sound of Will's transit pulling into the drive. Weak with relief, she was at the front door before he had even got out of the van, but she could tell as soon as he got out that something was wrong.

'Good gig?' she asked as he brushed past her and into the hallway.

'It was different,' he said, dumping down his things. He turned to glower at her before going into the kitchen, where he opened the fridge and took out a beer.

She trailed him in there. 'How do you mean?' Lucy asked. This sounded personal, though she couldn't imagine what it could possibly have to do with her.

'Thanks to you, I've been under surveillance from the police all night.'

'What? How do you know?'

'One of them introduced herself to me at the end and said that she knew you.' His voice was even but the fury was evident in the twitching muscle in his jaw. 'Why didn't you tell me you went to the police? I hate being put on the spot like that.'

'Because I didn't–' Lucy whimpered. 'At least I did, but then I thought about what you said, about it probably being just kids, and realised how stupid it all was and I asked them to forget it.'

'So what were they doing there?' Will demanded.

'Maybe it was just coincidence.' She gave a nervous laugh. 'Maybe they like folk music.'

Will just looked at her. 'You think I was born yesterday?'

Lucy capitulated, her resistance gone. 'Someone reported us to them,' she said listlessly.

'What? When?'

'When we had that row on Tuesday night,' Lucy said weakly. 'The police got a phone call from someone saying that I was being attacked. Someone must have been watching. Someone *is* watching me, Will. It's what I've been trying to tell you. The policewoman, Millie–'

'An Asian woman?'

'Yes, she came to see me. I've been getting all these things in the post, and all these emails. They think there's something going on.' *They believe me,* she wanted to say, but something in Will's expression stopped her.

'And what exactly do they think is "going on"?'

'That someone is trying to frighten me!' she exclaimed.

'And they think it's me?'

'Of course not!' Did the denial sound as false to Will's ears as it did to her own? 'They're talking to everyone I know. It's what they do.'

'Well, now they've talked to me,' Will said. 'And it's not going to happen again any time soon.'

'What do you mean?'

'This situation is getting too crazy for me. I need to get some stuff off the computer then I'm out of here.'

'You can't.'

Will regarded her coolly. 'I think you'll find that I can.'

'No, I mean the computer. They've taken it away to look at.'

'What?' Will took a step back and Lucy couldn't help it, she flinched in anticipation.

'It's because of the emails I've been getting,' she said. 'They had to take it away to trace them.'

Will's expression had changed subtly. Could she see panic in his eyes now? 'The details of the band's itinerary, the confirmations are on there.'

'Is that all?' Instantly she regretted the question.

'What kind of a fucking question is that?' He moved towards her, but then changed his mind, turning and storming out into the hall, where he picked up his bag and jacket again. 'Jesus, Lucy, I don't know what's got into you. Or maybe you always were this way but I didn't see it before.'

'Where are you going?' Lucy pleaded, hating the desperation in her voice. 'I was going to run you a nice hot bath.'

'I'm going some place I can relax,' Will said. 'Where I don't feel persecuted.'

'Back to Tess?'

He stopped in his tracks and turned back to her. 'Oh, so that's what this is all about. You're jealous, of Tess?'

'No, I'm sorry, I didn't mean–'

But he didn't wait for her explanation. He marched out of the house, slamming the door hard behind him.

Wrenching the door open again, Lucy called after him. 'Will, please, I didn't mean it! Come back so we can talk about this!' But he was already reversing out of the drive. As she watched the tail-lights of his van disappearing round the bend in the road, Lucy shuddered. A gust of wind blew up and, feeling suddenly exposed, she stepped back in and slammed the door, then leaned her back against it. Was he out there? Were the police about to arrive on her doorstep again? Part of her hoped they would, because at least then for a moment she'd feel safe again.

CHAPTER ELEVEN

Kat wasn't about when Mariner got up on Friday morning, the indulgences of the night before taking their toll, no doubt. He wondered if he should call her; she might be late for work otherwise, but her hours were flexible some days and in truth he was glad to be spared the embarrassment of facing her. He was still trying to work out what had happened last night.

As soon as he got into his office, he ran a check on the sports car he'd seen Kat getting into. A misuse of privileges perhaps, but Mariner didn't feel too guilty about it. He was merely protecting her. The car's owner was registered as Giles Ridley-Coburn. What's more, the Police National Computer told him that Giles had form. Millie knocked and came into his office.

'Would you trust a bloke called Giles Ridley-Coburn?' Mariner asked her.

'Who's he?' Millie came to look over his shoulder at the screen.

'He's the guy Kat went out with last night.'

'She went on a date? That's brilliant,' Millie enthused.

'Is it?'

'Of course it is. It means that she's getting back to normal. Does she know you're checking him over?'

'Not exactly,' Mariner confessed.

'So how did you get his name?'

'I didn't, I got his registration number.'

'He picked her up from the house?'

Mariner said nothing.

Millie's eyes widened as she pieced it together. 'You were spying on them. That's where you were before the gig last night.'

'You sound as if you don't approve.'

'Of you following Kat? It's what we call stalking.'

'I'm just watching out for her,' Mariner said defensively.

'That's probably what Will Jarrett would say about Lucy. You're not her dad, you can't police who she sees.' Despite her reservations, Millie peered over Mariner's shoulder at the screen, curiosity overriding propriety. 'Has he got form?'

'Not much; a couple of endorsements for speeding, and one for possession of cannabis, though nothing recent. It doesn't say anything about his associates, though.'

'It's a pretty up-market address,' Millie noticed. 'Isn't that the old insurance building that was converted into luxury penthouses? They don't come cheap.'

'That's what I thought,' Mariner said glumly. 'He looks far too young to be earning that kind of money legitimately. And Kat was dressed provocatively yesterday evening.'

'How do you mean, provocatively?'

'She was wearing a short dress, sort of clingy, and not much to it, if you know what I mean.'

'It was a mild evening.' Millie laughed. 'And she's a young woman with a great figure. My God, if I was her shape I'd be showing it off too. Perhaps all it means is that she's feeling confident about her body again and doesn't need to hide it away under baggy clothes. I think it's a good sign.'

'Is it a good sign that she hit on me too?' Mariner explained what had happened the previous night.

'OK, that's something different. But surely that was just the drink talking.'

'You mean, why else would she come on to a sad old git like me?'

Millie smiled. 'You took the words right out of my mouth. You need to relax a bit and let her be herself.'

'Yeah, maybe you're right,' Mariner conceded. 'While we're on here, let's take a look at our obsessive Will Jarrett fan.'

Millie typed in the registration number she'd noted down the previous night, and the record unfolded.

'Sally Frick,' he read. 'Address in Kings Heath, as she told us.' He did a swift mental calculation. 'Aged forty-one, and clean as a whistle.'

'No previous stalking convictions?' Millie asked hopefully.

'Sadly not,' said Mariner. 'But it might be worth paying her a visit.'

'On what grounds?'

'You could try openness and honesty,' Mariner said. 'Tell her what's going on and see if she knows any other fans who might do this sort of thing. While you're there you can get a sense of what she does all day, and at least establish whether she's computer literate and has access to a machine.'

A wolf whistle out in the bull pen caught their attention and they looked up to see Tony Knox, looking uncharacteristically formal in a dark suit, giving the V sign to Charlie Glover.

'Blimey,' said Millie. 'What's the occasion?'

'Nina Silvero's memorial service,' said Mariner.

'Ah.'

Nina Silvero had been cremated that morning in a small family service that even Mariner felt unjustified to intrude upon for the purposes of the investigation. But the memorial celebration that followed was at the Oratory, also known as 'Little Rome', the huge Baroque-style edifice on the Hagley Road, built as a memorial to Cardinal Newman, and was altogether a different affair.

'Wow, what a place,' murmured Knox, gaping up at the ornate high ceiling, as he and Mariner accepted hymn books from an usher and took a couple of seats towards the back, the better to observe the mourners.

By the time the proceedings began, the transept of the church was full, and not just with ordinary folk. Among the various low-level dignitaries, Mariner watched a couple of high-ranking police officers make their way down the aisle towards the middle of the church. Family and close friends occupied the first couple of rows, including Rachel and Adam Hordern, and Mariner pointed out Estelle Waters, elegantly dressed in a grey wool suit. In addition, there were a number of couples, some accompanied by teen and pre-teen daughters, who Mariner deduced to be from the ballet school, past and present. A number of mature women, grouped together, Mariner surmised could also be ballet-school officials. Rachel Hordern was the epitome of the grieving daughter and spoke movingly about her stepmother.

'If she did have anything to do with it she's putting on one hell of an act,' Knox whispered to Mariner.

As he spoke they became aware, as did those around them, of a commotion on the opposite side of the church as a woman, apparently in some distress, jumped up and began forcing her way from her seat in the middle, to the end of the row; no mean feat as she was a large woman, wearing a bulky duffle coat and carrying a capacious handbag. People turned to stare as, in her haste, she practically fell into the side aisle before recovering and hurrying out of the church. Mariner, placed on the end of the row, quietly got up and followed her out, catching the closing door before it slammed shut. But, when he emerged into a squally shower, the woman had vanished.

The service ended with a rousing hymn, after which Rachel and her entourage proceeded out of the church. Mariner turned to watch them go, and as he did so locked eyes with another familiar, albeit older figure at the very back of the church on the opposite side. Nodding an acknowledgement, he turned to tell Knox. 'See who's over there?' But when he turned back again, Jack Coleman, his old DCI, had gone. On their way out of the church there was the familiar meet and greet line. Mariner scanned the crowd ahead for Coleman, but he'd disappeared, leaving Mariner wondering if he'd been mistaken.

'Thanks for coming, Inspector,' said Rachel, as they approached. 'I hope you and your sergeant will be able to join us at the reception.'

'Thank you, we'd be pleased to.' Mariner

didn't like to say that they had been planning to come along anyway, invitation or not.

Nina Silvero's wake was held just down the road at the Clarendon Suite and many of the guests were choosing to walk there, Mariner and Knox included. They caught up with Susan Brady.

'I still can't believe she's gone,' she said. 'I keep expecting her to pop up. All other things being equal, I think she'd have rather liked it; the music, the friends. I can't imagine how we're going to get on without her.'

'Not all bad, though,' Mariner said. 'We have had a look at her will. In some respects it's worked out well for you, hasn't it?'

Susan's colour rose. 'Look, if you think I had anything to do with–'

'How well do you know Rachel?' Mariner asked.

'Before today I hadn't seen her in ages, but we used to dance together when we were younger. We weren't close. Rach is a couple of years older than me, and moves in rather different circles.'

'Did you notice the woman who left the church halfway through?' Mariner asked.

'Yes, overwhelmed by it all, I suppose.'

'Did you know her?'

She shook her head. 'She might have been a ballet-school mum, though I couldn't be sure. There are so many of them. And there are plenty of people here today that I don't recognise.' They had arrived at their destination and Susan excused herself to go to the Ladies.

Mariner and Knox were directed, along with those around them, to a windowless, airless room that looked as if it was designed for sales conferences. It couldn't have been further removed from the church, but perhaps that was the intention. Helping themselves to the proffered mineral water, Knox and Mariner hovered on the fringes doing what they did best – watching people. Rachel was working the room expertly, though she looked drawn and tired. There must have been a hundred people there at least, and it was her task to go through the same routine with them all. Mariner's eyes roamed constantly, but Coleman wasn't here. Assistant Chief Constable Bennett was, though, and eventually came up to them and shook hands. 'How's the inquiry going?' he asked Mariner.

'There are a few leads emerging,' Mariner replied. 'But nothing yet that stands out, sir. We're still doing all the leg work.'

'Well, keep on it. This is one we need to crack, and as quickly as possible, and without dragging up any old skeletons if at all possible, if you get my drift.' Bennett's none-too-subtle way of saying he didn't want the media spotlight casting its beam once more on Ronnie Silvero's death.

'Yes, sir.'

Towards the end of the afternoon people began to drift away, and Mariner noticed Rachel for once standing a little apart. Seizing the opportunity, he picked up a glass of sparkling water and swooped in on her. 'Here.'

She took it gratefully. 'Thanks, I'm parched. It's rather exhausting, all this.'

'As you said, your stepmother was popular,' Mariner observed. 'She had a lot of friends.'

'Even I had no idea how many,' Rachel agreed. 'This probably isn't the time to ask, but is there any news?'

'Nothing concrete,' Mariner said. 'But we're following up on a number of things. Actually there was something I needed to ask you about.'

'Go ahead. It'll make a change from what I've been talking about all day.'

'I understand you and your stepmother had a disagreement a couple of weeks ago.'

She hadn't been expecting that. 'How did you...?'

'One of the neighbours overheard you.'

'Oh I might have known. Bossy Patterson next door. Just happened to have her glass to the wall, did she?'

Mariner was taken aback by the acid tone. 'She was working in her garden,' he said. 'It

210

doesn't sound as if you were particularly discreet.'

Rachel sighed. 'Well, in the end there wasn't much to be discreet about. Mum turned me down flat. She said that the key to starting any business is to know your limitations, and that, if she just handed over the money, we would have an unrealistic idea of what they were. Never mind that actually most of it is my dad's money.'

'What kind of business were you starting?' Mariner asked.

'Organic bath products, soap, shampoo, that kind of thing. We were going to market them over the Internet, still are as a matter of fact.'

'So you raised the capital elsewhere?'

'Not as much as we'd have liked,' she said.

'But that hardly matters now, does it?' Mariner couldn't resist it.

She gave him a quizzical look.

'We've had access to Nina's will. It's all part of the investigation.'

Having placed her glass carefully on an adjacent table, Rachel held out her hands towards Mariner, wrists together in preparation for handcuffs. 'It's a fair cop,' she said. 'You've got me bang to rights.' But, despite the levity of the words, her tone was hard. She let her hands drop, and for a second Mariner thought she might hit him, but instead her eyes narrowed a little. 'Today of all days,' she said, with great control. 'How dare you?' She turned and walked away.

Mariner watched as Adam approached her, offering some comfort and they both glared accusingly across at him.

It was time to go. But all the mineral water had caught up with Mariner and he went to find the Gents. As he passed back through the room on his way out, afterwards, he couldn't help noticing that Rachel was no longer in conference with her husband. Instead she had moved along the room and was deep in conversation with Susan Brady.

'Let's go to the crematorium,' Mariner said. He and Knox had retraced their steps to the car.

'She was cremated this morning, boss,' said Knox, getting into the driver's seat. 'There'll be no one there.'

'I want to look at the flowers,' said Mariner. 'It might be interesting to see who's left them. If our killer sent her some while she was alive, perhaps he's done the same again now that she's dead.'

The floral tributes for Nina Silvero took up the whole of one bay, from modest wreaths to elaborate floral creations spelling out her name, but Knox and Mariner were the only ones there to see.

'What a waste,' said Knox. 'A couple of days and all this lot will be dead, too.'

Mariner walked slowly along the line. 'Look.' He pointed out the wreath from Jack and Glenys Coleman. 'The gaffer must have known Ronnie Silvero. That's why he was in the church.'

'Would he have worked with Silvero?' Knox wondered, and Mariner realised that he probably did. The message on a nearby wreath was simple: *Cherished, loved and much missed,* but was unsigned. With a jolt, Mariner recognised the handwriting, but Tony Knox had already moved on, so no need to draw his attention to that one. There were no others that stood out, and certainly at this point no arrangements of dead flowers. Maybe Rachel Hordern was right, and that had been a mistake. It had begun to drizzle again and Mariner caught up with Knox sheltering inside the crematorium entrance where the book of remembrance lay open on this date for previous years. He stopped to scan the pages. 'Christ,' he said to Knox. 'There's a woman here in her twenties.' He traced his finger along the protective glass case. 'Makes you think about how little time you've got, doesn't it?'

'In that case can we stop wastin' time here freezin' our arses off, eh?' his sergeant retorted.

'Yeah, let's go and find a pub.'

They settled for a swift half at the Bell in

Harborne, before returning to Granville Lane in the late afternoon. Mariner almost didn't go back into the station, but at the last minute changed his mind. Up in his office he put through a call. Jack Coleman picked up on the third ring.

'It's Tom Mariner.'

'Hello, Tom.' After all this time Coleman wasn't surprised.

'I saw you at the service,' Mariner said.

Coleman's tone was guarded. 'I used to work with her husband.'

'Can I come and see you?'

'Come tomorrow morning, after ten o'clock.'

Mariner drove out to Stourbridge on Saturday morning with mixed feelings. In many ways he still missed the old man. Jack Coleman had been his boss when he started in CID at Granville Lane as a DC and they'd been through the ranks, albeit Coleman one level higher, together. They'd had a great professional relationship and Mariner had always looked up to Coleman, who he considered to be the epitome of a good copper. He'd also come to be the father figure Mariner had otherwise lacked. But Coleman's behaviour yesterday had been odd. He'd seen Mariner, there was no question of that, so why had he disappeared so swiftly? And then there was the wreath.

As he pulled into the drive, the gaffer came to the door and seeing him close to reinforced Mariner's initial reaction yesterday afternoon; that he looked old. He seemed to have shrunk in the time since he'd retired, and there was a pallid tone to his complexion. In a hot rush of emotion, Mariner thought, he's ill. He's got something awful and he hasn't told me. That's why he couldn't face me yesterday.

The thought merely compounded his guilt – he'd promised to keep in touch with Jack Coleman to keep him up to speed with what was going on, but this was the first time – second if you counted yesterday – he'd seen him during the last year, and this was only because he wanted something from the old man.

'Listen, I'm sorry I haven't been out sooner,' Mariner began awkwardly, from the comfort of an armchair in the large, traditionally furnished lounge. Strange to see Coleman in this environment with all its flounces and frills. Stranger too, to have Jack Coleman making coffee for him, arranging it on the occasional table beside him and fussing over the coaster. His movements were slow and unhurried, giving weight to Mariner's theory about an illness.

'Don't worry about it,' Coleman said, taking the sofa across from him. 'I know what the job's like, remember? Socialising isn't a high priority. Still, you and Anna must come over sometime.'

'Anna and I aren't together any more.' It came out as a distressed cry, Mariner only then realising that Coleman didn't know.

'Oh?' Coleman was confused. 'I hadn't heard.'

'Why would you? We split just over a year ago.' *Fourteen months two weeks and three days, but who's counting?* 'Just as we were bringing Goran Zjalic to justice.'

Coleman shook his head wearily. 'Oh, Tom, Tom, what did you do?'

Mariner was affronted. 'She walked out on me!'

But Coleman knew him too well; he simply waited patiently for an answer.

'OK,' Mariner conceded. 'I probably messed her about a bit. She wanted to settle down, house in the country, kids and all that.'

'And you couldn't make up your bloody mind.' Christ, it was terrifying how well Coleman knew him. 'How could you let her go? She was bright and witty, and so right for you. You were right for each other.'

'You should get a slot on daytime TV,' Mariner said sulkily. He could have told Coleman about the miscarriage, but he knew that was only part of the problem.

'I'm only stating what's obvious,' Coleman pointed out. 'Any idiot could see it, apart

216

from you apparently. Who's she gone off with?'

'A quack from Wales.'

'Gareth what's-his-face?' Mariner had forgotten that Coleman had been around when his rival first came on the scene. 'You should have seen him off.'

'Well, I didn't,' said Mariner. 'So there we are.'

Coleman gave a wistful sigh. 'It's a crying shame. I really liked Anna. And Glenys will be devastated.'

So that makes two of us. There was a lengthy pause.

'I was surprised to see you yesterday,' Mariner said, moving the conversation around to where he wanted it.

Coleman shifted in his seat and stared into his coffee mug. 'Just paying my respects.'

'You didn't come to the bash afterwards, though.'

'No.' Coleman inspected his shoe. 'I had to get back.'

'I went to the crematorium afterwards,' Mariner said carefully. 'I couldn't help but notice the wreath.'

'Nina was a friend of ours,' Coleman said evenly.

'I mean the other one,' Mariner said. 'The one you hadn't signed. *Cherished, loved and much missed?* That sounds like more than friendship to me.'

Coleman gazed out through the windows at the freshly mown lawn. 'I visited Nina a few times after Ronnie died. She was having a hard time. She'd just lost her husband, yet the press were still saying terrible things about him. She needed taking care of. One thing led to another...' He tailed off and now Mariner understood partly why he looked so terrible.

'Christ. Were you still–?'

Coleman closed his eyes briefly and gave a shake of the head. 'It didn't last long, mostly because I still love my wife and Nina had loved her husband. I think it was just a little comfort that got both of us through a tough few months.' He looked up at Mariner. 'Glenys doesn't know,' he added. The question was in his eyes.

'I've no reason to share that information with anyone,' Mariner said. A thought occurred to him. 'Do you remember once running into one of Nina's friends while you were with her?'

'We did have a couple of narrow scrapes, yes,' Coleman admitted.

'She introduced you as her cousin?'

'I think that was how it went.' Coleman rubbed a hand over his face. 'I can't get over what's happened to Nina. It's a terrible thing. Is it true, what was reported in the press, that she was forced to drink sulphuric acid?'

218

Mariner nodded grimly. 'There aren't any signs of a struggle, so "duped" is looking more probable. Her killer brought along a doctored bottle of Chardonnay.'

'Jesus, that's nasty.' Coleman's words caught in his throat.

'Nasty and personal,' Mariner said. 'Someone wanted to do Nina Silvero serious damage. Trouble is, no one we've spoken to yet has a bad word to say against her, so we're left wondering who the hell would want to do it. We've got people who might have been after her money, but it doesn't seem to give us the right motive for such cruelty. How well did you know Ronnie Silvero?' Mariner asked.

'We worked together for a while at Steelhouse Lane – I was a sergeant while he was in CID.'

'What was he like?' Mariner asked him.

'Well, if he was still alive I'd have said that Ronnie could easily have been a target for this kind of thing. Nowadays he'd probably be tagged as a bully; sexist, racist and about everything else-ist. Though of course back then we didn't have to worry about things like political correctness. He was an old-fashioned copper; some of his methods might occasionally have been questionable, but he got the job done.'

'He did all right too,' Mariner remarked. 'Made it to chief inspector.'

'I said he was a bully, not that he was stupid. Ronnie was a shrewd strategist. He knew exactly how to behave in certain situations, and who were the important players,' Coleman said wryly. 'Belonged to the right lodge.'

'He was a Mason?'

'Oh, yes, he was thick with them. It all appealed to his sense of self-importance.'

'Did you like him?' Mariner asked.

It was a leading question and one Coleman preferred to evade. 'We worked OK together. I don't think Nina or the daughter – what was her name?'

'Rachel.'

'Of course, Rachel, that was it. Well, I don't think they had an easy life of it.'

'What about the investigation that was going on when Ronnie Silvero died? Did you know anything about that?' Mariner asked.

'I couldn't help it. Despite what the media think, the death of a prisoner in custody is always regrettable and of course it caused a stir.'

'Justifiably?'

Coleman suddenly seemed uncomfortable. 'As far as I understood it, the officers involved were doing their job and made decisions based on what they thought was the right thing at the time. You know how it is when something like this happens. Half the time you're thinking, there but for the grace... That line between too much force and not enough is paper thin, and you know that as much as I do. Billy Hughes was asthmatic and no one knew it. If they had, things might have been handled differently – or they might not.'

'You think the CPS would have gone all the way with the prosecution?'

'They had every reason to. Hughes' family were applying a lot of pressure and had the press behind them, and Butler had just come out, criticising the failure to prosecute in previous instances. This would have been a high-profile case to show that things had changed.'

'And Silvero definitely died of a heart attack?' Mariner verified.

'As opposed to what?' As Coleman fixed his gaze on Mariner, the room temperature seemed to drop a couple of degrees.

Mariner had seen that expression on Coleman's face before, but rarely directed at him. It told him he was overstepping the mark, but it wasn't in his nature to back off. 'He must have been under a lot of pressure,' he said meaningfully.

'Ronnie Silvero died of a heart attack,' Coleman said coldly. 'Christ, Tom. You think he could have staged that?'

'Yeah, OK. I had to ask,' Mariner said lightly and the tension in the air seemed to ease a little. 'What was the reaction of Hughes' family when Silvero died?'

Coleman sighed, as if dredging all this up was taking enormous effort. 'Like I said, they gave Nina a hard time about it. Some of them thought Ronnie had got what he deserved, and others felt cheated by it. Of course they did. They'd lost their scapegoat.' Coleman looked up as if something had occurred to him. 'You're thinking Nina's death might be some kind of posthumous revenge thing?'

'I'm thinking I'd just like to find some kind of motive for such an obscene attack on an otherwise universally popular middle-aged woman,' Mariner said. 'At the moment we're clutching at any old straw we can find.'

'Well, it's a pretty flimsy straw. It happened twenty years ago. Why on earth would anyone want to start digging it all up again?'

'I'm going to have to talk to the Hughes family,' Mariner said.

'You must do what you have to, just like we all do.' But Coleman didn't sound happy about it.

Mariner drained his cup. 'Did you know the first Mrs Silvero?'

'No, she was long gone when I met Ronnie. He was a single dad. It was like a dream for him when Nina came along.'

'How was the relationship between Nina

and Rachel?'

'I don't remember it being an issue, though it might have been in the early days. Half the time I used to forget that Nina was her stepmother.'

'Nina Silvero would have been pretty busy, what with the ballet school as well,' Mariner said. 'Did you know her well, I mean before?'

'We'd met a couple of times at social functions, but Glenys would have talked to her more. She's shopping in Worcester today, but when she gets back I'll ask her what she remembers, and, if you want to come back and talk to her, that'll be fine.'

Mariner raised an eyebrow. 'You sure?' The Glenys he remembered hated the way the job had taken over her husband and probably wouldn't be keen on him getting involved again.

'I'm sure. She'd want to do what she can to help. It'd be good to find the bastard who did this.'

'Yes,' said Mariner. 'It would.'

The rest of the conversation was small talk, Mariner updating Coleman on the station gossip.

'How's your new gaffer working out?' Coleman wanted to know.

'She's good. Could never fill your shoes, of course, but she's OK. You'd like her.'

As Coleman was showing him out, Mariner had to ask, 'Do you ever miss it?'

'Do I miss being up to my elbows in paper-work, trying to juggle a budget that covers about half of what we need and all with the brass breathing down my neck about targets? Do I miss standing in a morgue looking at what some lowlife has done to a woman like Nina Silvero?' There was a catch in his throat and, to recover, Coleman feigned reflection for a moment. 'Can't say that I do,' he concluded, his voice still hoarse.

'No, when you put it like that.' Mariner extended a hand and as the two men shook, as if to underline the point, a blackbird sang out joyfully from a nearby tree.

On his way back to the city, Mariner went for a walk on Holly Hill, before dropping down to the Holly Bush, an unpretentious working-men's pub, for a pint of M&B mild. In the late afternoon it was quiet, those who had been for lunch were drifting away, and it was too early for the evening drinkers. The Holly Bush was also one of those pubs that would have suffered from the smoking ban. A gazebo had been erected at the back of the pub in the car park, but it was question-able how many people would be prepared to drive out to a country pub only to spend large chunks of the evening shivering out-side under canvas.

But the lack of activity suited Mariner very well, allowing him the peace and quiet to mull over what Jack Coleman had told him and, equally significant, Coleman's mood. He'd remained studiously objective about the death of the prisoner, though not without some sympathy for the family, but he was right about the timing. Could the attack on Nina Silvero really hark back to something that happened twenty years ago? As Tony Knox had pointed out, Nina Silvero had been afraid of something. But, if it related to that death in custody, why now? At the very least it was a possibility that would need to be ruled out. And it would be interesting to know what the dead man's family were doing now.

CHAPTER TWELVE

On his way home, Mariner considered picking up a DVD, but decided to consult Kat first on what she might like to watch. They could get a takeaway to go with it. But Kat had other plans. He arrived back to find her all dressed up and hunting around for her bag.

'You're going out again,' Mariner said, stating the obvious. 'With Giles?'

'Yes, we go to Broad Street.'

'Is he picking you up?' Mariner asked hopefully.

'No, I get the bus.'

'I can take you,' Mariner said impulsively. 'If you can wait while I get changed. I'm meeting someone too.'

Kat smiled. 'A woman?'

'It's work,' Mariner said vaguely, cutting that one off at the pass. Anything else and he'd be committed to the full post-mortem the following day. 'Where are you meeting Giles?'

'Mambo's is a bar on Broad Street.'

She waited, and a little later Mariner joined the line of taxis flooding into the city centre, their passengers heading for Saturday-night entertainment. After dropping Kat off by the Hyatt, Mariner turned into Gas Street and parked in the first multi-storey he came to. Bearing in mind Millie's remarks the previous night about blending in, he'd worn a short-sleeved shirt, which he pulled outside the waistband of his jeans. It took ten years off him, but getting out of the car he shivered as the easterly wind cut right through him. He made his way back to Broad Street. He'd never heard of Mambo's and had to ask directions. Once he'd located the bar, he waited till a large and noisy group of young men was going in, and hooked on to the back of them, hoping that, if Kat was still there, he would see her before she saw him.

The place was packed and dimly lit which

both hindered and helped his cause, but Mariner was able to secure a spot at the end of the bar with his back to the wall that gave him a wide view through the heaving mass of bodies. Finally he saw Kat, and in the nick of time too, as she was on her way out, being shepherded through the crowds by Giles, his guiding hand at her back. Mariner followed them as best he could, weaving a path through the closely packed bodies. Out on Broad Street the crowds thinned a little, though gangs of youths and young women cluttered up the pavement, some of them already the worse for drink. Mariner was grateful that Giles was tall and he was able to follow the dark mop of hair back in towards Brindley Place. Then suddenly Giles ducked into a doorway and Mariner followed, descending a dark stairway in their wake and into his idea of hell.

The club was dark, but for a web of laser beams and a cinema-sized flat screen on one wall showing random images cut from old news footage of the sixties; flower power and mushroom clouds, JFK on a grin and grip. The music was a heavy dance beat that battered his ear drums and Mariner stood back and watched as Giles and Kat joined the mass of people thrashing in the middle of the room. Mariner's dancing had never been up to much and he couldn't help envying someone like Giles who could throw himself into the music with such abandon while still looking pretty cool. Mariner couldn't help wondering what he might be fuelled on. Kat was more restrained, a little dazed, Mariner thought, but she still moved well. For a while Mariner was mesmerised, but, when his back started to ache from standing in one place for too long, he strained to see his watch. He'd been here more than two hours tracking their movements between the dance floor and the bar, and so far it had been a total waste of time.

He was about to give up, when suddenly the whole enterprise became worthwhile. Kat had retired from the dance floor for a drink and was standing to one side, leaning, as Mariner was, against the wall, sipping her drink and watching the revellers. Giles had disappeared, but returned after a few minutes. He towered over Kat as she leaned in against him and their faces got close as they seemed to be talking about something. Then, as Mariner watched, Giles shifted his position to retrieve his wallet from his back pocket.

He opened it and took out a small packet, from which he shook something into the palm of his hand, closing his fingers around it, as he replaced his wallet. Giles held out his hand for Kat to see. Looking up at him, she nodded and Mariner watched as she picked up the item from Giles' palm between finger and thumb, threw back her head and stood poised to drop it into her mouth. In seconds, Mariner had covered the ground between them, shoving aside anyone and anything in his path, and grabbed Kat's arm before she could swallow the pill.

Giles was big but Mariner had outrage and intent on his side. 'You, outside, now!' he spat in Giles' face and, seizing the young man's arm, launched him towards the exit, vaguely aware of Kat trailing helplessly behind them. Mariner propelled Giles up the dark stairwell, battling against the downward surge, and out on the street where it seemed blissfully cool and quiet. Retaining his firm grip, Mariner dragged Giles into a side alley, slamming him none too gently against the wall.

'What the hell is going on?' Giles demanded, though Mariner could see the fear in his face.

Kat looked terrified. This was a side of him that she'd never seen. 'What are you doing, Tom?' she pleaded.

'Tom?' Giles was incredulous. 'Fuck it. You're Tom Mariner?'

'*Detective Inspector* Tom Mariner actually,' Mariner said evenly. 'You just chose the wrong customer to screw with.' Mariner drew out his warrant card. 'I'm arresting you for the possession of a Class A drug with intent to supply.'

'What?'

'You do not have to say anything—'

'It's not a fucking Class A, you moron,' Giles cut him off. 'It's a paracetamol!'

His indignation was enough to make Mariner waver for a second.

'I have a headache,' Kat wailed in corroboration, tugging on Mariner's arm. 'Giles is give it to me for the pain, and then we go home.'

Putting his face close to Giles', Mariner hissed. 'Don't you dare *move*.' Then, relaxing his hold on the young man just a little, he fished in his pocket for the small torpedo-shaped pill that he'd taken from Kat. He held it in the light cast from the street lamp, to examine it more closely. It did look bigger than any ecstasy tablets he'd seen before. And it did appear to have the letter 'P' stamped on the side.

'I can show you the rest,' Giles offered.

Reluctantly taking his arm off the boy's chest, Mariner nodded acquiescence. Giles took out his wallet once more and retrieved from it a small blister pack, the foil backing imprinted with the name and logo of a national high-street pharmacy. He passed it to Mariner. There was a single empty compartment and Mariner opened a second to reveal a pill identical to the one he was already holding.

'It's as Kat said,' Giles told him calmly. 'She had a headache, so she was going to take that and then we were calling it a night.'

For the first time Mariner looked carefully at Giles and tried to weigh him up. What he said didn't seem entirely implausible. And embarrassing as it might be, his gut feeling was that Giles was telling the truth. He fished in another pocket for the evidence bag he'd brought for this very eventuality and slipped in the pill and the blister pack. 'Well, I won't arrest you this time, but I will be getting this tested, to make sure what you're saying is true. And I wouldn't leave the city any time soon.'

'I wasn't planning to,' Giles snorted. 'You can suit yourself of course, but that won't contain anything you can't buy over the counter. I gave all that up a long time ago.' He shot Mariner a meaningful glance, well aware that he'd been checked up on. 'Look, I don't really understand what you are to Kat, but you should know that I really like her and I wouldn't do anything to hurt her.' Stepping away from the wall, he slipped a protective arm around Kat. 'You want to go home, sweetheart, don't you?'

'She can come with me,' said Mariner, looking across at Kat, 'if you like. I mean, I've got the car here anyway, so you may as well–'

Giles looked at Kat who nodded, and Mariner had to stand by and watch them hug and kiss, before he bid an awkward goodnight to Giles. In normal circumstances he might have shaken the man's hand but somehow on this occasion it didn't seem quite appropriate.

Leaving the buzz of Broad Street behind them, Mariner and Kat walked back to the car park in painful silence. Not until they were driving out of the city along Bristol Street could Mariner bring himself to venture grudgingly, 'I'm sorry, I spoiled your night.'

Kat was looking away from him and out of the window. 'Is OK. Is like Giles say. I want to go home soon anyway. My head is bad.'

The silence recommenced, and continued all the way out to Kingsmead. Mariner pulled up outside the house and cut the engine. They sat for several seconds not moving.

'Giles is a nice guy,' Kat said suddenly.

'I'm sure he is,' said Mariner, still smarting from having made such an idiot of himself.

'He knows what happened to me. I tell him all about it. He understands.'

'Where did you meet him?' Mariner asked.

'At a cancelling group.'

It took Mariner a few seconds to decipher what she meant. Finally he got it. 'A *counselling* group?' he said.

'Yes. Is for rape victims. I go there every week.'

232

Wow. 'I didn't know that,' Mariner said. 'So Giles is a counsellor?'

'No.' Mariner was still working it out when she added quietly, 'Giles is raped too, when he was a boy.'

Sunday dawned grey and drizzly. By mid-morning Kat still hadn't surfaced, for which Mariner was grateful. And he decided that the best policy might be to stay out of her way, the truth being that he was embarrassed to face her. After putting on his walking boots and waterproof jacket, he opened the back door of his house and stepped out on to the canal towpath. Today, with the absence of any sunlight, the air was tangy with damp vegetation. Mariner followed the canal for a mile or so until it cut through the Primrose Hill estate, where he surfaced and picked up the footpath taking him out into the countryside skirting the Blues training ground and on to the North Worcestershire Way. Out in the open fields the mud stuck to his boots, making them heavier with every stride. The Peacock at Wetheroak was packed with families noisily enjoying a late Sunday lunch, so Mariner had a quick half and then walked home again. When he got back to the house Kat had gone out, and thus they successfully avoided one another for the whole day.

Millie had been visiting her in-laws in Dudley, where Suli was helping his brothers with some decorating to the family home. Dal was going to drop him off later, leaving Millie free to go home in the evening. Driving up through Northfield, she realised she was not far from Lucy Jarrett's, and wondered what kind of a weekend she'd had. Millie was pretty sure that Will was away. She'd also been driving around with her own wedding snaps in her car for a couple of days, with a view to taking them round to Lucy sometime; awkward to fit that in with professional concerns. But perhaps tonight would be a good opportunity. Having taken a slight detour along the Bristol Road, she turned into Lucy's estate.

Although there was no transit van on Lucy's drive, there was another car tucked in behind Lucy's Mercedes, and when Millie rang the doorbell she was surprised to hear music coming from inside the house, as if a party had already started. And for once, when she came to the door, Lucy was smiling, glass of wine in her hand.

'Hi.' Millie smiled brightly, and held up the photo album. 'I've brought pictures, but it looks like you're busy. If you want me to come back another time…?'

Lucy's hesitation was momentary and her smile returned, if a little tightly, as she stepped back to let Millie in. 'No, that's great, Julie-Ann's already here. You can join the party.'

Millie followed Lucy through to the kitchen. There was something she had to confess to before they could relax. 'We went to see Will's band,' she said.

'I know.' It was said with feeling and Millie had a sudden sense of foreboding.

'Will told you?'

'Yes, just before he stormed out again, accusing me of suspecting him,' Lucy said pointedly.

Shit. 'Oh, Lucy, I'm sorry, that was my mistake. I thought it would be a good idea for us to let him know that we were keeping an eye on things, making sure that you were OK, especially since he's away such a lot. He obviously didn't take it that way.' Millie wondered again where it was that Will stormed off to. It seemed to be a habit of his.

'No, he didn't,' Lucy said, leaving Millie to wonder if she'd given any thought to why that might be. But she had to keep Lucy on side, so she said nothing more. 'And he was furious that you'd taken the computer.'

'Well, we should be able to let you have that back soon.'

'Did you find anything?' Lucy asked.

'We're still following up on the spam,' Millie said, suddenly aware that she'd let that slide.

'So what did you think?' Lucy asked.

'Of?'

'The band?'

'They're good,' Millie said truthfully. 'I mean, not really my kind of thing, but Will's obviously a talented musician – they all are. And that young woman – Tess, was it? She's got a great voice.'

'Yes, she has, hasn't she? Anyway, what would you like to drink?'

'Have you got a coke or something? I'm driving.'

Lucy retrieved a can from the fridge and poured it into a glass.

'Forgiven?' Millie asked, taking it from her. 'Believe me; I was only trying to help.'

Lucy smiled, this time a warm and open smile. 'You are forgiven, DC Khatoon. Cheers.'

Julie-Ann appeared and regarded Millie warily. 'Hey, what's going on?'

Lucy grinned. 'All the best parties happen in the kitchen. But, yeah, let's go somewhere more comfortable.' She picked up the wine bottle and led them into the lounge.

'This a bit above and beyond, isn't it?' Julie-Ann said to Millie. 'I'm impressed.' Though Millie got the distinct feeling that the opposite was true.

'I was just bringing Lucy up to date,' Millie said. 'We met one of Will's fans the other night.'

'Oh, not Sally!' shrieked Lucy, plonking

herself down on the sofa, and curling her legs underneath her.

'You know about her?' Millie asked, taking an armchair across from her and Julie-Ann.

'Yes, Will thinks it's hilarious. The poor woman's obsessed.'

'Has he ever been concerned about her?'

'No, it's just a joke.' Lucy stopped in her tracks. 'You don't think she…?'

'It's a possibility,' said Millie, staying casual. 'No more than that. I agree that on the face of it she seemed harmless. I'll probably go and talk to her. Where's the band playing tonight?' she asked, to change the subject.

'Oh, they're up in the north, Will called me from Bolton.'

And from that point the talk of the investigation ceased, and, thanks to a bottle of Merlot or two, Julie-Ann seemed to relax and Millie saw a whole new side to Lucy. When she let her hair down, she and Julie-Ann were wild together. They drooled over Millie's photographs, and listened sympathetically to her account of her rocky relationship with her parents which had all come right in the end.

'I need a man,' said Julie-Ann, as they finished Millie's pictures. 'Here's both of you settled down and I haven't even got a bloke.'

'Millie's boss is pretty hunky,' Lucy said drunkenly.

Millie pulled a face. 'He's all right, but hunky isn't really a word I'd use.'

'Oh, he is. He's tall, slim, still got all his own hair.' She turned to Millie. 'Unless you know something I don't?'

Smiling, Millie shook her head.

'You'd really like him, Jules,' Lucy went on. 'A bit on the serious side, but he's got these amazing blue eyes. Is he married?'

Millie sighed. 'No, as a matter of fact he's not, but I think he might be seeing someone.'

'Serious?'

'I don't know. It's none of my business really.'

'There we are then,' Lucy said triumphantly. 'We could fix you two up. What's his name again?'

'Tom Mariner.'

'Tom and Julie-Ann, Julie-Ann and Tom. Yes, I like it.' And to Millie's great relief she seemed content with that.

What Julie-Ann and Lucy had in common was their shared history and inevitably they got around to reminiscing.

'Your mum showed me all your cheer-leading trophies,' Millie said.

Lucy cringed. 'The burden of being an only child,' she groaned. 'Mum collects and archives everything. She and Dad must have recorded my every breath from the time I was born. Did she take you up to the spare room? It's entirely taken up with photo albums. And those trophies really should go.'

'No!' Julie-Ann cried. 'They remain a shrine to your achievements. The cheerleading was so much fun!'

'How on earth did you get into it?' Millie asked, knowing that nothing like that ever went on at her own school.

'We came up with it ourselves,' said Lucy. 'They had some cheerleaders on *Blue Peter* or something, so we decided to set up our own troop.'

'Only because "Foxy" Foxton disapproved,' put in Julie-Ann. 'And it looked so cool! We did it all ourselves; held the auditions – only the prettiest girls allowed to join.'

'Oh, come on,' Lucy objected. 'It makes us sound really exclusive.'

'It's true,' Julie-Ann contradicted her. 'You might be all politically correct now, Ms Health Visitor, but, at the time, the whole point of it was to attract boys! God, we were so shallow then. And the costumes only came in one size, so everyone had to be thin enough to get into them.'

'Oh, that was terrible,' said Lucy, suddenly shamefaced. 'The poor girls we had to turn away.'

'It was only fair,' Julie-Ann insisted. 'You had to be fit enough to do the routines. They were really energetic. And you had to

239

be able to dance a bit of course, even though neither of us was much good. The auditions were hilarious. Everyone was desperate to join so it was such a feeling of power. I don't think I've ever had a buzz like that since.'

'We were good for a while,' Lucy admitted.

'You won enough competitions,' Millie said. 'So why did you stop?'

'The exams came along so it kind of fizzled out.'

'We grew up,' Julie-Ann reminded Lucy. 'Maybe we should start it up again.' She giggled. 'I bet we can still do it. Come on, I'm sure Millie would love to see one of the routines.'

Millie was caught up in their enthusiasm. 'Oh, yes! A demonstration!'

It was pretty impressive, even though they were rusty after all this time, and, when they did the final leap and whoop at the end, Millie clapped and cheered unrestrainedly, to make up for being the sole member of the audience.

But the excitement was short-lived. Lucy had gone a funny colour. 'Oh, God, I think I'm going to be–'

She ran to the bathroom and they heard the sound of the lovely Merlot being regurgitated. Julie-Ann was staying the night, so, having ensured that Lucy was OK, Millie left them to it and drove home.

First thing on Monday morning Mariner called through to Tony Knox.

'We've got something else to work on.' He filled Knox in on what he had learned from Coleman. 'I want to look at all the archive material we've got on that case and find out what the dead man's family are up to now.'

'Oh good,' his sergeant said, and Mariner pictured him eyeing up the pile of paper on his desk. 'I could do with something to read.'

'Don't worry,' Mariner said. 'This is one for me. If anyone needs me I'll be at Lloyd House all morning.'

Hughes' CPS case file would be stored alongside the thousands of others in the basement of police HQ in the city centre. It was the early morning rush hour, and the journey in took Mariner a protracted hour. As he inched his way through the Queensway tunnel, he thanked God he didn't have to make this journey every day.

It took the archivist some time to retrieve Hughes' file. Mariner couldn't begin to imagine how many records were stored here, but the one he was given was pretty substantial. He settled himself in one of the half-dozen booths designed for the purpose, and began to read.

The first thing that smacked Mariner in the face was the date of Hughes' death.

According to the CPS report, Billy Hughes, aged nineteen, had been arrested by officers, Ronnie Silvero among them, called to a brawl outside a nightclub, and in police custody in the early hours of the morning of Saturday, 3 April 1988, exactly twenty years ago last Sunday, he had slipped into a coma. His life-support machine was switched off a week later. That was interesting, or might be if they could pin down the exact date when Nina Silvero received the flowers. Last year dead flowers, this year murder?

Mariner began with Ronnie Silvero's version of events, as taken in his statement that fateful night. It was, according to the report, the day of a Midlands derby, Notts Forest had travelled to the city to play Birmingham City in an FA Cup semi-final, along with thousands of fans. Trouble had been expected, which explained why Silvero, by then an inspector, was out on the streets at all. But the expected hooliganism never kicked off, and all that was reported that night were a series of minor scuffles, the usual Saturday-night fodder.

Ronnie Silvero had been in the vicinity of a nightclub when he and the two constables he was with were called to a fight outside the Dome. Hughes was drunk and abusive, behaving in a violent and aggressive manner towards the officers, and had resisted arrest. It took the three of them to restrain him, handcuff him and get him into a squad car, using batons and at one point even CS gas. Reading the report, it seemed ridiculous that all that should be needed for just one man, but Mariner had been there enough times. Some men and, increasingly these days, women could behave like wild animals in that context, and generally speaking the aggression was directed at the arresting officers. Mariner had no trouble at all envisaging the scene.

Back at Steelhouse Lane, Hughes was briefly uncuffed while being processed, but turned his aggression on another detainee, so again he was wrestled to the ground, his hands cuffed behind his back in the classic 'prone restraint', and he was removed to a cell to cool off. So far so routine. But the detail that followed in Silvero's report became suddenly skimpy, making reference instead to the duty sergeant's log. Hughes was checked, he said, at 'regular intervals', but when the duty sergeant looked in at two forty-five, the prisoner was found to be apparently unconscious. The alarm was raised and the sergeant attempted resuscitation, but at eight minutes past three an ambulance was called and Hughes was taken into intensive care at Dudley Road Hospital. A week later he was pronounced brain dead and the machinery keeping him alive was turned off.

What surprised Mariner was that the inquest that followed, considering all the evidence, had so definitively reached a verdict of unlawful killing. There were a number of reasons why Hughes might have died, including injuries sustained during the brawl. The prosecution was two pronged; the officers had used undue force on the hapless Hughes, and that they had neglected him when he had been left in the cell. One of the cornerstones of the prosecution case was the evidence from Arthur Rhys, the only other man arrested on the same night, who had been occupying the cell next door to Hughes. Rhys had given a statement, from where he was, by that time, on remand for burglary, about what he'd heard on that night. He claimed that, shortly after Hughes was placed in the cell, he heard a rasping noise, and Hughes calling for help and shouting that he needed an inhaler. The duty sergeant came and looked at Hughes, said, 'I'll see what I can do.' And went away again.

According to Rhys, the rasping noise continued for several minutes, then there was a noise like choking, before everything went quiet. Rhys claimed to have yelled, 'We need help in here. I think he's in trouble,' and banged repeatedly on his cell door. He claimed that nothing happened until about ten to fifteen minutes later, when he heard the duty sergeant open the viewing hatch on

Hughes' door, and say, 'Oh fuck,' before pressing the emergency bell. During the commotion that followed, Rhys claimed to have heard an officer saying, 'We shouldn't have left him like this, we shouldn't have left him like this.'

The problem with this particular piece of evidence, of course, was that it was unlikely to be unbiased. Rhys himself was also under the influence of alcohol at least, and, as he didn't have any form of timepiece, the chronology couldn't be relied on.

So what had happened during the time in between the duty sergeant's visits to Hughes' cell? For enlightenment, Mariner rifled through the file for the duty sergeant's report. Finding it, he gave a start. The name at the top of the report in distinctive handwriting was that of Sergeant John Coleman. Christ, so Coleman had been personally involved with this. That was why he'd been so reluctant to talk about it. But he must have known that Mariner would find out at some point.

Mariner read Coleman's report carefully. Everything tied in with what Silvero and Rhys had recorded. It was when he got to the part about leaving Hughes in his cell that things got tricky. At this point, according to Coleman's notes, he had gone back to the custody desk and rung through to Inspector Ronnie Silvero, who was, by this time in the canteen for R&R.

I told Inspector Silvero that I was concerned about Hughes remaining in that position, suggesting that, now he was in a cell and could do no more damage, the cuffs should be removed. We discussed the situation. There was some concern about whether the prisoner might harm himself and it was felt that he could reasonably be left in the restrained position a little longer. I also had concerns about the prisoner's breathing and asked if anyone knew if he was asthmatic. No one did. A fellow officer, I can't remember who, also suggested that Hughes might be 'playing to the gallery'. Inspector Silvero suggested I relax, have a cuppa and then check on Hughes, at which point we would remove the handcuffs...

And by which time, it was too late.

So Coleman had done what he could to avert the tragedy. The responsibility for the decision-making had been Ronnie Silvero's and Silvero's alone. The statement from a WPC who had been present in custody at the time corroborated Coleman's version of events, confirming that the conversation had taken place, and that Coleman had proposed removing the handcuffs from Hughes. The subsequent prosecution would have put Coleman in an impossible situation. Tell the truth and incriminate Silvero, or protect Silvero and incriminate himself?

Coleman had chosen the way of common-sense and integrity, but he wondered what Ronnie Silvero had thought about that. Was that why Coleman had been so attentive to Nina Silvero after Ronnie's death, because he, too, felt responsible?

There had been an outcry, of course, with Hughes' family and their supporters calling for a public inquiry, which an apology from the then chief constable didn't dampen. The subsequent inquiry concluded that 'errors of judgement' had been made and the CPS began assembling a case against the three officers involved; Silvero was charged with manslaughter and suspended from duty, and the two arresting constables faced lesser charges. Jack Coleman, Mariner noted, was not charged. Eighteen months on and shortly after the date for the trial was set, Ronnie Silvero had died. There was no detail, just the simple words 'deceased' and 'file closed'.

Also contained in the file were copies of the hate letters that Rachel Hordern mentioned had been sent to her stepmother. They didn't make pleasant reading, the general themes being that Ronnie Silvero had got off lightly and that the hope was that he would rot in hell. They were not very imaginative, but the subject was definitely Ronnie and not Nina. They were also handwritten and Mariner took them to compare with the handwriting on the florist's card. The letters were unsigned but the next of kin recorded on file were Eva and Eric Hughes who had an address in Rubery, once a village, but now the southernmost suburb of Birmingham. Alongside notes he'd already taken, Mariner wrote it down together with the phone number and, for the moment, closed the file on Billy Hughes.

Mariner rubbed his eyes. He was getting a headache; the sooner he picked up those glasses the better. Leaning back in his chair, he considered the single most useful piece of information he had gleaned from all this; that Billy Hughes had died of asphyxiation, and Nina Silvero died a similar, choking death.

CHAPTER THHIRTEEN

Even though she had only been drinking coke and tea, Millie still arrived outside Sally Frick's house on Monday morning feeling as if she had partied the night before. She felt slightly queasy and shivery as if she might be going down with something.

Sally Frick lived with her elderly mother in a terraced house off Kings Heath High Street. The front door was in need of a coat of paint, and when Sally showed Millie in there was an odd smell, the smell of old age. She took Millie through a dim and narrow hall past a closed door behind which there were murmuring voices. The sitting room at the back of the house overlooked a narrow stone yard, and the interior of the house was decorated like something from the nineteen forties.

'We have to sit in here as Mummy's room is in the front,' Sally explained. 'She can't manage the stairs any more. The nurse is here getting her up. Would you like a cup of tea?'

Millie declined. 'How long have you been following the band?' she asked.

'Oh, ages, about four years. Since I first saw them at the Red Lion and fell in love with Will.'

'And you go to all their gigs?' Millie asked.

'The ones in the Midlands, yes. Sometimes it takes me all afternoon to get there.'

'You must have an understanding boss.'

'Oh, I don't work any more. Caring for Mummy is very demanding so I gave up work some time ago. My neighbour is very good, though. She comes and sits with Mummy when I want to go out.' Her face creased to a frown. 'I don't really understand why you're here. How can I help?'

'We're investigating some nuisance phone calls that Will Jarrett's wife has been getting,' Millie said.

'Oh dear.' She didn't sound too put out by the idea.

'Do you know anyone who might want to do that?'

'No, I can't think of anyone,' Sally said straight away.

'Could I use your bathroom?' This time it wasn't a ploy, Millie genuinely felt quite queasy. But it did give her the chance to peep into each of the three small bedrooms. On the bedside table in what appeared to be Sally's room was a framed photograph that caught Millie's attention. It was framed in the way that most people would a picture of a close family member, but within this frame was a picture, clearly printed from the Internet, of Will Jarrett. Disappointingly, however, unless Mummy had one in her room, Sally Frick did not appear to own a computer. Just to be sure, Millie asked anyway, when she returned to the sitting room.

'Oh no,' Sally said. 'I wouldn't really have the need for one, though I used to use one at Cullen's, where I used to work, and they did once send me on a course for beginners. And I sometimes use my brother's computer to keep up to date with what the band are doing.'

'What about a mobile phone?' Millie asked.

Sally chuckled. 'Whatever use would I have for one of those?'

Back in the office, Millie was struggling to concentrate on what the young and eager IT technician, Max, was telling her about the Jarretts' computer. She was distracted too by the array of studs in his ears and the elaborate sculpture of his jet-black hair. It must take him longer to get ready in the morning than it takes me, she was thinking.

'There's a lot of music on there, which I guess you'd expect,' Max was saying. 'The guy's into some pretty obscure stuff; bands I'd never heard of.'

'He plays in a folk-rock band,' Millie enlightened him.

'Right.' Max nodded, understanding. 'That explains it. And someone's visited a few porn sites, but nothing hard-core and there's nothing that's been deliberately downloaded. This is a summary of the other sites that have been visited.'

As he said, there seemed nothing to arouse suspicion.

'The only other thing is the emails,' Max was saying.

'Is there a way of working out who sent them?' Millie asked.

'We can trace them back as far as the IP but–'

'IP?' Millie queried.

'Internet provider,' Max helped her out. 'After that it's down to them. They have agreed to help, but they'll have thousands of records to go through, so we're going to have to be patient. It could take several days. If it's any help we've run an analysis of the dates and times–' he paused to pass Millie a further sheet of data '–and, as you can see, most of them have been sent in the late evening, for some reason a lot of them on a Wednesday.'

Millie was studying the list of sites again. 'Someone has a big interest in Huntingdon,' she said. 'Isn't that somewhere near Cambridge?'

'John Major's old constituency, for what it's worth,' Max added. 'I thought that maybe the band played a gig there, or is due to.' It seemed a reasonable explanation.

Before driving back to Granville Lane, Mariner sat in his car and put through a call to the address in Billy Hughes' file. Unsurprisingly, Billy Hughes' parents no longer lived at the house in Rubery, but helpfully the woman who inhabited it now had bought the house from them when they moved away from Birmingham to the south coast six years ago.

'The daughter still lives around here,' she said. 'We had her address to forward any post to.'

'Do you happen to still have that?' Mariner asked.

It was a lot to ask, but she did remember that it was somewhere on Rea River Drive.

Mariner phoned Tony Knox. 'It's your lucky day,' he said. 'You're going on a little outing.' On the way Mariner filled Knox in with what he'd found out. 'See if you can pinpoint the exact address of a Tracey Hughes, Rea River Drive, and I'll pick you up in the car park in half an hour.'

Tracey Hughes located, they were driving away from Granville Lane towards Kingsmead.

'Christ, so the gaffer was all set to testify against a CID colleague?' Knox said.

'What other choice did he have?' Mariner pointed out. 'All he was going to do was stand up and tell the truth. And all this time on, he still feels bad about, and still partly blames himself for, Silvero's death, I could tell.'

Tracey Hughes' house was a typical, boxy eighties detached, so narrow that it really should have been a semi – all Georgian windows and tiny box rooms. The front door was uPVC with an extravagant brass knocker.

Mariner rang the bell. 'Tracey Hughes?' he asked the thirty-something young woman, with spiky bleached-blonde hair who came to the door.

'What do you want?' she asked in response to Mariner's warrant card, but the tone was

253

wary rather than hostile.

'Just to ask you a few questions,' said Mariner.

'Is it about that copper's wife?'

So she kept up with the news. 'Yes, it is. Can we come in?'

It wasn't exactly a gracious welcome, but she showed them into a lounge where another young woman was overseeing a gaggle of pre-teen children.

'It's the police,' Tracey said. 'Can you take the kids outside for a bit, Shel?'

Shel regarded the two men with an added layer of suspicion. 'Sure. Is everything all right?'

'It's fine,' Tracey reassured her.

Politeness compelled her to invite them to sit, although Mariner sensed she would have preferred them not to contaminate the beige leather sofa.

'You heard about Mrs Silvero then,' Mariner said.

'Couldn't really miss it, could I?' she said. 'The name's engraved on my brain.'

'How did you feel when you heard about it?'

'I just thought it's a shame, like you do when you hear about anything like that.' She reached for a pack of cigarettes and lit one, blowing smoke away from them, towards the window.

'There wasn't part of you that thought,

"I'm glad she's dead"?'

She had no difficulty meeting Mariner's gaze. 'No. I might have thought that when her old man died. It was him was responsible for our Billy, and he went before justice could be done, but that wasn't her fault. None of it was her fault. So I just felt sorry for her. It sounded nasty.' There wasn't much warmth to her sympathy.

'What about the rest of your family? Have you seen your mum and dad lately?'

'Yesterday afternoon.'

'They're back in Birmingham?' Mariner was surprised, though of course there was a good explanation.

'They always come back up here this time of year; they like to go to our Billy's grave.'

'For the anniversary.'

'There's no crime in that. It's all they've got left.'

'How long are they staying?' Mariner asked.

'About ten days. They came up a week last Saturday, go back the day after tomorrow.'

'Quite a long visit then,' Mariner observed.

'They've got a lot of friends and family up here still,' replied Tracey.

'And where are they staying?'

'With Auntie June, Mum's sister. They always stay there.' She recited the address and Knox wrote it down.

'Have you ever been round to Nina Silvero's house?' Mariner asked.

'Till I saw it in the papers I didn't know where she lived.' The response came out glibly, almost as if she'd rehearsed it.

A small child came running into the room. 'Mum, Mum, can I have a lolly? Shel said we can have lollies.'

'Are we finished?' Tracey asked, absently stroking the child's head.

Mariner got up to go, and Knox followed suit. 'One more thing,' Mariner added. 'Where were you last Sunday evening, between seven thirty and midnight.'

'We all went out for dinner; about twenty of us.'

'Thanks,' said Mariner. 'We can see ourselves out.'

Back in the car Knox had doubts. 'It doesn't make sense, boss,' he said. 'Surely the last person Nina Silvero would let into her house is a member of the Hughes family.'

'Unless they persuaded her that they wanted to bury the hatchet,' Mariner said. 'After all she'd suffered a loss too and, as Tracey said, what her husband might or might not have done wasn't down to her. The twenty-year anniversary is a significant one. Maybe somehow they persuaded Nina Silvero that they wanted to put it all behind them. Nina might have even seen it as an opportunity to clear her late husband's name. It might explain why they didn't get any further than the kitchen, too. Nina Silvero could have been uneasy about the approach but not wanting to be impolite.'

'But why now?'

'Like I said, the anniversary for one thing, and perhaps someone in the family saw the announcement in the paper; Nina Silvero getting her MBE. It probably didn't seem much like justice to them.'

'Tracey Hughes doesn't seem to bear any grudges,' Knox pointed out.

'She'd hardly let it show in front of us,' Mariner countered. 'And she's not the only member of the family, is she?'

The address Tracey Hughes had given them was for a house in West Heath, just a mile away, but when Mariner and Knox arrived there was no one there.

'We'll come back later,' Mariner said. 'We've got a couple of days.'

After Max had gone, Millie sat quietly, glad of a few minutes to rest her aching eyes, when her phone rang.

It was a woman's voice. 'Hello, I don't know if you'll remember, but you came to talk to me the other day. I do some cleaning on the Manor Farm estate.'

The silver Honda driver. 'Yes, of course,' Millie said. 'You've got a vacancy?'

The woman laughed. 'No, sorry, it's not that. It's probably nothing at all, but the person at number nineteen getting these calls – her name wouldn't be Lucy, would it?'

'Why do you ask?' Millie sat straighter in her chair.

'When I parked my car as usual this morning at the top of Hill Crest, I had one of those *déjà vu* things that you get, and remembered a man who came up to me a couple of weeks ago. He wanted to know where Lucy somebody lived. I said I didn't know, because, well, I didn't. It may be nothing, of course, and I'm sorry I didn't think of it before, but I thought I ought to let you know.'

Millie fought to suppress her excitement. 'You've done the right thing–'

'Pam.'

'Pam. Thanks. Do you remember what this man looked like?'

'Well, that was it,' Pam said. 'It's why I should have thought of it before. He wasn't at all the sort of man you generally see around here.'

'In what way?' Millie asked.

'Well, he was a big man, tall I mean, not fat, and he was unshaven and quite scruffily dressed, one of those shirts without a collar. And his jacket, it was like a suit jacket, but well worn and not too clean. My first thought was that he was–'

'What?' Millie prompted gently.

'Well, I was going to say "gypsy" but that's not PC, is it? What's the word we're supposed to use now?'

This got better and better. 'A traveller?' Millie offered. *Or perhaps a man who travels a lot?*

'That's right, a traveller. And he had some kind of brogue, Irish I think.'

Millie's heart did a somersault. Most of Leigh Hawkins' band were Irish, including, presumably, their roadies. She cast her mind back trying to remember anyone who might fit the description. There had been a couple of men tinkering about on stage before the show started, but neither had struck her as being particularly tall. 'How sure can you be about that?' she asked.

'Well, I'm not very good at accents,' Pam admitted. 'But he sounded like my cousin Martha's husband, Bill.'

'Did you feel threatened by him?'

'Oh, no, he was perfectly polite, although I suppose I did feel slightly intimidated, mostly because of his size, and because he looked a bit rough.'

'And how long ago was this?' Millie asked.

Pam thought for a moment. 'A couple of weeks, maybe three.'

'Can you remember the exact day or the time?'

A pause while there was further thought. 'I think it was a Thursday because I was just about to go into Mr Coyle's house, and it would have been at about nine thirty.'

'Thank you,' said Millie. 'That's been really helpful.'

So was someone doing Will's dirty work for him?

Lucy Jarrett would be at work. Millie tried phoning but the line was permanently engaged, so she drove straight to the health centre. This couldn't wait.

Lucy and Paula were both in the office. Nodding a greeting to Paula, Millie went over to Lucy's desk. She looked terrible, pale with dark circles under her eyes.

'Hi,' said Millie. 'Great night last night.'

Lucy gave a wan smile. 'It was, but I'm paying the price today.'

'Bad head?' Millie queried.

'Not just that.' Lucy lowered her voice so that Paula wouldn't hear. 'I haven't stopped throwing up all morning.'

'Maybe you should have stayed at home,' Millie said sympathetically.

'For a hangover? I couldn't do that. I'll be OK. What are you doing here?'

'The other day, when I was leaving your house, I bumped into the woman who cleans for some of your neighbours,' Millie told her.

'A cleaner? Really?' Lucy brightened.

'That sounds like a great idea, I wonder if she'd do our house too?'

Millie shook her head. 'Don't get your hopes up. She told me she's full.'

'Shame. That's the other thing about having such a ridiculously big house; all the cleaning. Sorry, you were saying?'

'This woman called me back this morning because two or three weeks ago, she was approached by a tall, scruffy Irishman, who was asking where you live. Have you any idea who he might be?'

Lucy wrinkled her nose. 'The only Irish I know are Leigh and the guys in the band. Are you sure it wasn't one of them?'

'The description doesn't fit Leigh,' said Millie. 'This guy was tall but with short dark hair. Is there anyone who fits that description; one of the roadies perhaps?'

Lucy shook her head slowly. 'Of course, they come and go, so I might not necessarily know, but the only ones I know are Dec and Rod and neither of them has short dark hair. They're both pretty average height, too.'

'This man looked scruffy too, like a traveller. There's no one else you can think of like that?'

They were speaking normally now and Paula Kirkwood must have heard from across the office. 'What about Michael Kerrigan?' she said to Lucy. 'Didn't you say he gave you a hard time about the social worker?'

'Oh, God, Kerrigan, yes, of course. It all makes sense now!' Lucy seized on the idea enthusiastically. So much easier to contemplate than that her husband or one of his friends might be behind all this.

'What happened?' Millie asked.

'Kerrigan was waiting for me in the car park one evening a couple of weeks ago. He started yelling at me, shouting abuse, but that was all.' After the initial fervour, doubts began to creep in. 'But he's all bluster, and he'd been drinking. I'm sure he wouldn't–'

'If he was waiting for you in the car park he could have watched you get into your car. He could also have followed you, at least as far as the estate. Why was he waiting for you?'

'To give me a piece of his mind, mostly,' Lucy said. 'Part of my job is to go into homes where there's a newborn, to make sure that the baby is being cared for and that there are no problems in the family. The Kerrigan family is on my caseload. They are settled travellers.'

'So what was Michael Kerrigan so unhappy about?' asked Millie.

'When I did the home visit, I had concerns about his wife. She was very low; I thought she might have postnatal depression. I think the money is a bit tight and there are some issues with the older children attending school, so all in all it seemed a good idea to make a referral to social services. It didn't go down very well with Mr Kerrigan.'

'When did this happen?'

'I suppose I did the home visit about a month ago and would have made the referral straight after that.'

'So it would be around the same time as the phone calls started?' Millie said, piecing it together.

'I couldn't be sure, but, yes, I suppose it was about then.' Lucy was warming to the idea again.

'But how would Kerrigan have got your personal phone number?' Millie wondered. 'You're not listed in the phone book.'

Lucy flushed. 'I gave it to his wife,' she confessed.

Paula couldn't restrain herself. 'Lucy!'

'Isn't that against your professional code or something?' Millie hazarded.

'It was stupid, I know, but I was worried about Mrs Kerrigan. I wanted to give her every opportunity to contact someone if she needed to. I thought it was possible that the relationship might be abusive. Michael came in while we were talking and she seemed afraid of him.'

'Where do they live?' Millie asked. 'I need to go and talk to Mr Kerrigan.'

Lucy gave her the address. 'Should I come

with you?'

'No, that's fine.' Millie was resolute. 'You can leave this one to me.'

But once out in her car again, Millie was torn by indecision. What she wanted more than anything was to solve this case herself and be able to deliver a result to Mariner that she'd achieved all on her own. But she was also a realist. If Kerrigan was a traveller, albeit a settled one, then it was likely that he'd be more forthcoming speaking to a man. And if Lucy suspected him of being abusive towards his wife, then he may be aggressive towards her, too. She recalled the advice Mariner had given her, and recognised this as one of those occasions when she could potentially get out of her depth. First, though, she drove back to Granville Lane to find out whether Michael Kerrigan had a history. He did. Kerrigan's convictions were mainly for petty theft and burglary, but he had also got himself into some scraps; a couple of assaults that were basically drunken brawls, outside various local hostelries. No arrests or convictions for some years.

Mariner himself was out with Tony Knox but luckily Charlie Glover was available, and what's more already knew the Kerrigan family, so would be able to smooth the way. And as far as Glover could recall there had never been any complaints of violence against the long-suffering Mrs Kerrigan.

'He's a lovable rogue,' Charlie said as they drove off the station concourse.

Millie liked Charlie Glover. A quiet and unassuming family man, Charlie would have seemed more at home as an accountant or a civil servant than a police officer. Solidly built, with thinning fair hair, he was also solid in a scrape and she was confident that, like the other members of the team, he wasn't about to try to steal her glory.

'Do you think he'd be up to stalking?' Millie wondered.

'It might depend on how much he thinks he's been wronged,' Glover said. 'And how much drink he's got inside him.'

The Kerrigan family lived in the heart of the Nansen Road sink estate in one of the larger council houses. Michael Kerrigan was in the garden tinkering with an ancient motorcycle when they got there. Even though it was a cool day, he wore jeans and a sleeveless T-shirt, his tattooed arms oily and a grimy bandana tied around his forehead. Pushing fifty he was rangy and strong; not a man you'd want to run into in a dark alley. Millie could understand why Pam had felt intimidated.

But Kerrigan seemed unperturbed to see them. 'Mr Glover,' he said evenly. 'This is a rare pleasure. What can I do for you, sir?' He picked up a filthy cloth and wiped his hands on it. Though he'd lived in the city for three decades, the Irish accent was as strong as any Millie had heard.

'I hear congratulations are in order, Michael,' said Glover pleasantly. 'You've got a new addition to the family.'

Kerrigan beamed with what seemed like genuine pride. 'I've still got it in me,' he boasted.

'What did the social services think?' Glover asked.

Kerrigan's face clouded. 'They had no feckin' business coming here, and that feckin' nurse had no right to send them in the first place.'

'She was only doing her job,' Glover reasoned. 'Making sure that your wife had all the support she needed.'

'I give her enough support. She doesn't want anyone else interfering.' Kerrigan's fists hanging loose at his sides, had clenched, the knuckles white.

'You seem upset about that,' Glover observed.

'They have no right to come sticking their noses in, the social. It's only because of who we are.'

'It still bothers you, doesn't it?'

Kerrigan's eyes narrowed quizzically.

'Is that why you're giving Mrs Jarrett a hard time?'

Kerrigan squinted at Glover uncertainly.

'I heard that you caused a scene outside the health centre a couple of weeks ago,' Glover continued, and the penny dropped.

'Yeah, well, she deserved it,' said Kerrigan petulantly.

'Did she deserve the phone calls too?' Millie interceded. 'Have you been trying to give her a scare?'

'What?'

'*You bitch, I'm going to make you suffer.* It's not very imaginative, Mr Kerrigan.'

Kerrigan directed his confusion at Glover. 'What the hell is she talkin' about?'

'So you haven't taken it upon yourself to make nuisance phone calls to Lucy Jarrett's house?' Glover said. 'We've got a witness who can put you in the vicinity of Mrs Jarrett's home about three weeks ago.'

'How the feck?' Kerrigan seemed mystified. 'I don't even know where the woman lives.'

'You know where she works, though. It would have been easy enough to follow her home,' Glover pointed out.

'Oh, and I can run at forty miles an hour now, can I? In case you hadn't noticed, Mr Glover, I don't have a car.'

'It doesn't mean you can't borrow one when you need it. Our witness saw someone fitting your description, including the accent, who says you were at Hill Crest three weeks ago on a Thursday at about nine thirty, asking where Lucy Jarrett lives.'

'I've told you,' Kerrigan insisted. 'I don't even know where that is.'

'Let me refresh your memory then. It's the estate off the Bristol Road, just down from the college.'

Kerrigan thought for a moment. 'Ah, I know the one. The big posh houses. Yeah, I was there. Can't remember when it was, though.'

'What were you doing there?' Glover asked.

'Knocking doors,' said Kerrigan. 'We had a load of tarmac, so I was askin' if anyone wanted their drive doin'. It was ages ago.'

'Our witness says you were asking for Lucy Jarrett's house.'

'Well, your witness is wrong, Mr Glover. It wasn't me he talked to. There was no one about, the place was like a bleedin' ghost town, and, anyway, I'm not anywhere at nine thirty in the morning. I don't get up till all the kids are off to school, maybe ten o'clock.'

'Is there anyone who can back that up?' Glover asked.

'Do you mean is there anyone there in bed with me at that time? Now whatever would the wife think, Mr Glover?'

'Have you got a computer, Mr Kerrigan?' Millie asked.

Kerrigan regarded her with suspicion. 'Aye, the kiddies need it for their school work, but I know nothin' about the thing.'

CHAPTER FOURTEEN

Millie walked back to the car with Charlie Glover. 'What do you think?' she asked. 'He's admitted to being in that area.'

'But not at that time of day. His kind of lifestyle, I doubt very much that he's up with the lark. And I don't think he's that vindictive.'

'But he is proud,' Millie pointed out. 'I can't imagine he'd like what it would do to his reputation if it got around that social services had been in. You saw how tense he was about that.'

'True,' Glover conceded.

'Do you think it's worth an ID parade?'

'Trouble with that is that he's admitted being on the estate. Your cleaner might well recognise him, but only because she's seen him at a completely different time.' Glover had a point. 'I mean, I wouldn't discount him straight away, but you're going to need more than circumstantial to bring him in.'

Still feeling ill, Lucy Jarrett had left work

early and arrived home late on Monday afternoon to find another package on the doorstep. She groaned inwardly. Mostly this was just becoming tiresome now. She picked up the long, narrow cardboard box, which was surprisingly lightweight, its label announcing that inside were flowers from Guernsey. Taking it into the kitchen, she actually considered consigning it straight to the bin, but realised that Millie would probably want to see it. Then she remembered Alice, who had started out with her as a health visitor and had moved to Guernsey just a few months ago; they must be genuine after all. With some relief she snipped open the tape and lifted off the lid. She cried out involuntarily. Inside were six roses, dried, withered and obscene like tiny skeletons lying side by side in a miniature coffin. There was a sheet of paper wrapped around them which she gingerly removed, and on it was one of her own wedding photos, but her face had been obliterated by the frenzied scribble of a black marker pen. The caption typed underneath read: *A flower that isn't nurtured withers and dies. I'm going to make sure it happens to you. Happy Anniversary.*

Bright lights flashed behind Lucy's eyes and she felt faint, bile rising suddenly in her throat again. Thank God for the downstairs cloakroom.

When the retching had finished, she threw

cold water on her face, and looked up into the mirror. Wither and die? It was already happening. Her skin was pale and her cheeks sunken. Lately she'd had to start wearing a belt with her favourite jeans, to keep them up. Last week alone three different people had asked her if she was all right, or told her how tired she looked. When she lifted the phone she was unable to control the tremor in her hand.

Millie had already left, so Lucy spoke to her voicemail. The message was simple: 'DC Khatoon, it's Lucy Jarrett. Something else came today.'

Millie picked up the message first thing on Tuesday morning and went straight out to see Lucy. She looked as grey and ill as she had the day before. 'Are you sure you're not sickening for something?'

'I don't know,' Lucy said wearily. 'I do feel lousy and I've been sick again this morning.' She glanced at her watch. 'I've got a doctor's appointment in an hour.'

'You're not–' Millie began.

'Oh, God, no. Could you imagine? I think Will would kill me.'

Millie wondered if she realised what she had just said. Lucy took her through to the kitchen where the box lay on the table.

'Where is Will?' Millie asked.

'They're in the north Midlands tonight,

he'll be back tomorrow. He called this morning. I think he's forgiven me.'

'For what? For being afraid and asking for help?' Millie was incredulous. 'You shouldn't let him make you feel bad.'

'I know. How did it go with Michael Kerrigan?'

'Well, he has admitted to being here on the estate, though not at the time we were told. He said he was canvassing for work, though, laying tarmac drives.'

'Maybe he was.' Lucy got up and went over to the kitchen drawer. She sorted through some leaflets. 'I had this through the door a couple of weeks ago.' She passed Millie a roughly printed leaflet offering just those services, complete with mobile number. Taking out her phone, Millie tapped in the digits. It rang a few times, then the unmistakable voice of Michael Kerrigan cut in, inviting her to leave a message.

'So, he has been around here. Perhaps he already knew which house was yours,' Millie said. 'But we'd need more evidence to bring him in. Did you mention to his wife that you weren't planning children?'

'I might have, I really don't remember. And what about these?' Lucy pushed the box across to Millie. Just looking at it put a catch in her throat.

Millie carefully lifted the lid. 'What's the anniversary?' she asked, examining the ruined picture.

'I don't know. It's way too soon to be Will's and mine. I've racked my brains but I can't think of anything else.'

'Who would have had access to your wedding photos?'

'Lots of people,' Lucy said. 'We had them put online and when we sent out thank-you cards for gifts we put the web address inside the card. Anyone who had that address could then access the photos and print off what they wanted. I gave the address to a couple of other people who wanted to see them.'

'Kerrigan's wife?' Millie asked.

'No, I'm sure I wouldn't have given it to her. I hardly know her.'

'I'll need the name of the photographer, and a list of your wedding guests.'

'I'll get it for you.' Moments later she was back with a business card. 'The wedding guests are on the computer. You'll just need to print them off.'

When Millie returned to Granville Lane armed with the information Lucy had given her, CID was still pretty deserted. The first thing she did at her desk was to phone the wedding photographers. They couldn't tell her there and then who had accessed Lucy Jarrett's photographs but promised to find out and get back to her later in the day.

Millie looked up and called a greeting as Tony Knox came in. As he walked past her desk to get to his own, he stopped in his tracks. 'What've you got there?' he asked, looking at the flower box in its evidence bag.

'Lucy Jarrett got sent them yesterday,' Millie said. 'Lovely, aren't they?'

But Knox was just staring at them.

'What is it?'

Ignoring the question, Knox went over to his own desk and sorted through the mess of paper till he came up with a copy of Nina Silvero's florist card. 'Snap,' he said, slapping it down next to Lucy Jarrett's box. 'Soon as the boss gets in we need to talk.'

Mariner spent the drive in to Granville Lane playing over in his head the fiasco at the weekend. Kat had stayed out until late again last night, and they had stepped carefully around each other once more at breakfast. Then, just as he was leaving, she'd fixed him with those huge grey eyes and said, 'I think I like to get my own place.'

His pathetic response had been a smile, at least he hoped that was how it looked, and 'Sure, we'll talk about it.' And after that he'd escaped as fast as he could. She hated him, he thought; him and his assumptions.

Millie would probably know what to do, but when he walked into CID his DS and DC were clearly waiting for him with urgent issues of their own. Along with three strong coffees, he called them both into his office.

Millie showed him the flowers that Lucy Jarrett had received. 'Tony says we need to discuss these but won't say why,' she said.

Taking the box in its evidence bag, Mariner turned it over in his hands. 'Birmingham postmark,' he said, to no one in particular. He glanced up at Millie. 'We haven't got Nina Silvero's flowers, and Rachel Hordern never saw them, but from her description they sound the same–'

'And this is definitely the same message.' Knox held up the card and the picture for comparison.

Mariner was still trying to absorb this development. 'Christ, this is too close to be pure coincidence.'

Millie too was looking stunned. 'So these cases are linked?'

'How else do we explain it?' said Knox.

'I didn't think much of it at the time,' Mariner said. 'It seemed almost incidental, but Rachel said her stepmother had some funny phone calls about this time last year, and then she received the flowers.'

'Well, Lucy Jarrett has been getting the funny phone calls, and now she's had the flowers.' Millie paled. 'God, does that mean someone's planning for her to meet the same end as Nina Silvero?'

'Let's stay calm about this,' Mariner said.

'Even if they are, we might have a bit of time. For Nina Silvero there's been a gap of a year between the flowers and her murder, though Christ alone knows what that means. But I'm not aware of anything else that links these two women.' A glance at his sergeant and constable confirmed that neither were they. 'We need to think about who we've got in the frame for each of these and try to find some kind of connection.' Mariner stood up, went over to the window and pushed it open a couple of inches. 'Make yourselves comfortable, we may be here a while.'

'We should get Charlie in on this too,' Millie said, seeing Charlie Glover out in the bull pen, at his desk. 'He's got previous experience of one of my possible suspects.'

'We could certainly do with the extra brain power,' Mariner said, and summoned Glover into the meeting, explaining briefly where they were up to. Then he turned to Millie. 'Take us through what you've got so far.'

Millie cleared her throat. 'As you know, the main thing I've been investigating is nuisance phone calls, post and emails, and the possibility that someone might be following Lucy. I still haven't ruled out her husband. He remains the person with the most opportunity to set everything up and, if we acknowledge the possibility that he and Tess Maguire have got something going on, he's also got the motive too.' She glanced up at Charlie. 'We also have an Irish connection. About three weeks ago an Irishman was on Lucy's estate asking where exactly she lived. Leigh Hawkins' band is essentially Irish. But there's only circumstantial evidence so far. We found nothing incriminating on Will's computer. Max is trying to locate the source of all the spam emails Lucy has been getting, so that will tell us more. And Asheville police have put him in the clear; he's not wanted for any criminal activity, nor does he have any other wives and families over there.'

'Mr Squeaky Clean,' Knox remarked.

'That's how it seems,' Millie agreed.

'And no connection with Nina Silvero that springs to mind,' added Mariner. 'I can't think how their paths might cross. The women are different ages, live in different parts of the city, different careers. I can't imagine Nina Silvero being a big folk fan. I seem to remember her CD collection being mostly classical works, though we can easily check with Rachel.'

'Rachel has a toddler, and Lucy's a health visitor,' Knox said. 'Could it be professional?'

Mariner shook his head. 'The Horderns have lived in Somerset since before Harry was born.'

'Also, if Will's motive is to get his hands on half Lucy's worldly goods, where does Nina

Silvero come in?' said Millie. 'The only possibility might be that Nina knew what he was up to, but, given that there's no evidence they even knew each other, that doesn't stand up.'

'What about the jealous friend?' Mariner asked.

Millie was doubtful. 'No, I'm not sure about Julie-Ann. She was round the other night and she and Lucy seemed pretty close.'

'So who else have you got?'

'Well, if the mysterious Irishman isn't a band member, there's also Michael Kerrigan.'

Mariner leaned forward, suddenly interested. 'I know that name,' he said.

'He's on our books for past misdemeanours,' Glover said. 'I've had a couple of run-ins with him, and he didn't take kindly to Lucy's referral to social services. He admits to being on Lucy's estate looking for work tarmacking drives, but not at the time our witness says.'

'Could she be mistaken?' asked Mariner.

'We're talking weeks ago, so, yes, she could,' Millie said.

'Nina Silvero's drive had been recently tarmacked,' Mariner recalled. 'It was still sticky.'

'But what's the motive, boss?' Knox asked. 'At a stretch I can see why Kerrigan might have had reason to be annoyed with Lucy

Jarrett. And perhaps he did a new drive for Nina Silvero, but what possible motive could he have for such a malicious attack on her?'

'Maybe she made some derogatory comment about travellers,' Glover speculated. 'He's pretty touchy about stuff like that.'

'He wouldn't kill her for it, though,' Knox said.

'I couldn't see Nina Silvero inviting him into the house either,' said Millie.

'Or Kerrigan as a Chardonnay drinker, for that matter,' Glover conceded.

They sat in silence for a moment, thinking.

'OK, let's approach this from the other angle,' said Mariner. 'What we've got for Nina Silvero. Tony, can you run through it for us?'

'Well, if we start with opportunity again, the most likely candidates are her step-daughter Rachel and dancing "partner" Susan Brady,' Knox said. 'They're the ones who had most to gain from the will, and they're the ones who would have had easiest access. We also know that Rachel quarrelled with her stepmother just a couple of weeks ago. She's given us her version of events on the evening Nina died; that she was on the phone to her stepmother when the un-known visitor arrived, but, since no one saw this person, we only have her word for it. Hordern and Brady could be in it together; Brady carrying out the murder. They looked pretty tight at the funeral, even though they'd said they didn't have much to do with each other any more, and Brady is definitely someone Nina Silvero would have invited in.'

'But the motive doesn't transfer,' Millie said. 'What possible reason could either Rachel or Susan have for terrorising Lucy Jarrett? There's no indication that they know each other.'

'Do we know that for sure?' Mariner's question was met with silence. 'They're all around the same age,' he went on. 'We need to check that out. Aside from them, the strongest lead we've got for Nina Silvero is Billy Hughes' family.' He described what he learned about the past case to Millie and Glover.

'They certainly have reason to hold a grudge against Nina Silvero, but again it doesn't tell us where Lucy fits in,' Knox said.

Mariner rubbed a hand over his face. 'Maybe we're looking for someone that doesn't exist.'

'But these exist all right, boss.' Knox picked up the flowers. 'Same MO; could be a coincidence. But same wording on the notes? It has to be more than that.'

'Ronnie Silvero was a Mason,' Mariner

said. 'But we probably shouldn't hold that against him.'

'Paul Copeland was a Mason, too,' said Millie.

'Paul Copeland?'

'Lucy's father.'

Mariner scrabbled around his desk until he found his notes from the Billy Hughes file, and flicked through until he found the right page. 'Gotcha,' he said. 'I knew I recognised the name. Paul Copeland was on the public inquiry into Billy Hughes' death. Which brings us back again to the Hughes family. I think we need to pay them another visit. Meanwhile, keep plugging away on the leads we've already got and we'll convene again later today.'

On the way out to West Heath, Mariner slammed on his brakes as a car shot out in front of him at a mini roundabout, allowing access from yet another brand-new housing estate. He only just missed the offending vehicle, and blared his horn and gesticulated.

'You're meant to give way to traffic from the right, moron!' he yelled.

'Don't think he heard you, boss,' said Knox drily.

The development was not dissimilar to Lucy Jarrett's estate; a mixture of detached executive properties, three-storey townhouses and flats, with wrought-iron balconies.

'Christ, where do all the people come from to live in these places?' Mariner said. 'They're springing up all over the place. What used to be there?'

'Some factory, wasn't it?' Knox said.

'That's right. What was it?' No doubt yet another product Birmingham can no longer boast. 'They must have knocked these up pretty smartish. It only closed a couple of years ago.'

When they got to the address Tracey Hughes had given them, they found a semi-detached, a generation or two older than hers. As Mariner parked up along the street, a car pulled on to the drive. The Hughes family were just returning from a shopping trip; two couples in late middle age and another younger man, late forties or early fifties. While three of the older occupants of the car got out, laden with numerous high-street-store carrier bags, the younger man went round to the remaining passenger door where he helped out the fourth passenger, passing to him the two walking sticks necessary for mobility.

Mariner and Knox watched and waited until everyone was in the house, allowed five minutes for good measure, then went and rang the bell. The younger man answered it, and this time, when Mariner produced his warrant card, only his speedy reflexes prevented the door from being slammed in his face.

'I understand Mr and Mrs Hughes are staying here,' Mariner said, keeping his foot firmly in place.

'What do you want with them?' The man was short and stocky with big shoulders and a thick neck, his eyes close together in a podgy face.

'And you are?' Mariner asked.

'Their son.'

'Ah, Billy's brother, George, I presume. I need to talk to your parents about the death of Nina Silvero.'

'This week of all weeks? You know what you can do.' Hughes pushed against the door but Mariner held firm.

'I understand that this is a difficult time, Mr Hughes,' Mariner said calmly. 'But if we don't do it now we'll have to come back. All we need to do is eliminate them from our enquiries. Then we can leave you in peace.'

An older man appeared, white haired and in checked shirt and cardigan. 'What is it, Georgie?'

'They're coppers. Want to talk to Mum and Dad.'

The man was resigned. 'Let them in, son. Let's get this over and done with.'

He stepped aside, but George Hughes made sure his presence was felt while

Mariner and Knox talked to his parents. Refusing to sit, he stood glowering in the corner of the room across from where the two policemen sat on the sofa. Neither Eric Hughes, who appeared to be in the early stages of Parkinson's disease, nor Eva, a mild woman, small and quietly spoken, appeared to object to the visit.

'I felt sorry for her,' Eva said, of Nina Silvero. 'She'd lost her husband, hadn't she?'

'Sorry for her?' interjected Hughes junior. 'Christ, Mum, after what he did? And she stood by him, denying that he'd done anything wrong, while my little brother lay dead in the morgue. I'm glad she's dead, and I hope she suffered in the way that our Billy did.'

'Don't talk to your mother like that,' barked Eric Hughes, his speech slightly slurred.

'Did you go to Nina Silvero's house after your brother died?' Mariner asked George.

'I think you know the answer to that one,' Hughes spat.

'So it was you who put a brick through her window?'

'We weren't going to get any comeback any other way, were we? You lot, you all close ranks and cover up for each other. It was a whitewash. Our Billy was dead and nobody gave a toss. Is that what you're here for, to charge me with criminal damage twenty years too late? You lot must be desperate for something to do.'

'Is that the last time you went there?' asked Mariner.

'What are you getting at?' Hughes' eyes narrowed.

'That you could have approached her recently, insinuated your way into her house and ensured that she suffered the same agonising death that Billy did.'

'I haven't been near the place in twenty years.' Hughes was defiant. 'I'd hardly thought about her until now.'

Mariner noticed the folded newspaper on the coffee table. 'You get the *Mail* regularly, do you?'

'June and John get it,' said Eva.

Mariner fixed his gaze on George. 'Told you about the announcement, did they? That must have provided a little reminder.'

'It made me sick,' said Hughes, with disgust. 'Bloody MBE. What's she done to deserve that?'

Mariner nodded slowly, understanding. 'So much anger and resentment,' he said. 'It's been festering away all this time, hasn't it? And the twenty-year anniversary of your brother's death might be just the right time to get justice once and for all.'

'Georgie?' Eva Hughes cast a doubtfiul look at her son.

'Where do you live, Mr Hughes?' Mariner asked.

'Down south with Mum and Dad. I got made redundant.'

'Where from?'

'The Rover.'

'And what did you do there?' Mariner persisted.

'I was in the paint shop.'

Mariner turned to exchange a brief glance with Tony Knox. 'What were you doing on Sunday evening between seven thirty and midnight?' he asked Hughes.

Hughes laughed and shook his head in disbelief. 'You're so way off beam, it's a joke. You haven't got a clue.'

And Hughes, it transpired, had a pretty good alibi. The family had all gone for a meal with other relatives, including sister Tracey, at a local restaurant. 'About twenty other people and the staff in the restaurant can confirm it,' Hughes finished smugly.

'Although there was nothing stopping him from slipping out for half an hour,' Mariner said to Knox, as they were walking back to their car.

CHAPTER FIFTEEN

Mariner was home a little late that evening, and as he pulled into the service road leading up to his house he came to a halt behind a Porsche he recognised. As he walked into the lounge, Giles jumped to his feet immediately. In the light Mariner had a better opportunity to study him, and gallingly he was even better looking than Mariner remembered. He matched Mariner for height and was lean and athletic looking, from what Mariner could tell through the well-cut jeans and pink candy-stripe shirt, and, despite what had happened the previous night, he had manners. They both remained standing, two stags weighing each other up.

But it was Giles who ended the stand-off. 'Hello again, sir.' The confidence and enunciation said public school. The 'sir' underlined both the breeding and Mariner's age.

Mariner took a few seconds to arrange the bullet between his teeth, then he clamped down hard on it. 'Look, I'm sorry about Saturday night,' he said. 'I jumped to some conclusions.'

'Apology accepted,' Giles cut him short. 'I admit that I was pretty annoyed at the time, but I know what kind of life Kat had before she came to stay with you, and I understand that you were only looking out for her.'

'Still, I made some assumptions about you that I shouldn't have,' Mariner said.

'Occupational hazard, I suppose.' Giles smiled. 'Really, it's OK. Forget it.'

'Thank you,' Mariner said awkwardly. He took the small evidence bag from his pocket. 'And you can have this back. I didn't get around to having it tested.'

'Thanks.' Giles took it from him and pocketed it.

Mariner gestured for Giles to sit, and they took up places opposite one another. 'I'm not sure that Kat will be so quick to forgive,' he said. 'She wants to move out.'

'I think she's wanted to for a while,' Giles said. 'She just didn't know how to tell you.'

'Well, I've certainly given her that opportunity. Is she moving in with you?'

'No.' Giles seemed surprised. 'It's not like that. I think she wants her own place, close to one of her friends at the centre.'

'Oh.'

'She'll get over this, sir,' Giles reassured him. 'She worships the ground you walk on, talked about you non-stop when we first met. It's her opinion that you saved her life.'

Mariner nodded; gratifying though it was, he wasn't sure of what to say to that.

Once again Giles rescued him. 'We're

going out for dinner. If that's OK.'

'Of course.' Mariner nodded. For an awful moment he thought Giles was going to invite him along, but thankfully he didn't. That would have made for an uncomfortable evening. 'So what is it that you do, Giles?' he asked.

Giles visibly relaxed, on safer ground. 'I'm in merchant banking, for my sins. It's something of a family tradition.'

That and polo at the weekends, Mariner guessed. At least it went some way towards explaining the affluence.

Kat rescued them from further awkward small talk, appearing at the top of the stairs. She looked frail yet stunning, dressing again to show off her best features, and Mariner wanted to rush over and cover her up. Instead, he just said, 'Have a good time,' as he got up and saw them out, hoping that the gritted teeth weren't too obvious. On her way past Mariner, Kat leaned up and kissed him on the cheek. Giles was right (again). They'd get over it.

On his own again, Mariner felt restless. He phoned Tony Knox, with a view to a possible early-evening drink, but caught his sergeant on his way out to the pictures with Jean. 'Want to come, boss?' Knox offered, but Mariner had no intention of playing gooseberry with Knox and his date either.

Instead, he got a sheet of paper and

divided it into two columns, Nina Silvero heading up one, Lucy Jarrett the other. Then he listed everything he knew about the two women, highlighting any possible connections between them. By midnight the paper was a mess of scribblings and arrows but, aside from a few question marks, he found nothing that connected the two.

On Wednesday morning, Mariner drove in early and caught up with Tony Knox in the car park. 'Good film?' he asked.

'It was OK,' Knox conceded. 'Jean liked it. I spent most of the time trying to work out what Nina Silvero and Lucy Jarrett have in common.'

'You and me both,' said Mariner. They climbed the stairs to find Millie already in CID along with Rick Fraser from forensics, who was outside Mariner's office, hopping from foot to foot like an errant schoolboy waiting to see the head teacher. A comical sight given that Fraser was a bear of a man, red faced with explosions of wiry ginger hair above each ear and fringing a completely bald dome of a skull.

'Sackcloth and ashes, Mr Mariner,' he said sheepishly, passing Mariner a manila folder. 'You should have had this a couple of days ago, but I wanted to tie up the loose ends before I gave it to you.'

'This is the crime-scene report?' Thanking

him, Mariner took the folder. 'Can you stick around in case we've got any questions?'

'Of course.' Fraser followed Mariner and Knox into Mariner's office, where Millie joined them too.

Sitting behind his desk, Mariner opened the report and scanned it quickly. 'It's as we thought,' he said eventually, glancing up at the three on the other side of his desk. 'The wine bottle had been rinsed, leaving no traces of white wine or paint stripper. Two wine glasses had also been recently used and rinsed. Looks as if it played out just as we surmised.'

Knox nodded thoughtfully. 'So the killer comes to the door with a celebratory bottle of wine, they go into the kitchen, two glasses poured.' He mimed the pouring of the wine. 'They toast the MBE.' He raised his imaginary glass.

'And the killer hesitates, allowing Nina Silvero to drink the fatal mouthfuls, while he or she watches,' Mariner added.

'Then he or she tips the rest of the paint stripper down the sink, rinses the bottle and his own glass, puts that glass away again and takes out the plastic drain-fluid bottle containing the residue of the paint stripper, and leaves that on the table.'

'There's nothing else?' Mariner was disappointed. These results only confirmed what they'd already worked out.

'In case you're interested,' Fraser added helpfully, 'the wine was part of a batch sold at Sainsbury's in Selly Oak between December last year and February this year. And there is one more thing,' he said tantalisingly. 'We've got a latent lifted from the base of the bottle.'

'There's a fingerprint?' Mariner remained cautious. 'I thought the bottle had been wiped clean.'

'So did we.' Fraser grinned. 'The killer must have overlooked it. In all the areas where you'd usually hold the bottle – the neck and body, it's been wiped, but the killer slipped up. There's a single print on the base of the bottle that's been missed. It probably got there when the bottle was first picked up in the supermarket to examine the label. Do you mind?' Millie was clutching a bottle of water. With her consent, Fraser took it from her and placed it on Mariner's desk. He then picked up the bottle, grasping it around the neck with his right hand, and resting the base on the fingertips of his left hand to demonstrate. Satisfied that they'd all seen, he held up the index finger on which the bottle had been resting. 'And that's the print that was overlooked.'

'It's not Nina Silvero's print?' Mariner allowed himself a glimmer of hope.

'Definitely not,' said Fraser, with an emphatic shake of the head.

Mariner hardly dared ask. 'Is it one we've got on record?' The print was useless if it wasn't already on file.

Three pairs of eyes fixed on Fraser. His face broke into its crooked grin. 'Indeed, it is. Of course it may not mean anything,' he cautioned. 'If that's the explanation for how it got there, anyone could have picked up the bottle from the supermarket shelf prior to the killer, then changed their mind and put it back again, but–' He broke off and shrugged.

'Come on then.' Knox's impatience was beginning to show. 'Give us the worst.'

'The print belongs to a Martin Bonnington, sixteen, Hill Crest.'

'Jesus,' Mariner said.

'You know him?' Knox wrinkled his nose, the information meaningless to him.

'Hill Crest is where Lucy Jarrett lives,' Millie put in. 'Number sixteen is just across the road from her house. I rang the bell there when she had a parcel delivered, but there was no one home.'

'So we've got ourselves another coincidence,' said Knox.

'And I'd say a possible suspect,' Mariner added. 'Do you know what Bonnington's on our books for?' he asked Fraser.

'About three years ago, he had an injunction out against him to stop him harassing a female work colleague,' Fraser told them.

'Which makes him well worth a look for Lucy Jarrett,' Mariner said. 'But where does Nina Silvero come in?'

When Fraser had departed with promises of a pint next time they were in the pub, Mariner brought up Bonnington's record on his PC, Millie and Knox standing at each shoulder. 'Do you recognise him?' he asked Millie, as Bonnington's mug-shot appeared.

She shook her head. 'I haven't seen him around there. When I rang the bell at his house there was no vehicle on the drive, though I did get a feeling that there could be someone in the house. Also, I think Lucy must know him too, at least just to say hello to. I'm sure that at the time she said, "That's Martin's house."'

The file didn't tell them much else, only that just under three years previously Bonnington had been accused of harassing a woman called Claudette Vernon, who had subsequently made a complaint to the police. Officers had gone to see him, at a different address from his current one, and presented him with the injunction. Bonnington, it appeared, had initially protested his innocence, but had then been penitent and had accepted the court order. Brian Mann had been one of the officers involved and Mariner made a note to go and talk to him about it. He printed off copies of Bonnington's photograph, hoping that it was still a good likeness.

Back at her desk, Millie phoned Lucy Jarrett's mobile. 'When would be a convenient time to come and see you?'

'I'm at home right now, if that's any good.'

'Not at work today?' Millie asked.

'No, the doctor has signed me off for a few days. Stress she says, but she's running some blood tests too.'

Twenty minutes later Mariner and Millie presented themselves at Lucy Jarrett's house. Mariner was shocked by her appearance. Since he'd last seen her she'd visibly lost weight, and her skin looked pale and sallow. They followed her into the lounge, where she sat across from them on the sofa, hugging a cushion to her for comfort. 'So what brings you here?'

'The flowers you had in the post,' Mariner said. 'We've come across something similar before.'

'Oh?' Lucy looked uncertainly from one to the other of them. 'What's going on?'

'Lucy, do you know a woman called Nina Silvero?' Millie asked her.

Her brow creased to a frown. 'The name is fam– Wait a minute, isn't she that woman who was killed recently?'

Mariner nodded. 'But had you heard of her before that? Did you know her?'

'No.'

'What about Rachel Silvero, or Rachel Hordern as she's called now, or Susan Brady? They're more your age.'

But Lucy knew neither of them.

'Did you ever have ballet lessons?' Mariner asked.

'No.' She glanced at Millie, her anxiety levels visibly rising. 'The cheerleading is the closest I got. Look, I'm sure I don't know any of these people. What is it? What's going on?'

Mariner chose his words carefully, knowing that what he was about to say would put the fear of God into her. 'Nina Silvero received some flowers packaged in the same way as yours, and with exactly the same message, about a year ago,' he said. 'It seems that she had been getting unwanted phone calls too, and there's evidence to suggest that she had fears for her own safety.'

'What kind of evidence?' Lucy made no effort to disguise her unease now.

'She'd taken steps to make her house more secure,' Mariner said.

'And you think it's the same person who's coming after me?' Lucy asked, her eyes wide.

Mariner took out the photograph he'd brought along. 'Do you know this man?'

'Yes, of course I do.' Now she was baffled. 'It's Martin from across the road.'

'How well do you know him?'

'Not at all really.' Lucy shifted uncomfortably. 'He was very helpful when I moved in to the house.'

'Helpful how?' Millie asked.

'He's a computer geek. He wired everything up for me.'

Millie and Mariner exchanged a surreptitious look.

'And since then?'

Lucy shrugged. 'Nothing much. We speak to each other when our paths cross but that's about all.' But she'd coloured. Something she wasn't saying.

'Lucy, if there's anything–' Millie bided her time and eventually Lucy cracked.

'It was just a misunderstanding, that's all,' she blurted out.

'What was?' Mariner wanted to know.

'Martin came over to look at my computer one evening, not long after I'd moved in,' Lucy said. 'He came on to me, but he'd completely misread the signals. He's a bit, well, old-fashioned looking and I didn't fancy him so I fielded it. And that was the end of it. It was all perfectly innocent and it was ages ago.'

'Do you know where he works?'

'From home mostly. He's freelance.'

'He's at home now?' Mariner asked.

'He comes and goes. If his car's there, he will be. If not, he shouldn't be long.' Lucy looked up at Millie. 'But I don't understand. You can't think that Martin's behind this? He's harmless.'

'Did he talk to you about his previous relationships?' Millie asked her.

'We didn't get that close.'

'So he didn't tell you that he was subject to an injunction to stop him harassing another woman?'

'Oh, God. No, he didn't.'

Leaving Lucy to rest, Mariner and Millie went together to interview Martin Bonnington. The way some men behaved towards women could often be telling, and Mariner wanted to determine his attitude towards Millie. But Bonnington's car wasn't on the drive and no one answered the door. They were in for a wait, so, sat in the car.

While they were doing so, Mariner put through a call to Tony Knox. 'When you were going through Nina Silvero's paperwork, did you come across any adverts for computer services?'

Knox couldn't remember seeing any.

'Bonnington's a freelancer and helped Lucy with hers,' Mariner told him. 'He might have done the same for Nina Silvero. Have another look, will you?' He ended the call.

'How's things with Kat?' Millie asked.

'We've called a kind of truce. I've apologised to her boyfriend and actually he took it surprisingly well. That's what breeding does for you, I suppose.'

'And you feel happier about him?'

'Sort of. Once Kat explained how she met him, it all made sense. I still think he's too worldly for her, but he does seem to genuinely care about her, and the bottom line is, it's none of my business, is it?'

'Is she still talking about moving out?'

'We haven't discussed it, but I think—' He broke off. A Renault Clio had just swung into the drive of number sixteen. They watched the man they assumed to be Bonnington get out of his car and let himself into the house. Several minutes later, they followed him to the door.

Bonnington took a little while to respond. At first glance he wasn't what Mariner had expected. He was small, probably about five six or seven, and his short dark hair was thinning slightly on top and neatly combed across from a side parting. He wore dark trousers, white shirt and a cardigan. Mariner could see what Lucy Jarrett meant about Bonnington looking old-fashioned. Good looking? He'd have to ask Millie later. The facial expression was one Mariner recognised; Bonnington was afraid they were going to try to sell him something, at worst a religion, and his greeting was mild but uncertain. 'Hello, can I help?'

Mariner held up his warrant card and made the introductions. 'Your neighbour,

Lucy Jarrett, is being harassed by someone making, among other things, nuisance phone calls,' he said.

'Oh. So she pointed you in my direction.' More than anything, Bonnington sounded hurt.

'We're checking out all friends and acquaintances, which means talking to neighbours as well,' Mariner said. 'It's just routine.'

'Uhu.'

'Can we come in?'

'Well, to be honest, it's not the most convenient...' He tailed off, the weak protest left hanging as Mariner and Millie walked past him into the house. 'In here.' He indicated the way into the front living room whose bay windows would have overlooked the street had the wooden slatted blinds not been half closed. A computer work station took up one wall, otherwise the room was sparsely furnished, tidy and spotlessly clean. Mariner remembered Knox's comment about Nina Silvero's obsessive compulsive tendency and, in a moment of idle speculation, wondered if this was something she and Bonnington had in common. Perhaps they'd met, like Giles and Kat, through some kind of support group. 'What are you working on?' he asked, though he had next to no interest in computers.

'I'm a freelance programmer,' said Bonnington. 'Though Lucy must have told you that. I'm working on an auditing programme for an accounting firm.'

Mariner sat on the white linen sofa with his back to the window, Millie beside him, leaving Bonnington the armchair opposite. All the better to see his face. But instead he chose to sit where he felt most at home, on the office chair beside the computer. He leaned forward, hands clasped between his knees.

'I understand you and Mrs Jarrett are friends,' Mariner said.

'Friends? Is that what she told you? That might be putting it a bit strongly.'

'So how would you characterise your relationship?' Mariner asked.

Bonnington shrugged. 'I helped her to move in, we went out for a couple of drinks and then she dropped me when she had no further use for me.' He flashed a brief, humourless smile. 'I'm not sure I'd describe that as friendship.' He seemed bemused, stating the facts blandly. Mariner was alert to any hint of bitterness, but there seemed to be none.

'Mrs Jarrett says you made a pass at her,' he said.

'Does she?' The puzzled frown looked real enough. 'That makes it sound a bit one sided.'

'You disagree?'

'She seemed keen enough, to a point,' said Bonnington. 'All I did was respond in the way that any normal man would.'

Mariner exchanged a fleeting glance with Millie. They'd both heard that one before. 'She says you misread the signals,' Millie said.

'Oh. Well, of course, she could be right about that,' he accepted. 'It wouldn't be the first time. I don't have a great success rate with women, generally speaking. But in Lucy's case–' he grimaced, straining to recall '–I did think it was obvious, even to me.'

'So why don't you tell us what you think happened?' Millie suggested.

'Well, as I said, we went out about three times. On the last occasion Lucy told me that her Internet connection was playing up. As I'd set up the system for her when she moved in, I felt responsible, so offered to go in and fix the problem. When we got back from the pub we went to her house and I went upstairs to where her computer is. It turned out to be quite simple; for some reason the configuration of the modem had–'

'You can spare us the technical details,' Mariner intervened.

'OK.' Bonnington seemed puzzled at the lack of interest. 'Well, then I came back down and Lucy had made tea and we sat talking. We seemed to be getting along well, and we were sitting quite close, so, at what I thought was an opportune moment I leaned over and kissed her. It was probably a bit clumsy, admittedly, but she kissed me back, which I took as an encouraging sign.'

'You're sure about that, she definitely kissed you back?'

Bonnington looked Millie in the eye. 'Oh, yes. I was pleasantly surprised. It doesn't always work out that way.'

'And then?'

'Clothing got unfastened, as I remember it.'

'Hers or yours?'

'Both; she worked on mine and I worked on hers, except that she was more adept at it than I was. She had these tiny buttons on her blouse that were impossible, so she progressed further than I did.'

'What do you mean by that?'

'She had her hand inside my trousers before I'd even got the top couple of buttons undone.'

'And then?'

For the first time Bonnington avoided eye contact, and his colour heightened a little. 'It was over before it started really.'

'Meaning?'

'I ejaculated. I couldn't help it. It just sort of happened. I suppose it had been a while since – anyway, I apologised and she said it was OK, which clearly it wasn't. And we both got dressed and I went home.'

'So that was the end of it?' said Mariner.

'Well, a couple of weeks later the man in the van appeared, so what do you think?'

'The man in the van?'

'Will drives a transit,' said Millie. 'Did you think you were still in with a chance?' she asked Bonnington.

'We seemed to get on quite well, and the sex would have improved, I'm sure, but I didn't get the opportunity to find out, did I?'

'How did you feel when Lucy "dropped" you?' Mariner asked.

'Let's just say it wasn't a shock. I could hardly compete, could I?'

'Do you like him, Will?'

'From what I've seen, I can't imagine we'd have much in common,' Bonnington said. 'And, for what it's worth, I don't think he treats Lucy very well.'

'What makes you say that?'

'I've overheard them arguing. He seems to do a lot of storming out. And I think he might be violent towards her.'

'That's quite an allegation,' Mariner observed. 'Did you contact us earlier this week?'

After a lengthy pause, Bonnington owned up. 'Yes, that was me.'

'You didn't give your name. Why was that?'

'I don't know. I didn't want to get involved.'

'Yet you were happy to report it. Where were they when this argument was taking place?'

'In the kitchen. Their house is laid out differently, and theirs is in the front. But I suppose you must know that.'

Mariner got up and went across to the window. 'That must be thirty feet away, and behind the shrubs and double glazing. How did you hear that?'

'I didn't, I saw it.'

Mariner strained his eyes. He could hardly see into the kitchen opposite, for one thing there was a thick conifer obscuring the view.

'From upstairs,' Bonnington added.

'And what did you see?'

'I saw Lucy and her husband leaning in towards each other, you could tell they were shouting, then suddenly Lucy fell to the floor and he stormed out. I tried ringing Lucy but there was no reply, and she didn't seem to get up again; I couldn't see her, so I thought the best thing was to call you. I thought I was helping.'

'How do you feel about Lucy now?' Mariner asked. 'Still fancy her?'

Bonnington shrugged. 'I still think she's an attractive woman, yes, but I got over it. You have to, don't you? There's more to life.'

'Like computer programming?' Millie ventured.

'Are you laughing at me?' Bonnington didn't sound in the least bit offended.

'Not at all,' Millie said. 'Are you seeing anyone at the moment, Mr Bonnington?'

He raised an eyebrow. 'Is that a proposition?'

'Just answer the question,' Mariner warned.

'No, I'm not seeing anyone. But that's pretty much my default setting.'

'Do you mind that?'

'It keeps life simple. Don't get me wrong – I like women, but in my experience they're complicated.'

'How well did you know Nina Silvero?' Mariner asked.

Bonnington didn't miss a beat. 'That's easy. I've never heard of her. Who is she?'

'She was a sixty-one-year-old widow. She was murdered several days ago in her home.'

Bonnington paused, his brow creased in confusion. 'What's that got to do with me?'

'That's what we're keen to find out,' Mariner told him. 'Someone gave her some industrial paint stripper to drink; sulphuric acid chiefly. It came disguised in a bottle of Chardonnay. The bottle had your fingerprint on it.'

Bonnington remained remarkably calm. 'I don't drink white wine,' he said, as if that settled the matter.

'All that tells us is that you might have bought this bottle specially,' Mariner said.

'Where do you usually shop, Mr Bonnington.'

'It varies, but mostly Sainsbury's.'

'Which one?'

'In Selly Oak,' Bonnington said, showing the first signs of impatience. 'Look, this is ridiculous. I told you, I've never even heard of this woman. Why would I want to – how could I – harm a total stranger?'

Mariner ignored the question. 'What were you doing last Sunday evening between the hours of seven thirty and midnight?' he asked.

'I would have been here.'

'On your own?'

'I think we've already established that,' Bonnington shot back.

'So no one can verify it?'

'Not really, that's kind of the point of being alone.'

'Do you mind if we have a look round, Mr Bonnington?' Mariner asked.

'Would it matter if I did?'

'It would only delay the inevitable.'

'Then you may as well get on with it. Can I continue with my work?'

'Could you show me first where you keep any cleaning materials?'

Bonnington kept them in the usual place, under the sink, but Mariner wanted him to be there while he examined them. Among the collection was a grey plastic bottle with an integral handle, containing drain fluid. It bore dire warnings about safety and was identical to the bottle found on Nina Silvero's kitchen table, though this one felt full. Bonnington did an impressive double-take. 'That's not mine,' he said. 'I haven't bought that. I never use it.'

Ignoring him, Mariner bagged it up. Bonnington's claim about the wine appeared to be true. The half-dozen or so bottles in the wine rack were all French reds. After the kitchen, Mariner and Millie continued their search of the rest of the house; the first floor, two bedrooms and a bathroom, and the top floor, further bathroom and a spare room.

'Well, looky here,' said Millie, reaching the doorway of the spare room. On a tripod stand, pointing out over the street below, stood a telescope. 'Something caught my eye when I was over at Lucy's the other day. He must have been watching us.' She shivered. 'What a creep.'

'This is where he'd have seen the fight from, too,' said Mariner, going over to the window. 'No wonder he could describe it so graphically.'

'I wonder how many hours he spends up here, spying on the neighbours.'

Back downstairs, Mariner tackled Bonnington about it. 'That's quite an impressive piece of kit you've got up there,' he commented.

'I like watching the stars,' Bonnington replied, unruffled.

'And your neighbours arguing?'

'I just happened to be up there. It drew my attention.'

'I'll bet it did,' Mariner said. 'You need to shut your computer down now, Mr Bonnington, we'll have to take it away with us.'

At last the composure went and there was panic in his eyes. 'You can't, I need it for my work.'

'We can, and you'll have to make other arrangements.'

'Can I just download some work material?'

This time Mariner just laughed. 'We'll let you have it back as soon as possible. Do you own a mobile phone?'

'Yes, but I need it for my business.'

Mariner held out his hand. 'We'll let you have that back too.'

CHAPTER SIXTEEN

'What do you think?' Mariner asked Millie, as they were driving back to Granville Lane.

'I kind of liked him.' She saw Mariner's expression. 'I know. But he seemed pretty honest and open. I don't know many men who'd confess their failings so easily. I mean, he virtually admitted to being a loser. How many other men would do that? And he's got a sense of humour, which I didn't expect.'

'It could be a ploy. He was polite about it but he doesn't seem to have a very high opinion of women. He seems pretty resentful of Will Jarrett, too. And he has the opportunity. He knows Lucy's address to send the unwanted post to, and he knows her computer system, so it would be easy enough to set up the incoming emails. Also, he can see when Jarrett is coming and going, so can time the phone calls.'

'So wouldn't he realise that we'd be straight on to him?' Millie pointed out.

'Except that he'd equally know that we have no proof. I'd be interested to know who he used to work for and why he left.'

'But if it's Bonnington, and this is all because he's still in love with Lucy, why wait until now? She got married six months ago.'

'He's caught them arguing,' Mariner suggested, 'seen some cracks in the relationship and is taking advantage.'

'So wouldn't a better strategy be to offer a shoulder to cry on, rather than making threats?'

'Not if it's all designed to incriminate Will Jarrett, or drive him away. Let's face it; that's who you've been thinking is behind it all, haven't you?' Mariner said.

'But Bonnington just doesn't seem the

type you'd expect to be stalking.'

'There isn't a type,' Mariner reminded her. 'Would women be attracted to him?'

Millie shrugged. 'He's intelligent, and not bad looking, even if his clothes are a bit nineteen fifties. I could see some women wanting to take care of him.'

'The thing I don't get is where the hell Nina Silvero comes into all this,' Mariner said. 'Say he did fix her computer, would he do it on a Sunday night, and would she then share a glass of wine with him?'

'Depends how well she got to know him. If she was the motherly type, perhaps she wanted to look after him.'

'It would be interesting to know if his name rings any bells with Rachel Hordern,' Mariner said. 'Give her a call and find out where she is.'

In the middle of the afternoon, Rachel and Adam Hordern had just returned to their hotel after a trip to the Sea Life Centre. 'I'll come down and meet you in reception,' she told Millie. 'We've just got Harry down for his nap.'

By the time Mariner and Millie got to the hotel, she was waiting for them in a quiet corner of the lobby. Mariner formerly introduced Millie and, as they sat, put the photograph of Bonnington down in front of Rachel. 'Have you ever seen this man, or

311

heard your stepmother mention a man called Martin Bonnington?'

Rachel studied the picture carefully. 'No. Who is he?'

Mariner bypassed the question for now. 'Who set up Nina's computer for her?' he asked instead.

'My husband,' Rachel replied.

'Do you know if Nina ever called anyone out for technical support?'

'Not as far as I know. She hasn't had the computer very long and I think she's hardly used it. We encouraged her to get it so that we could keep in touch by email.'

'Her history shows that she had explored one or two Internet dating sites,' Mariner said. 'Do you still feel sure that she hadn't been meeting men at all?'

'I'm absolutely sure.' She gave Mariner a pointed look. 'It has about as much credibility as the idea of me murdering Nina for her money.'

Mariner ignored the comment. 'Have you ever heard your stepmother talk about a Lucy Jarrett or Will Jarrett?'

'No.'

'Did Nina like folk music?'

That made Rachel smile. 'Absolutely not. She was strictly Brahms and Vaughan-Williams. Why all these random questions, Inspector?'

'We're just verifying some background

information,' Mariner said.

'My,' said Millie when she and Mariner got back in the car. 'She's a bit prickly, isn't she?'

En route back to Granville Lane, Millie remained in the car while Mariner went up to Estelle Waters' flat to ask the same 'random questions', but Nina's friend similarly had no recognition of the name or picture of Martin Bonnington. Nor could she recall Will or Lucy Jarrett ever being mentioned in conversation.

'Did she ever talk to you about her computer?' Mariner prompted.

'Only to say that the whole contraption was a complete waste of money,' Estelle told him.

Back at Granville Lane, Tony Knox had found nothing among Nina's things relating to Martin Bonnington, but there was a note on Millie's desk from technician Max, along with a list courtesy of Lucy Jarrett's Internet provider listing the addresses from which the spam emails had been sent to her machine. Millie took it through to Mariner's office.

'This might help us, sir.' With a brief explanation, she handed Mariner the list. By far the most frequently listed name and address was Mr M Bonnington, sixteen, Hill Crest.

'At last this is starting to look like a case,' said Mariner.

'And we know the flowers were sent from Birmingham,' Millie reminded him. 'Is it enough to bring him in?'

'The fingerprint itself isn't conclusive,' Mariner said. 'But triangulate it with these emails and the flowers, posted locally, and I think we've got more than enough. Before we do, though, I want to talk to the other woman he harassed; Claudette Vernon. Let's get to know as much about Martin Bonnington as we can. He played it pretty cool this afternoon and I'd like to get one step ahead of him if we can. We also need to keep working on the Nina Silvero connection. Unless we can come up with some kind of motive for her, we've only half got him.'

When he had explained the urgency of the situation, Claudette Vernon invited Mariner and Millie to call round and see her at her flat that same evening. They turned up promptly at six o'clock, the agreed time. Bonnington must have something, Mariner thought, when she came to the door. She was mid-forties, Mariner would have guessed, olive-skinned with fine features and sleek black hair. Her movements were graceful and unhurried as she showed them into the sitting room of her flat, the ground floor of a detached Georgian villa in a smart area not far from the University. When they'd declined her offer of drinks, she picked up her own wine glass and positioned herself opposite them, curling into the armchair like a contented cat.

'You met Martin Bonnington on an Internet dating site, I understand?' Mariner said, quoting from the file.

Claudette smiled, a perfect, white smile, and her voice, when she spoke, was deep and husky. 'Yes. His postings on the website were funny. That's what attracted me to him in the first place, and he just seemed a nice guy. Some of them stand out as creeps right from the start; they try too hard. My initial reaction when I met Martin, and got past the wardrobe issues, was that he was a sweet guy, if a bit nerdy. And he knows that. He never tried to sell himself as anything he wasn't, and that honesty was very appealing. We built up a rapport quite quickly. I loved his dry sense of humour.'

'We had a taste of that,' Mariner said wryly. 'How well did you get to know him?'

'What do you mean?' She tilted her head to one side.

'Was there any kind of physical relationship?'

She drew back a little. 'Is that really necessary?'

'We're investigating a particularly nasty

murder, Miss Vernon. We wouldn't ask if it wasn't central to the case.'

'Oh my God, and you suspect Martin?' She was incredulous.

'We're just trying to find out a little more about him,' said Mariner. 'We've no reason to believe that you're in any danger.'

'OK, well, yes, it did get physical, almost straight away. I think it surprised both of us.'

'And how was it? Really, this is crucial,' Mariner added, seeing the look on her face.

'It was fine!' she said. 'OK, well, it wasn't earth-moving. He wasn't terribly experienced, so I had to take the lead quite a bit, but he was very responsive, if you know what I mean.'

'Did Mr Bonnington have any difficulties in that area?' Mariner asked.

'Not difficulties as such. I mean, the first time wasn't that great but after that it got better. He learned fast.'

'How long did your physical relationship last?'

'About a couple of months, no more than that.'

'So what went wrong?' Mariner wanted to know.

'Not the sex,' Vernon said quickly. 'That was getting better all the time. It was the other stuff. It was getting too intense emotionally; claustrophobic. Martin wanted to be with me all the time and I began to feel hemmed in. He used to send me dozens of emails every day, and leave messages on my mobile. I started to realise that emotionally he was quite–' she broke off, searching for the right word '–needy. It became clear that he hadn't had many relationships with women and, having found me, he clung to me desperately. I have other friends, and I like to go out with the girls at the weekend too. We had a couple of fairly public arguments about it, and in the end I felt that the fairest thing was to finish with him.'

'How did he take it?' said Mariner.

She sat back. 'It was a horrible conversation to have. He was upset. I actually think he thought we had a long-term future together, but in reality we hardly knew each other. He's a nice guy and I felt terrible, but it had to be done. We had very different approaches to relationships.'

'And after that?' Mariner asked.

'I thought that would be it, but he kept ringing me. Usually it would start off on the pretext that he thought there was something he'd left at my flat, or he'd been given tickets for something that I might like, but from there it would always turn into a discussion about what he'd done wrong. He didn't seem to grasp that fundamentally we're different kinds of people. I'd started seeing someone else, and he asked some very intrusive questions. Then he began hanging around outside the office where I work, waiting for me to leave, and a couple of times he came up to me while I was out with friends. He was clearly following me and it was getting creepy, so I went to the police.'

'And since the injunction was served?'

'Actually I feel quite bad about that. In retrospect, it probably was a bit heavy-handed. It shocked him. I'm not even sure that up until then he'd realised what he was doing. But he took the hint and it stopped.'

'How about in the last six months or so?' asked Mariner. 'Has he tried to contact you?'

She shook her head. 'Not at all, I mean, I saw him once when I was in the super-market and that freaked me a bit, but I think that was a genuine coincidence. We just smiled and said hello and moved on. It was fine. In fact, he told me he was seeing some-one else, too.'

'Did he tell you her name?'

'No. I wasn't even sure that I believed him. What's all this about? What has he done?'

Millie put away her notebook as Mariner stood up to go. 'We don't know yet if he's done anything,' Mariner said. 'But thank you for your help, Ms Vernon.'

'So Lucy Jarrett is the second woman to have turned him down,' Mariner observed, when he and Millie were back in the car.

'And she gets the stalking treatment too.'

'But what about Nina Silvero?' Millie wondered.

'Maybe she was the person he really vented his frustration on,' Mariner speculated. 'Tomorrow we could use some kind of break.'

Mariner opened his front door that evening to be greeted by the smell of Kat's home-made beef goulash from the pot that was simmering on the cooker. Hearing him come in, Kat herself appeared on the stairs, in one arm a bottle carrier, which she passed to him. Six different varieties of ale. 'We can watch this too?' She held up a copy of *The Big Easy*, one of Mariner's all-time favourite films, and one that he knew she didn't really like, because of the violence.

'That would be good,' he said, gratefully accepting the olive branch.

'We are friends again?' She smiled tentatively.

'Friends again,' Mariner agreed.

It was almost like the old times, but there was a conversation they needed to have.

'So, tell me about this flat,' Mariner said, when the film had finished and he was mellowed by the food and beer.

'My friend Saira at the language centre, she haves one,' Kat said. 'Is in Moseley near to the cricket pitch.'

'I think you mean the cricket *ground*,' said Mariner.

'Yes, and it haves one bedroom and a lounge and a kitchen and all the furnitures.' Her enthusiasm grew as she spoke.

'And you can afford this?' Mariner asked. But he already knew the answer to that. Albanian translators were in demand in a city as culturally diverse as Birmingham, and Kat was paid handsomely for her services, which he knew because she occasionally worked for them at Granville Lane. And she had thought it through.

'Saira, she have not such much money as me, and she can do this. She help me. Wait.' She disappeared up to her room and returned moments later with a glossy folder containing property details and notebook, in which she'd worked out all the sums. The flat would be rented but well within her means and, after all, she pointed out, she may not be in this country for ever.

'It looks great,' Mariner said, saddened by that thought. 'Do you want me to help you to apply for it? You'll need to get hold of an application–'

Sheepishly, Kat sorted through the pack to produce application forms already completed in her neat hand. 'Is all done,' she said. 'Will you referee for me?'

Despite himself, Mariner smiled. 'Yes, I'll referee for you.'

At Mariner's request, DCI Sharp joined them for the briefing session first thing on Thursday morning. If they were to bring Bonnington in, Mariner wanted her to hear what the grounds for it were.

Knowing what they were up against, Max had worked overnight on Bonnington's computer and he joined them as well. 'Bonnington's taste in porn is a tad disappointing,' he told them, 'very tame. And there are a few legitimate emails sent to Lucy Jarrett months ago, but I can confirm that most of the spam emails and the catalogue requests were triggered by his machine. He's also accessed Lucy Jarrett's wedding photos on several occasions. And I found this.' He passed round a sheet that bore a printed label: *flowers from Guernsey*. 'He must have mocked it up himself and stuck it to the boxes to make them look legit. Stupid git saved the document to his hard drive.'

'Isn't that odd?' queried Sharp. 'He's a computer expert himself, yet he's made no attempt to hide any of this?'

Max shook his head. 'He must have thought he was safe. He hasn't made any attempt to conceal any of this, and there are plenty of steps he could have taken. Ultimately we'd have found it of course, so it wouldn't make any difference, but it means that I could just lift all this off straight away.'

'He panicked when we said we were taking the machine,' Mariner told her. 'He even asked if he could download some "work material" before we took it away. Maybe he just got lazy and didn't bother at the time.'

Sharp nodded, seemingly satisfied with that explanation. 'Can we pinpoint the times when the emails were sent?' she asked.

Max responded by producing a data printout. 'This is a breakdown of dates and times. Bonnington's a "night prowler". Most of the stuff is done in the late evening, a couple of times in the early hours. His mobile is clean, by the way, no calls to Lucy Jarrett's number. Most of the numbers coincide with the numbers for client accounts on the computer, but he could have another one he's not telling you about.'

'Is Nina Silvero on his client list?' Mariner took the printout that Sharp handed him.

''Fraid not,' said Max. 'Only similarity with her is that they've both used Internet dating sites, but they're not even the same ones.'

'So what now?' Sharp asked Mariner.

'I'd like to bring him in,' Mariner said. 'Voluntarily, if he'll come. I want to get him on to our territory, where I think he'll be less sure of himself. There's enough to question him about Lucy Jarrett, and maybe in the course of the interview the link with Nina Silvero will become clear.'

Sharp nodded agreement. 'Best of luck, and keep me posted.'

Mariner took Millie with him to collect Bonnington. She'd done a lot of work with Lucy Jarrett and deserved to take the credit.

Bonnington continued to maintain his innocence. 'There must be some misunderstanding,' he kept saying. But he put up no resistance, and didn't feel the need to have a solicitor present. Entering the interview suite, Mariner felt the familiar nervous anticipation that came with the end game. The most satisfactory outcome, as always, would be a confession from Bonnington, preferably with a clear explanation of his motives. It was seldom what they got, of course, and Bonnington was continuing to play the 'confused' card, which could be genuine, or preferably meant that he had simply convinced himself that he had done nothing wrong. Either way, he was pretty calm, confident that the misunderstanding would be rectified. He looked smaller than ever in the interview room, Mariner and Millie on the opposite side of the table.

'I really don't understand why I'm here,' he said, for the umpteenth time. 'A fingerprint on a wine bottle? I mean, that could be anyone's.'

'Tell us about Claudette Vernon,' Mariner said.

'Ah.' Bonnington looked directly into Mariner's eyes. 'You obviously know all about her. That's the other reason I'm here, is it? That I happened to be a little over-enthusiastic in my advances towards Claudette, let me see, three years ago? Hm, I can see how that might make me an automatic suspect for harassing a married neighbour whom I hardly know, and murdering a middle-aged woman I've never heard of.'

Mariner ignored the sarcasm. 'Were you harassing Ms Vernon? Is that how you'd describe it?'

'That was your word,' Bonnington corrected him. 'You told me yesterday that Lucy Jarrett was being harassed.'

'So why don't you tell us about your relationship with Claudette Vernon?'

'You really do have an unusual preoccupation with my sex life, Inspector, which I probably could understand if it was a particularly salacious one, but I think we all know that you're in for a disappointment.'

'Just get on with it, Mr Bonnington.' Mariner tried to quash his rising exasperation.

'All right.' Bonnington shrugged. 'I met Claudette through an Internet dating site. She turned out to be a very attractive woman and, quite amazingly, she seemed to feel the same way about me, at least to begin with. No signals misread there, I can assure you.'

He looked from Mariner to Millie. 'We went out for two or three months, usually to a film or to the theatre, or for dinner. After the first couple of dates we started fucking, and I think we fucked on most occasions subsequent to that.' Spoken in such a polite conversational tone, the words sounded obscene and Mariner felt sure that Bonnington's intention had been to try to shock them. He'd have to try a lot harder than that.

'And how was it, the fucking?' asked Mariner.

'Not up to much to begin with, if I'm brutally honest, but Claudette was prepared to give it a chance, and it got better, for both of us.'

Mariner had to admire his honesty. 'You must have missed it then, when she ended your relationship.'

'I did. And not just the sex, but the conversation, the evenings out. She's a lovely woman. I think I'd fallen for her.'

Mariner searched Bonnington's face for signs of irony, but for once they were absent.

'So you stalked her.'

'I wasn't stalking her,' Bonnington said impatiently. 'I admit that I found it difficult to accept our relationship was over. I couldn't understand how her feelings could be so intense one day and non-existent just a few days later. I had to be sure that she really thought it was over, and that there wasn't something I could do to rekindle the interest. I can see now that at the time my behaviour must have seemed odd, and that I might have frightened her.'

'Did it give you a buzz, frightening her?' Mariner asked. 'Is that what you get off on?'

'No.' Bonnington seemed offended by the question.

'Did you find it difficult when Lucy Jarrett finished with you too?'

'Finished what? I've already told you; with Lucy there wasn't anything to finish.'

'Must have been tough, though; two women dumping you within such a short space of time,' Mariner said. 'And both because of your inadequacies in bed. That's pretty humiliating, isn't it? Did you wonder what they might be saying to their new partners: *Poor old Martin, nice guy but can't really cut it?* Did you think Lucy and Will were laughing about you behind your back?'

'The thought never crossed my mind.'

'So, why have you been sending her hundreds of emails, and ordering dozens of products on her behalf?' Mariner put the data sheet down on the table in front of him.

Bonnington took his time, studying the list for a couple of minutes, before looking up again, directly into Mariner's eyes. 'I didn't make those requests,' he said.

'Can you explain, then, how we've traced

them back to your home computer?' asked Mariner.

'No, I really can't, because I didn't send them.' He appeared completely ingenuous.

'That's not good enough, Mr Bonnington,' Mariner told him. 'We have the techno-logical proof that they were sent from your computer, and what's more we can tell exactly when you sent them.' Mariner cast his eyes down the list. 'For example, what were you doing on March the ninth at eleven fifteen pm, when the appointment was made with this nursery-design company?'

'I would have been at home, I expect, but I didn't do it.'

'For the record: you live alone, Mr Bon-nington?'

'You know I do.'

'And no one else has access to your computer.'

'That's right.'

'So you must see how, logically, if this request was made on your computer at that time, it must have been made by you,' Mariner said patiently.

'I can see that, but it wasn't,' Bonnington reiterated. 'I've never even heard of this company.'

'So how else can you explain what we've found?'

'Maybe I've got a hacker,' said Bonnington.

'Our technician told us that your machine is one of the most secure he's ever come across,' Mariner replied. 'You're an IT consultant. You trying to tell us you'd be that careless?' He glanced down at the list again. 'A lot of these have been sent on a Wednesday evening. What's so special about Wednesdays, Mr Bonnington?'

'My house is clean,' Bonnington offered, helpfully.

Mariner ignored the cryptic remark, not sure if Bonnington was being facetious. 'What were you doing on Tuesday evening at eleven forty pm?'

'I was at home.'

'More specifically, you were on the phone to our emergency team.' Mariner took another sheet of paper from the folder in front of him. *'I saw him attack her'* he read. *'She fell on the floor, and now he's gone out and she's not answering her phone.'*

'I've already admitted to making that call,' Bonnington said, the first signs of frustration beginning to show. 'I was looking through my telescope at the Great Bear. I saw my neighbours having an argument, which looked violent, so I phoned the police. I was genuinely concerned for Lucy Jarrett's safety. I was being a good citizen.'

'Hm, your telescope,' Mariner said. 'Do you use that to spy on other neighbours, or is it solely for Lucy Jarrett?'

'I've told you I have an interest in astronomy.'

'But you just happened to have it directed at the Jarretts' house that evening,' Mariner said. 'Is that how you can be sure when Lucy's husband is out? So that you can make your other phone calls?'

'What other calls?' Bonnington frowned.

'The silent calls made to Lucy Jarrett when her husband is out. The ones in which you don't speak, oh, except the first time. *You bitch, I'm going to make you suffer.* Wasn't that how it went? What have you done with the phone?'

'What phone?'

'The mobile that you made those calls from.'

Bonnington glanced across at Millie. 'I have no idea what you're talking about.'

'Did you go to Lucy Jarrett's wedding?' Mariner asked, changing tack.

'I wasn't invited,' Bonnington stated baldly.

'Were you disappointed about that?'

'I didn't expect to be invited. Particularly after what happened between me and Lucy. Anyway, I hardly know them, I just happen to live nearby.'

'But you've seen the wedding photos?'

'I've looked at them online, yes.' Bonnington blushed.

At last, something. Mariner almost sighed with relief, and he and Millie exchanged a brief look.

Bonnington looked from one to the other. 'I don't see what the problem is with that. I gave the happy couple a gift, just to be neighbourly, and when Lucy thanked me she told me about the web link. I assumed her intention was that I could look at the photos. They were very good. Very professional. Lucy looked very pretty.'

'How did they make you feel?' Mariner asked.

'What do you mean?'

'Did they make you feel angry that it wasn't you in those photos; that Will Jarrett was standing where you should have been?'

'No,' Bonnington protested. 'I thought they were nice photos.'

'Nice enough to print them off?'

'No.'

'How do you explain this then?' Mariner put down the doctored photograph. We can prove that it was printed on your printer at ten twenty-five pm on March the twentieth. Remember what you were doing then?'

'No, but I was probably at home.' An edge had crept into his voice. Mariner was beginning to needle him.

'Alone?'

'Yes. All right, all right!'

'All right what?' Mariner asked, with a surge of relief.

'I printed it off. I don't remember when,

330

but I printed off a picture.'

At last! Mariner wanted to crow; instead, he asked, 'What for?'

'Nothing, I just did!'

Finally, they were getting to him.

'But what did you do with it, Martin, when you'd printed it off?'

'Nothing! I– It–'

'What?'

'It turned me on.' Bonnington had blushed crimson. 'It reminded me of that evening and it was a turn-on. I printed it off and I masturbated.'

'That's it?' said Mariner.

'That's it,' said Bonnington.

'Jesus,' Mariner sighed with disappointment. 'Did you talk about anything else when Lucy came to thank you?'

'I can't remember. I probably asked her something banal, like whether she was enjoying married life, and she probably said yes. I think I must have asked her when we could expect the patter of tiny feet.'

'And what did she say?'

'I can't really remember. That she and Will weren't planning a family.'

'When was this?'

'How the hell would I know? A few months ago. It was just a neighbourly conversation, that's all. I wasn't threatening in any way.'

'But you knew that they weren't having children.'

'Yes, but–'

'So is that why you started sending Lucy items through the post?'

'What kind of things?'

Mariner threw a selection down on the table.

'I didn't send those. I don't even know what that is.' Bonnington picked up the Clear Blue test and examined it closely.

'I think you know exactly what that is, and, having found out that Will Jarrett doesn't want children, you arranged for these things to be sent so that he and Lucy would fall out about it.'

'I really don't know what you're talking about.' Bonnington fixed Mariner with a steady gaze. 'I didn't know that Will didn't want children; only that they weren't planning to have any.'

'We have more than enough here to charge you with harassing Lucy Jarrett, you know. It really would help your case if you started to come clean about it.'

'I haven't been harassing her.' By now, Bonnington was looking increasingly desperate, flicking his gaze between Mariner and Millie.

'What's the anniversary?' Mariner asked.

'What?'

'Fifth of April. Does it relate to when you first met Lucy, when you first started going out, or first saw her and lusted after her?'

332

'That date means absolutely nothing to me.'

Mariner picked up the box of dead flowers in its new polythene wrapper, and threw it on to the table. 'So I suppose you're going to say that you don't know anything about these either.'

'Yes, because it's the truth!'

'And this?' Mariner put down the fake florist's label.

Bonnington peered at the message. 'That's not very nice,' he said.

'So why was it on your computer?' Mariner asked.

'I have no idea.'

'Your mysterious hacker again?'

But Bonnington only shrugged. They were hitting a brick wall again.

Feeling drained, Mariner suspended the interview and he and Millie got up and walked out. They needed to regroup. Up in CID Tony Knox and Charlie Glover waited expectantly.

'He's good,' Millie told them. 'He's just playing the wronged innocent and denying everything.'

'Though he can't offer much in the way of explanation either,' said Mariner. 'Are we any further forward with Nina Silvero?'

'Nothing so far,' Knox said. 'We've checked with all the family and friends, but no one in the Silvero camp knows Lucy Jarrett, and no one in her camp knows Nina Silvero, except for what they've heard or read in the news. And none of them except Lucy, and Will to a lesser degree, knows Martin Bonnington. It just doesn't make sense.'

'We still haven't identified the mystery visitor to Nina Silvero's house that night,' said Mariner. 'We need to find something that places Bonnington at Nina Silvero's house. Get forensics to go over the kitchen again for prints or fibres that we might be able to tie to Bonnington.'

CHAPTER SEVENTEEN

There was another possible association that hadn't yet been explored. With reluctance, Mariner picked up the phone and called Jack Coleman.

'How's it going?'

'We've picked up a Martin Bonnington. There's some overlap with another case we're working on and Bonnington has come up for both. But all we've got on him for Nina Silvero is a single fingerprint, and that's not watertight. I just wondered if it was a name you recognised, especially from the Hughes time? Bonnington would have been in his late teens when it happened. A friend of the family perhaps, a mate of George's?'

'It doesn't ring any bells,' Coleman mused. 'What's he like?'

Mariner described Bonnington as best he could, but it still didn't mean much to Coleman. 'He doesn't much sound like one of Georgie's friends,' he remarked.

'You didn't mention that you were there the night Billy Hughes died,' Mariner said.

'It's not something I'm proud of,' Coleman admitted.

'That was why you felt you had to support Nina.'

'I felt guilty.'

'Why?' Mariner said. 'You didn't do anything wrong. You were following instructions from a senior officer.'

'I felt guilty because I thanked God when Ronnie Silvero died. I was relieved that an impossible decision had been taken out of my hands. You don't have to disclose at an inquest, but if it had gone to trial I would have been called as a witness for the prosecution. I would have had to stand up in court in front of Ronnie and Nina and tell the truth; that mistakes were made that night and it was Ronnie Silvero who made them.'

'I've read your report,' Mariner said.

'We never should have left that boy in the cell handcuffed, and he didn't deserve the

335

level of restraint that was imposed. Sure, he was a live wire, but he wasn't violent, not in the way that officers tried to say, and not in the way that some of them are.'

'So the Hughes family were justified in their complaints.'

'If I'd been in their position, I'd have felt exactly the same way.'

Mariner ended the call with a vague promise that he would get out to see Coleman soon, but he wasn't sure how soon he'd be keeping it.

Mariner was anxious to get down to the interview suite to have another go at Bonnington soon, before he got too comfortable, but when he looked up Millie was standing in the doorway, Tony Knox at her shoulder. 'Something you need to hear, boss,' she said. 'Line two.' Stepping forward, she pressed a couple of buttons on Mariner's phone. 'Dr Chohan?' she said. 'Please could you tell Inspector Mariner what you've told me?'

A woman's voice, precise but heavily accented, came over the speaker phone, introducing its owner as Lucy Jarrett's GP.

'Lucy came in to see me earlier in the week,' she said. 'She's been feeling ill for some time and described a range of symptoms including nausea, occasional vomiting, headaches and tiredness. She told me she had been under some stress and that she'd been getting some nuisance phone calls and that you were involved. She gave me your constable's name. From her symptoms I thought we could be looking at anything from stress-related illness to glandular fever so I sent off some blood samples as a precaution. The results have come back and I thought I should get in touch with you. This is going to sound a little far-fetched, but it looks as if she's being poisoned.'

Glancing up, Mariner saw the fear in Millie's eyes. 'Do you have any idea what with?' he asked.

'The samples are being further analysed,' said Dr Chohan. 'And I've flagged them up as top priority, so we should know quite soon, but meanwhile I would like to get Lucy into hospital so that we can monitor her food intake and her condition and run some more tests. I'm making an emergency referral to the Queen Elizabeth.'

'Would you like one of my officers to escort her there?' Mariner offered, holding Millie's gaze.

'Until we find out what's going on, I think that would be most helpful.'

'Thank you, Dr Chohan. We'll keep in touch.' Mariner ended the call.

'I can't believe I didn't see it!' Millie shook her head in disbelief. 'She was obviously ill, she looks terrible.'

'This isn't your fault.' Mariner was firm.

'None of us had any way of knowing about this.'

'Will she be all right?' Millie asked.

'Well, until we know what we're dealing with it's hard to say, but the important thing is that now we know. I want you to pick up Lucy, take her to the QE and stay with her. Until we've identified what is poisoning her, she needs to be kept isolated. I'll speak to the DCI and get the toxicology specialists into Hill Crest and the health centre. Both locations will have to be sealed off, again until we can identify the source. Rachel Hordern told us that over the last year her mother had been suffering ill health and exactly the same symptoms: nausea, vomiting and tiredness.'

'So, if this is Nina's killer, is he likely to try to finish the job?' Millie asked, wide eyed. 'Is Lucy in any immediate danger?'

'Obviously we can't take any chances,' Mariner said. 'But the whole thing about this is that it's slow and drawn out. Nina Silvero received her flowers a whole year before she was eventually murdered. This is not just about killing, it's about suffering.'

'But if they know we're on to them the killer might feel under pressure to finish this one off sooner,' Knox pointed out.

'Like I said,' Mariner repeated, 'we're not taking any chances. We'll post an officer on Lucy's door.'

'Where does this leave us with Bonnington?' said Knox.

'He's not off the hook yet. Until we know what we're dealing with we don't know how the poison has been administered, or who would have the opportunity to do it.'

'It must bring Will back into the picture though,' Millie said.

'Do we know where he is?'

He's away, but– No, wait, Lucy said he was coming back yesterday. He must be home by now.'

Lifting his jacket from the hook, Mariner spoke to Knox. 'Time we had a chat with him.'

Lucy looked dazed and ill when Millie picked her up from the health centre late on Thursday morning. The place was in uproar as the toxicology team had arrived and was in the process of sealing off the building. Millie caught a glimpse of Paula Kirkwood looking anxious and harassed, carrying boxloads of files to where they were to be shipped to temporary accommodation, in a different part of the building. But she broke off for long enough to come over to Lucy. 'You take care of yourself and get well,' she said, giving her a hug.

'There's an irony for you,' Lucy joked weakly, as she and Millie walked out past the health centre sign.

'At least now we know why you've been feeling so lousy,' Millie said. 'And the doctors can work on making you better.'

The staff having been forewarned by Dr Chohan, the check-in at the hospital was quick and efficient and saw Lucy settled in isolation on a side ward adjacent to the infectious diseases department.

'What about Will?' she said, arranging her belongings in the bedside cupboard. 'I need to call him, let him know.'

'It's all right,' Millie reassured her. 'Someone's going round to see him.' Millie saw the look on her face. 'We have to, Lucy, this has become too serious.'

'But he wouldn't do this to me.'

Millie came to sit beside her. 'Lucy, think about it. Isn't it strange that you've been feeling ill and Will hasn't?'

'But that could be because he's barely home,' Lucy pointed out.

She had a point and Millie didn't want to distress her further, so she simply nodded affirmation. 'Where do you do your shopping, Lucy?'

'Sainsbury's Selly Oak usually.'

'Do you ever bump into Martin Bonnington there?'

'Yes, I have done from time to time.' Lucy looked up, her attention caught by the woman in uniform who had just taken up a position outside the door.

340

'There's going to be a police officer keeping an eye on you,' Millie told her.

Lucy scraped her fingers through her hair. 'Oh, God, this is unreal. Why would anyone do this? I haven't hurt anyone.'

Millie put an arm around her shoulders. 'I know.'

Before going out to pick up Will Jarrett, Mariner updated DCI Sharp on this latest development.

'Is there any chance that this is more than just Lucy Jarrett?' she was asking.

'We've no reason to think so at this stage,' said Mariner. 'The men in white suits are going to her home and workplace to gather evidence. We should know more in a few hours.'

The forensic team had waited on Hill Crest until Mariner and Knox arrived.

Banging on the door, even though it was midday, they apparently roused Will Jarrett from his bed. Dazed, scruffy and unshaven, he was, though, still undeniably handsome.

'Jesus, what's going on?' He blinked towards the motley collection of people on his drive. He squinted at Mariner. 'Do I know you?'

'We'd like you to come with us to answer a few questions, Mr Jarrett,' Mariner said, brandishing his warrant card. 'And, while we do, the forensic team is going to need to search your house and take away some samples.'

'What?'

'We'll need the keys to your van, and you need to come with us to the station. Your wife is being poisoned, Mr Jarrett. But perhaps you already knew that.'

Twenty minutes later, Jarrett was dressed and in the back of a car being driven by Tony Knox, while Mariner occupied the front passenger seat.

'Has Lucy told you this?' Jarrett wanted to know. 'Because she's been imagining all kinds of things lately. I don't think she's well right now.'

'That's true,' said Mariner. 'She isn't. But it's her doctor who told us. It's a fact, Mr Jarrett. Lucy is being poisoned.'

'Jesus. Where is she?'

'One of our officers has collected her and taken her to Queen Elizabeth Hospital.'

'But I need to see her.' Whether out of concern for his wife, or what she might say, Jarrett was suddenly animated.

'All in good time,' said Mariner. 'We need to have a little chat first.'

'You think I'm doing this, don't you?' he said, with disbelief. 'You really think I would poison my own wife? I love her.'

'We'll talk at the station,' said Mariner simply.

By the time Jarrett had been processed at Granville Lane, Millie had returned from the hospital.

'How is she?' Mariner asked.

'Scared,' said Millie. 'But her mum got there just before I left, so she's being taken care of.'

'You ready for this?'

'Oh, yes, sir.'

Mariner and Millie were ready and already waiting in the interview room when Jarrett was shown in. Although sitting beside her, Mariner was allowing Millie to take the lead, and she felt almost as nervous as Jarrett himself must have been.

'I should be with my wife,' he said, reluctantly taking a seat opposite them.

'You will be, very soon,' Millie reassured him. 'But we just need to ask you some questions. You haven't known Lucy very long, have you?'

Jarrett's eyes narrowed. 'By some standards I guess not, but we were attracted to each other straight away.'

'What was it that attracted you to her?'

'She's smart and she's thoughtful, and she's pretty; she doesn't look her best right now.'

That was the understatement of the year, Millie thought. 'She's also wealthy,' she said. 'How soon did you find that out?'

Jarrett had no problem returning her gaze. 'She took me back to her place after our first date. I guess I could tell then that she was pretty loaded. She told me that her dad had left her some money.'

'So was that part of the appeal?' Millie asked.

'No, it wasn't,' he replied evenly. 'I had already fallen for her by then.'

'So the new van, all the other gifts, they didn't influence your feelings for Lucy.'

'You take a pretty shallow view,' Jarrett said. 'Relationships aren't about material stuff. Sure, they were nice, but I didn't ask for any of those things. They were more important to Lucy than to me. She wanted to give them. Have you asked her about that?'

Millie flushed slightly, realising that she hadn't. 'What's your relationship with Tess Maguire?' she asked.

'You know about my relationship with Tess,' Jarrett reminded her. 'She sings with the band.'

'Is that all?'

'What do you mean?'

'Are you lovers, too?' Millie asked.

Jarrett glared at Mariner. 'Jesus Christ, what is this?'

'You seemed pretty close when we came to watch you,' Millie said.

'It's professional. You think it would be a better performance if we stepped around

344

each other on stage? That stuff, it goes with the music. Lucy knows that.'

'How do you explain her telling you to *"Kiss me, baby"*? Is that professional too?'

'What are you talking about?' Jarrett seemed genuinely baffled.

'Lucy overheard Tess Maguire say that to you, in a bar after the show, so that clearly wasn't just for the audience.'

For a moment Jarrett seemed floored, then he broke into a wry grin. 'It's the line from a song. We were playing that game where someone says a line from a song and the next person has to come up with the line that follows. We were all playing it in the bar that night. *"Kiss me baby, hold me, baby..."*'' he recited. 'Jesus.' He gave a derisory snort. 'That's what you have on me, the line from a song? Tess wasn't even talking to me. You can ask the other guys.'

'We will,' Millie said. This wasn't going well. She needed to move things along. 'Tell me about the evening of April the fifth. Last Tuesday,' she said.

Jarrett didn't even have to think about it. 'I was home,' he said. 'I got back in the afternoon, Lucy came in from work and we watched TV–' he smirked '–among other things.'

'And later?'

'We argued.' He was remarkably candid.

'Why?'

'Lucy had sent for some stuff in the post; at least I thought she had,' Jarrett said. 'I was upset.'

'What was it that upset you?' Millie asked.

'I found a pregnancy test.'

'Why would that be upsetting?' Millie acted confused. 'You'd just got married. Most people would say it's the next logical step.'

Jarrett shifted in his seat, this was less comfortable ground. 'Lucy and I had agreed that we wouldn't try for kids.'

'Why was that?'

There was a new tension in his voice. 'I don't want kids. I never have. We discussed it at length before we married. It was important to me and I needed to be clear that Lucy felt the same way, or at least understood and was happy to go along with it.'

'How did Lucy feel about that?' asked Millie.

'She said it didn't matter. I think maybe at one time she wanted a family, but it was more important that we were together.'

'That's a huge sacrifice,' Millie observed.

Jarrett glared at her. 'Yeah, you think I don't know that?'

'Why is it so important to you to not have children, Will? Not part of your long-term plan?'

'What long-term plan?' His tone was defensive now.

'The one in which you leave Lucy, taking half her possessions, and go off with Tess.'

'What? Are you nuts?' he reacted angrily. 'Is that what you've been saying to her? No wonder she doesn't trust me any more.'

'Or is it that you already have kids?' Millie speculated, even though she had no evidence for it yet.

Will Jarrett was speechless, and for a couple of seconds Millie thought they had him. When he eventually spoke, they could hardly hear him. 'If you must know, the reason I don't want kids is because I don't want them dying a slow and painful death, before their time. I saw what my parents went through with my younger brother. I can't put Lucy through that.' He looked straight into Millie's eyes. 'I carry a hereditary disease.'

In the silence that followed, Millie suddenly pieced together the information Max had given her and it all made terrible sense. 'Huntingdon's disease,' she said.

Jarrett sniffed. 'How d'you know?'

'You'd used your computer to search for support groups,' Millie said. 'I thought it was about the place, but it was about the disease.'

Jarrett rubbed his unshaven chin. 'I was looking for something for Lucy. I thought that once she knew she may need some help.'

'Shouldn't you have told her before you married her?'

'I guess I should, but it all happened so fast, and it never seemed like the right time. I thought as long as she was OK with not having kids that I could tell her the rest when the time was right. In the past, women I've dated have gotten freaked by it, and I didn't want to scare her away.' So that was what Will Jarrett was guilty of – protecting his wife. The tension in the room had evaporated, leaving Millie unsure of which way to go now.

'How well do you know Martin Bonnington?' Mariner intervened.

'Who?'

'Martin Bonnington, your neighbour.'

'The guy across the road? Hardly at all,' Jarrett said. 'I've said hi to him. I think Lucy went out with him a couple of times and he got the wrong idea, but that was finished a long time ago. Has he been saying something? Was it him reported us?'

'How about Nina Silvero?' Mariner asked. 'Do you know her?'

Jarrett shook his head. 'Who is she?' It was said quite naturally.

'Where were you on the evening of Sunday, April the third?'

There followed a pause while Will Jarrett mentally reviewed his schedule. 'I'm pretty sure we were in Reading that night, and I have plenty of witnesses.' He consulted his watch. 'Are we done here? I'd really like to go and see my wife.'

Millie glanced across at Mariner who nodded almost imperceptibly.

'For the moment, Mr Jarrett; we'll get someone to take you to the hospital. But we may need to speak to you again.'

Jarrett levelled a gaze at him. 'I'll cancel my gigs. I'm not going anywhere.'

'Shit,' said Millie, when Jarrett had gone. 'That didn't exactly go to plan.'

'It rarely does,' Mariner consoled her. 'You did fine. Don't beat yourself up about it. What do you think about him now?'

'I don't know,' Millie sighed. 'He seems – plausible, doesn't he?'

'He does,' Mariner agreed.

'And it certainly makes sense of why he's not in a hurry to be a father. Made me feel pretty stupid – and insensitive.'

'Don't,' Mariner said. 'You took a perfectly valid line of inquiry. It was his secrecy that created the suspicion.'

'And he's still the one with the best opportunity,' Millie said.

'As far as we know,' said Mariner. 'Let's wait and see what's been killing Lucy Jarrett.'

They were soon to find out. Emerging from

the interview suite, Mariner learned that he had a message from Dr Gail Hudson, head of toxicology within the forensic science unit. She was brusque and professional on the phone and got straight to the point. 'Lucy Jarrett has been poisoned with thallium,' she said.

'Which is what exactly?' Mariner's ignorance of chemistry was pretty far-reaching.

'It's a metallic element, a bit like lead or mercury, but actually more poisonous than both and relatively easy to use. The salts are soluble in water and virtually tasteless, so it can easily be added to drinks like tea and coffee. In that respect you might say that thallium's pretty much the ideal poison.'

'So it has to be someone close to Lucy who's doing this?' Mariner's thoughts instantly returned to Will Jarrett.

'It's the most likely scenario,' Hudson said.

'How would someone get hold of thallium?'

'It's hard to say,' said Hudson. 'It used to be found in some pesticides, rat poisons and ant killers, but because the salts are so poisonous they were banned in Europe and the US years ago. They might be still used in some developing countries, so I guess anyone visiting there might be able to get hold of it. Some pharmacies here might be able to get hold of it. Some pharmacies here might still stock thallium salts, but anyone buying them would be required to sign the poison book. It would be a risk, but you could ask around to see if anyone's done that. The other context for use is in some manufacturing processes; dyes, paints, glass, that kind of thing.'

Paints again. 'How much thallium would Lucy have needed to ingest to do the damage?' he asked. 'Would it have to be every day?'

'No, it's a cumulative thing, so if the dose is right it could be taken intermittently and still have the same effect. We've traced at least one of the sources; it's in the milk we found in Lucy's fridge.'

'Christ.' Mariner immediately thought of the ubiquitous plastic bottles stacked at the supermarket. 'This is milk that she's been buying off the shelf?' Mariner felt queasy. If a major supermarket chain was involved with this, then it wouldn't just be Lucy Jarrett, and suddenly they'd have a massive food scare on their hands.

'Don't panic,' Hudson reassured him. 'The milk was in bottles, so she must have been taking doorstep deliveries from a dairy. Unfortunately there was no milk at Nina Silvero's house that we could take for comparison.'

'That's unusual, isn't it?' Mariner said. 'Most people drink milk in some form or another.'

'It must have been removed. Didn't you say that she's got a daughter? Perhaps she cleared it out after her mother died. I guess milk is the first thing to go off.'

Except that the house had been preserved as a crime scene. If Nina was being poisoned, then the poisoner was also her murderer, and would have got rid of the milk on the night she died.

'There is another way to establish whether Silvero was being similarly poisoned,' Hudson was saying. 'Thallium's like arsenic, it's retained in the body cells, especially the hair and we would still be able to detect it, even after cremation. It depends if the family is prepared to part with a sample from her ashes.'

'It's a formality, I'm sure, but I'll see if we can arrange that,' Mariner said.

'I'll keep in touch,' Hudson said, and concluded the call. When she'd rung off, Mariner called Rachel Hordern. 'Have you scattered your stepmother's ashes yet?' he asked.

'No, why?'

'We need to test a sample from them, if you wouldn't mind.'

Rachel's tone was immediately suspicious. 'What for?'

'You told us that she had been suffering with her health in the months before she died,' Mariner recalled. 'We now have reason to think she was being poisoned.'

'What? How do you know that?'

'We don't, for certain, that's why we need the sample.'

'But my mother lived alone. Who could do that?'

'We're keeping an open mind,' said Mariner diplomatically. No reason to tell her that she was a suspect, at least not until after they had secured her cooperation. 'It's possible that the poison was added to the milk. How did your mother buy her milk?'

'She had a milkman, the same one she'd had for years. Why on earth would he want to poison my stepmother?'

'I'll send over an officer to collect the sample,' Mariner said. 'Thank you for your help, Mrs Hordern.' And he rang off.

After calling in Millie and Knox, Mariner brought them up to date with what Hudson had told him.

'It has to be Will,' Millie said straight away. 'No one else would have access to the fridge.'

'He'd have to be careful not to drink it himself,' Knox pointed out.

But Millie had the answer. 'He's lactose intolerant,' she said. 'Lucy told me. The organisers had to accommodate that when they planned the wedding breakfast.'

'Well, that certainly makes a perfect fit,'

Mariner agreed.

'And it must take Bonnington out of the equation,' added Knox. 'He wouldn't be in a position to do it.'

'Are we sure about that?' Mariner was reluctant to rule him out completely. 'Is there any way he could get hold of a key? Lucy isn't one of these people who keeps a spare under the doormat, is she?'

'I can't imagine so,' Millie said, 'especially lately, when she's been so nervy anyway. But I can soon find out.'

'So, unless Bonnington took a bottle, and removed and replaced a bottle top without anyone noticing–'

'It wouldn't be impossible, though, would it?' said Knox suddenly.

'Christ, if you're right that would open it right up again,' said Mariner. 'It could be anyone: Kerrigan, Hughes, Sally Frick. We need to find out for sure. How does the milk get delivered here?'

It took time, but eventually Mariner was able to track down a bottled pint of milk and have it sent up to his office. 'Right,' he said. 'Who wants to give it a go?'

'No good asking me,' Knox grumbled. 'I'm ham-fisted at the best of times.'

'Here, I'll try.' Millie came forward and, sliding a thumbnail under the foil, worked her way around the rim, loosening the skirt, and successfully removed the top without tearing it. Replacing it was easier, though it was by no means as snug a fit as before.

'It could be done,' Millie said. 'But you'd have to do it carefully, and it's not going to look perfect afterwards.'

'Would you notice, if you had no reason to suspect that the milk is being tampered with?'

Knox regarded it sceptically. 'I think you would,' he said.

Millie nodded reluctantly. 'Yeah, I think Tony's right.'

'Which means it has to be Jarrett,' concluded Mariner.

'But what about Nina?' said Millie. 'Will doesn't appear to even know her.'

'I've made an assumption that Nina was being poisoned in the same way,' Mariner pointed out. 'But we won't know until the tests on her ashes have been done. And Will Jarrett definitely has an alibi for the night she died. And none of this explains Nina's mystery caller, nor Bonnington's fingerprint.'

Knox shook his head slowly. 'If it is Bonnington, I can't believe that Nina's friends haven't heard of him, or her stepdaughter for that matter.'

'Which brings us to Rachel herself,' Mariner said. 'According to the neighbour, she visits her stepmother every couple of weeks. Given that Nina's symptoms sound less severe, if she has been poisoned, it's possible that her stepdaughter could have been doctoring the milk. She's agreed to give us a sample, but she wasn't happy about it.'

'This is beginning to look like a conspiracy,' said Knox.

'Among total strangers?' Millie said. 'That just doesn't make sense.'

They were interrupted from further speculation by Mariner's phone. It was Gail Hudson again. Mariner put the phone on speaker; they all needed to hear.

'Thought you might like to know, we've determined how the thallium was added to the milk,' Hudson said. 'Examination of the bottle top exposed a tiny puncture mark the size of a needle, so it was probably injected into the bottles.'

'That means that it could have been added any time after the milk was bottled,' Mariner said.

Hudson concurred. 'Both women were taking doorstep deliveries from dairies, but we've established that they were two different ones, so I doubt that the source goes that far back. You're looking at someone doing this while the bottles are on the doorstep.'

'Christ, so now it could be anyone,' said Knox, when Hudson had rung off.

Mariner nodded agreement. 'Injecting the thallium wouldn't be that difficult, if you pick your moment. Holding the syringe in your hand, maybe concealed in a pocket; you walk up to the step, stick in the needle, squeeze out the contents, walk away. The whole operation could be undertaken within half a minute, and we've already seen that Lucy Jarrett's ground floor is pretty well concealed by the shrubs in the garden.'

'It'd be early in the morning before many other people are around, too,' Millie pointed out. 'Depending when Nina and Lucy are up and about, there could be a window of at least a couple of hours when the milk is sitting on the step just waiting to be doctored.'

'Easy to invent a cover story too,' said Knox. 'Like, putting something through the door on the way to work.'

'Pity we've got no CCTV in either of those areas,' said Mariner.

'And does this make Bonnington the favourite again?' Knox wondered.

'It must do,' said Millie. 'He's the one we've got most evidence against, and he's the handiest.'

'Although realistically the milk tampering could be any of them; Rachel Hordern, Susan Brady, Kerrigan, the Hughes family,' Mariner reminded her.

'Bonnington's the strongest, though.'

'But, apart from that fingerprint, we still don't have anything to connect him to Nina Silvero,' Knox pointed out. 'Or to give us a motive for her.'

'So we should let him go,' Millie said.

'All in good time,' Mariner said. 'There's something we're missing here.'

'Why don't we look at it the other way round?' said Knox. 'The only person who really fits the stalking scenario is someone out for revenge. Who have Lucy and Nina both wronged?'

Millie snorted. 'That's a great question when we can't even find any common ground between them. Both Lucy and Rachel Hordern went to independent schools but not the same one. Paul Copeland and Ronnie Silvero were both in the Masons but not in the same Lodge. They both worked on the Hughes case, but not at the same time.'

'And as far as we know Paul Copeland did nothing to upset the Hughes family,' said Mariner.

'They're both prematurely dead,' Knox offered.

'But for different and transparently non-suspicious reasons. Anything come of the list of parents from the dancing school?'

'Nothing that I could find,' said Knox. 'The ones I've spoken to all seem pretty shocked by what's happened.'

'Lucy Jarrett definitely wasn't involved in that?' Mariner asked Millie.

'No. She was a cheerleader at school but she never had formal lessons.'

They all sat for a moment, each lost in thought, trying to find a way out of the conundrum.

'What we need to do is catch the poisoner in the act,' said Millie suddenly. 'So far the only one of our suspects who knows Lucy is in hospital is Will, and it seems to me that we've more or less ruled him out now.' She looked to Mariner for affirmation, which he gave. 'So why can't we send a decoy back with Will, to send out the message that Lucy's home and everything's normal, set up surveillance op, and just wait until the poisoner strikes again. Dr Hudson said that it's probably a weekly occurrence, so it wouldn't have to go on for ever.'

'It's a bit close to Bonnington. What if he runs into our decoy?' Knox said.

'Maybe we don't even need the decoy,' Mariner said. 'We still have Bonnington here. All we need to do is get Lucy's car back on the drive and, if Will draws the upstairs curtains, it will give the impression that Lucy's ill in bed, which is the line he can give if anyone asks. Whoever is doing the poisoning would expect that, after all. Then we can let Bonnington go.' He had been about to dismiss the idea as far-fetched but the more Mariner thought about it, the more sense it seemed to make. It was frighteningly simple.

'I still think we should go with the decoy,' said Millie. 'We're not certain that it's Bonnington, so we don't know who else might be watching the house.' It was a fair point.

'Tony?'

'It'd be easy enough to do,' Knox said. 'I think it's not a bad idea.'

'OK then. Millie, you contact Will and explain what's going on. He needs to get his story straight from the outset. Tony, you need to get in touch with the dairies and check the timing of the deliveries.' Now all Mariner had to do was sell it to the DCI.

'We're going round in circles with everything else,' Mariner told Sharp a little later. 'This would be a way of settling it quickly and decisively.'

'What would it involve?' Sharp was understandably dubious; she was thinking of the budget.

'Martin Bonnington is still one of our suspects,' Mariner said. 'So when we let him go we'll send Will home in Lucy's car with our decoy; a female officer who roughly resembles Lucy. Once in the house, Will closes the bedroom curtains and the story is that Lucy has gone down with a bug and is ill in bed. The decoy can then leave the house at an appropriate time under cover of darkness. Knox has checked the milk delivery time, which is between three and four, Monday to Friday, so all we need then is surveillance on the front of Lucy's house during that time and a few hours either side, along with a couple of officers on the ground to make an arrest. We'd start the early hours of Monday morning.'

'There's going to be a lot of movement,' Sharp said. 'Are you sure you can keep this covert?'

'It's small scale,' Mariner said. 'As long as we're observant and we use the opportunities presented by visitors to the house, I think we can handle it, ma'am. Meanwhile, we keep following up the other leads and, if nothing has happened within the week, we call it off.' Mariner knew that the prospect of it being a short-term surveillance would make it a more attractive proposition, and Sharp took the bait.

'OK. If you can find a suitable officer to pose as Lucy, you can give it a go. But only for a week, and then we review it.'

The first thing to do was to release Martin Bonnington, who was clearly bemused about what was going on. Millie had already identified an officer, and PC Jodie Ryan was a willing volunteer. Friday was spent briefing her, after which she and Will returned to Hill Crest, in Lucy's car. The surveillance team of two uniformed officers, rota'd in with Millie, Knox, Charlie Glover and Mariner from CID for the surveillance, would arrive at the house each evening, under cover of darkness. For now Lucy Jarrett was safe, and at the end of Friday Mariner suggested that they all take the weekend off and prepare for a busy week ahead.

CHAPTER EIGHTEEN

Mariner's first task on Saturday morning was to collect his new glasses. They were fine – basic wire frames – though they made him look older, he thought, and increased his resemblance to his late father. Now he'd just have to get into the habit of wearing them. Already he could anticipate the jibes in the station on Monday morning.

They were tucked in his pocket as he walked back up Corporation Street, and without them he almost made his usual old mistake. The woman up ahead of him looked from the back exactly like Anna. Same build, same hairstyle and colour. But this time he wasn't about to make an arse of himself. Allowing himself a smile, he turned to note the traffic prior to crossing the road, when a voice from behind halted him.

'Tom?' She had turned and was looking right at him. Christ, it *was* Anna. And she looked so happy to see him. He thought his heart would explode from his chest. 'How are you?' she was asking.

'I'm fine.' Recovering from the shock, Mariner stepped nearer, fighting the urge to throw his arms round her. 'What are you doing here?'

She inclined her head towards Brackleys department store. 'Got a meeting with the wedding planner.' She smiled.

Mariner's smile remained fixed in place. His facial muscles seemed to have frozen. 'Wow. Congratulations,' he managed to say.

'Oh, God, not for us!' Anna shrieked, playfully smacking his arm. 'That would be a bit premature. It's for Charles and Lottie, you remember them? Lottie wanted some support so I agreed to come, but this is clearly the season to arrange weddings because so far all we've done is wait in a massive queue, so I've popped out to do a couple of things, while Charles is being measured for his suit.'

'Have you got time for coffee or something?' Mariner asked, weak with delight.

'Yeah, I probably could steal away for a few minutes. Let me just text Lottie to let her know.' And she tucked her arm into his as they walked.

They ended up at one of the many new eating places in the Bull Ring and sat overlooking the concourse that led down to St Martin's church; two cappuccinos between them. It was just metres from here that they'd both been caught in an explosion that had ripped through the church, nearly eighteen months before. Mariner wondered if she'd thought about that. 'How long have you got?' he asked.

'Hours, I would think. I know what these wedding people are like. They'll want to know the ins and outs of–'

'–the cat's behind,' said Mariner finishing off one of her favourite expressions. He felt heady from the look of her and the faint smell of her perfume and had to consciously restrain himself from touching her. 'I was gutted for a minute there, you know, when I thought it was you and Gareth.'

Anna smiled. 'I could see that. You haven't got any better at disguising your feelings.'

'So, how's it going, the two of you?' The words almost choked him.

'It's fine.' She picked up her spoon and skimmed a little froth off her coffee, unable to quite meet Mariner's eye. 'We're um–'

'What?'

'We're taking it slowly, you know?' Her reply was careful, measured.

Mariner was euphoric, and for several seconds he had the wild idea of suggesting they get a room in a hotel. 'How's Jamie?' he asked to distract himself from that thought.

'He's great, doing really well,' she said. 'I mean, he's still autistic, and he still can't do much for himself, but it was the right thing to move him out to Towyn. The farm community suits him; he's strong and healthy,

364

and I think he's happy.'

'I'm glad,' Mariner said truthfully, even though it had helped to take her away from him. He knew that Anna had struggled to do the right thing by her younger brother.

'How's all the Granville Lane gang?' she asked.

'Tony Knox is still seeing his science teacher, Millie is loving married life. The DCI just got engaged.'

'And Katarina?'

'Even she's got a bloke,' Mariner said ruefully. 'It's just me who's billy no mates.'

She laughed. 'Oh, poor old you. My heart bleeds. What about Stephanie? Isn't that her name?'

Mariner was momentarily speechless. 'What do you know about her?'

'She called me.'

'What?'

'She rang me last week on my mobile. She said that you and she had started going out; she'd realised that I was important to you, and wanted to know just how important. I did think it was a bit strange, but understandable, I suppose.'

'Christ, she must have picked up your number from my mobile. I thought I was losing my marbles, because she mentioned your name and I felt sure that I hadn't talked to her about you. What did you tell her?'

'The truth,' Anna said, with a shrug. 'That

we were an item, but that now I'm with someone else. She seemed satisfied with that. Is it serious?'

'No! It's nothing, it's finished, I mean, it never was anything; one night plus her imagination,' Mariner babbled on. 'I actually thought I had a stalker on my hands at one point but I think she was just lonely.'

He paused. 'I really miss you,' he said, his voice catching. 'I fucked up so badly.'

'You did,' she said, holding his gaze. 'Still, now we've both moved on. And who knows how long it would have lasted anyway? Maybe it was for the best.'

Maybe? 'What if–'

Anna checked her watch. 'God, I should go back to Lottie,' she said, gathering her bags. 'She'll think I've abandoned her.'

Reluctantly, Mariner walked her back to where they'd met.

'It's been great to see you.' Stretching up to kiss his cheek, she rubbed his arm affectionately, her touch lingering, Mariner thought, for a moment longer than necessary. 'Take care, eh?'

'You too.' It was the most he could manage.

'Byee.'

Mariner watched her disappear through the glass swing doors and into the store. She didn't look back, but nonetheless he felt a sudden surge of optimism.

CHAPTER NINETEEN

Seeing Anna had been a welcome distraction from Mariner's Sunday undertaking, which was to help Kat to move her things to her new flat. Concealing his disappointment as best he could, he helped her to load up his car with her few boxes of possessions, and drove her over to the flat in Moseley. He was re-running in his head yet again his encounter with Anna when, in a momentary lapse of concentration, he overshot a roundabout.

'Tom!' Kat yelled, and Mariner slammed on his brakes just in time. The oncoming driver blared his horn and could clearly be seen mouthing obscenities. Mariner was tempted to get out of the car with his warrant card and teach the bastard a lesson, but he calmed himself, well aware of how these things could escalate. Only a few minutes earlier they'd caught the news headlines, dominated by a couple who had been attacked the previous night.

'I think your head is in the clouds today,' Kat said mildly.

'I saw Anna yesterday,' Mariner told her.

'Ah, I think you miss her.'

'Yes, I do.'

Kat's new home was compact, modern and airy; a far cry from Mariner's traditional canalside cottage. It wasn't what he would have chosen, identical as it was to the hundreds of others in the complex, but it was ideal for a young woman starting out, and Kat was thrilled with it, proudly showing him round everything. Mariner unaccountably got a lump in his throat, but all the same it took him by surprise when she dissolved into tears, 'I think my mum and dad would like this very much,' she said suddenly. 'Is better than the place they live in Tirana.'

Mariner put a comforting hand on her arm. 'They'd be very proud of you,' he agreed. 'But maybe they will get to see it. Are you still thinking of contacting them?' he asked.

She sniffed. 'Yes, one day, I think.'

'In the meantime, lunch.'

Mariner took her to the Selly Park Tavern, then afterwards they went for a blustery walk around Cannon Hill Park, where they walked past the models of the Elan valley dams. It had rained on and off all day, but there were plenty of families enjoying the park and feeding the ducks. When they returned to her flat, Giles was there, waiting in his car with a big bunch of flowers.

'I'll leave you to it then.' Mariner felt suddenly awkward.

'But you come and see me soon.' Kat smiled. 'Is not so far.' Tentatively she put her arms on his shoulders and hugged him. 'Thank you,' she whispered in his ear.

Back home the house seemed very empty without Katarina. Over the years the place had seen a number of lodgers, among them, at one time, Tony Knox. But maybe this had all worked out for the best. Now if Mariner needed to sell up at short notice he could. It would all depend on Anna. OK, she hadn't outright admitted that things were not going well with Dr Gareth, but he was sure he'd detected some uncertainty there. He still had the contact number for her in Herefordshire. Maybe his next weekend walk would be out there and he'd just 'drop in' to see her. He could phone her now and pave the way, but when he tried the number there was no reply. On a Sunday afternoon they'd be in the pub probably, Mariner thought, remembering the very attractive village inn. Still, he had the rest of the week to get hold of her.

The thought of Anna's local turned him to thinking about a drink. Mariner's nearest pub, the Boatman, had been recently refurbished, all the rooms knocked into one, children and families welcome. But sometimes desperation prevails and, having grabbed his coat and keys from the hook in the hall, he slammed the door behind him.

Mariner was in reasonable spirits driving in to Granville Lane on Monday morning. The Boatman hadn't been as bad as he'd feared, the novelty of the new facilities clearly wearing off, and leaving the pub as quiet on a Sunday evening as he had ever known it. He'd even managed a couple of games of dominoes with one of the old regulars. He missed Kat being around, but it didn't mean that he'd be on his own for long. All that was needed to consolidate this new-found optimism would be for the surveillance op to reap its rewards.

But the day didn't start well. On Mariner's desk was an urgent message for him to contact IT technician Max. Knox appeared while Mariner was making the call, and his slight incline of the head told Mariner that it had been a no-show. He confirmed as much when Mariner hung up the phone.

'We have to be prepared for that,' said Mariner, though he could tell that Knox was disappointed. 'It's not our only setback.'

'What else?'

'That was Max on the phone,' Mariner said. 'They've just realised that Martin Bonnington's computer clock is twelve hours adrift, which means he has an alibi for a lot of the computer activity. It's looking like he might have had a hacker after all.'

'Shit,' said Knox.

'That's two pieces of crap news,' said Mariner cheerfully. 'And here's DCI Sharp with the third.'

Sharp had appeared in the doorway, her face grim, and Mariner's remark failed to raise a smile. 'Could you give us a moment, Tony?' she said.

'Yes, ma'am.' Knox got up from where he was perched on a low filing cabinet. He walked out into the bull pen, curious that everyone seemed to be standing around waiting expectantly. 'What's going on?' he asked. But before anyone could tell him, an agonised howl ripped through the air from Mariner's office behind him.

'You heard about that road-rage incident on the M5 on Saturday night?' Millie said quietly.

'Yeah, I caught somethin' about it on the news,' said Knox, puzzled. 'But they hadn't named–'

'It was Anna Barham,' said Millie.

'Christ almighty,' breathed Knox, turning to stare at Mariner's office.

'I'm so sorry, Tom,' Sharp said.

Mariner sat at his desk, head in his hands, clawing at his scalp. 'I don't understand.' He looked up at Sharp, beseeching her to say it wasn't true; that she'd made a mistake; that

371

it was a cruel prank. 'I just saw her,' he said, as if that could change things. 'What happened?'

'She was a passenger in a Porsche driven by a Dr Charles Morse,' Sharp said, quietly. 'They were driving from Birmingham back to Hereford on Saturday evening, and got into some altercation with another driver. He and his mates followed them to the exit junction, waited until they were out in the wilds before forcing them off the road and attacking Morse. It looks as if Anna tried to intervene. They each died from multiple stab wounds, Morse at the scene and Anna on the way to hospital. Another woman survived the incident. I'm really sorry, Tom.' Going round to where Mariner sat, she placed a hand on his back. 'Is there anything I can do?'

'No,' Mariner whispered, 'thank you, ma'am.' And as Sharp closed the door behind her Mariner jumped up from his seat and swept the contents of his desk on to the floor.

'Anything you want us to do, ma'am?' Knox asked, as Sharp walked past them to return to her office.

Gazing in at Mariner, Sharp shook her head sadly. 'Just keep doing your job,' she said. 'Is everything in hand for tonight's surveillance?'

'Yeah, it's my shift, ma'am.'

'Well, at least let's try to get a result for him, eh?'

For some time CID remained unnaturally quiet; everyone kept their heads down trying to ignore the raging figure that could be seen pacing from side to side.

After forty minutes Mariner's door opened and, staring straight ahead, he walked purposefully across the bull pen, down the stairs and out of the building. All they could do was watch him go.

Throughout, Mariner had remained dry eyed, the overwhelming pain in the centre of his chest, like a vortex, sucking him dry. He got in his car and drove too fast up to Monument Hill where he could park and look out over the panoramic view south, towards the Malverns and beyond, to the place where she had perished. As he switched off the engine the tears came, and once they came they would not stop.

He must have sat there for hours gazing numbly out at the horizon because suddenly he became aware that it was getting dark, and his limbs were stiff with cold. His head felt muzzy with grief. Mariner got out of his car and walked in the dusk up to the miniature fortress that marked the top of the hill, immune to the cold wind that cut through his shirt. Pinpricks of light were beginning to appear in the urban sprawl below. He and

Anna had stood up here to watch the new year fireworks. It seemed a lifetime ago. 'We've everything to look forward to,' she had said at the time. How wrong could anyone be?

The next hours were a blur. When Mariner got home there were messages from Knox, wanting to know if he was all right, and from DCI Sharp. 'I've arranged compassionate leave,' she said. 'Take as long as you need.'

Mariner had abused his position and harassed West Mercia police for details of the incident, but they could tell him little more than was on the news. Already the story was starting to drop off the national cycle completely, and he was reduced to searching the Internet for scraps.

On Tuesday morning he got up and dressed at six in the morning. In his car, he retraced Anna's last journey, down the motorway, off the exit and on to the country lane where it had happened. He had no trouble finding it. On this sunny early spring day the narrow lane running between tall hawthorn hedges was bursting with life, the bright-green leaves beginning to push through the buds. A bedraggled strand of crime-scene tape provided an obscene counterpoint. Just beside it, on the road, was a dark stain. It could have been anything, but to Mariner's experienced eye it was unmistakable. He crouched on his haunches and again his vision blurred.

Afterwards he drove on into Upper Burwell, the village where Anna had made her home. His plan had been to offer his condolences in person to Gareth, but now he couldn't bear to even think of another man grieving for her. Instead, he drew up outside the chocolate-box cottage that he remembered as Becky and Mark's. Becky, Anna's former assistant, had been the catalyst for Anna's longing for the rustic life. They'd stayed here once for a few days, back when it was 'Tom and Anna'. It was when she had started to pull away from him.

'Tom.' Becky was shocked to see him and momentarily Mariner thought he'd made a terrible mistake, but then her arms were around him and she was weeping into his shoulder. 'I can't believe it,' she said. 'It's just too awful.'

'I want to find out exactly what happened,' Mariner said. 'Do you think Lottie would talk to me?'

'We can try.'

Mariner wondered if Lottie would even remember him, they had only met on one occasion. In the event it didn't seem to matter. Lottie was too dazed to notice and he couldn't begin to imagine how she must be feeling. But there was little she could tell him beyond what he already knew.

'If there's anything I can do...' Mariner found himself saying to this woman who was a stranger.

He repeated the mantra to Becky as they walked back to the house, though it was said automatically; a futile gesture. So, it was unexpected when she said, 'Actually, Tom, there might be. The thing is, nobody's cancelled the wedding coordinator. I don't think anyone can bring themselves to do it and I daren't raise it with Lottie. As you're up in Birmingham anyway, and in your official capacity, could you call in on your way home and explain to them what has happened? I can give you all the details.'

It was, in truth, the last thing that Mariner wanted to do, but he'd made the offer, how could he possibly refuse, despite the gaping hole in his world? Armed with his warrant card, he made his way into the city centre. He would make himself useful and do what Becky had asked. Retracing his steps along Corporation Street, between the high buildings, Mariner had to pass by the spot where he'd bumped into Anna just a few days ago. He lingered on the pavement for a moment, remembering the way the sun had glinted on her hair, the animated expression on her face, the image so powerful he felt he could reach out and touch her. Only when he saw an elderly woman staring up at him did he realise that he was weeping. Wiping his eyes, he ventured into Brackleys, running the gamut of the aftershave sales girls, and caught the escalator up to the fourth floor.

The wedding department staff were upset and sympathetic. They'd had no reason to connect a random news item with their client. It was unprecedented, and the young assistant Mariner spoke to had to go and fetch the manager, leaving him to wait in one of the private booths that they used. This was clearly big business and Mariner idly wondered how much was charged for this service. Restless and unable to settle, he paced the tiny enclosure. Certificates on the wall announced the awards for past Wedding Coordinators of the Year. Designed to impress customers, no doubt, but what the hell did it mean? His attention was drawn to one in particular.

'Inspector Mariner, I'm so sorry to keep you waiting.' The manager appeared, in a tight-fitting suit and too much make-up, with a range of paperwork for Mariner to sign, and in ten minutes it was all over. Charles and Lottie's wedding plans scrapped for ever. Travelling down again to the ground floor, Mariner felt a wave of sadness for poor Lottie. Walking down past the railway station, Mariner made his way through the exclusive Mailbox, Anna's favourite shopping centre, and to Brindley Place where he dropped down on to the canal.

Anna was living near here when they'd first met. It seemed that everywhere he went there were stinging reminders. It took him a couple of hours to walk back along the waterside, away from the city centre and to his house, and once there he felt un-accountably tired. The remaining bottles in the beer carrier that Kat had bought him sat untouched and inviting in the kitchen, and, after a couple of bottles to ease the pain, he fell asleep on the sofa.

When he woke up it was dark, and after a while he dropped back to sleep again. Then something woke him with a jolt. This time he found his watch. It was three in the morning. Christ, he'd been asleep for nearly eight hours. As he lay in the dark Mariner heard a milk float rumble by. He thought about the surveillance op and wondered who was on shift tonight. Were they just wasting time and resources with that? His mind skimmed over all their suspects, and for some reason came to rest back on those wedding planner awards. There had been something about that one. And that was when it came to him.

CHAPTER TWENTY

After scrambling for his mobile, Mariner called through to Tony Knox. His sergeant was groggy when he answered, woken from his own slumber.

'What day is it?' Mariner asked.

'Jesus. That you, boss? Are you–'

'What *day* is it?' Mariner demanded again. 'And who's on surveillance?'

'It's Wednesday, and I think it's Millie, boss, but–'

Mariner cut him off and punched in Millie's number. She answered almost immediately.

'I know what we've missed,' he said. 'I know who it is, and they're coming today. I'm coming over. I want you to let me in.'

'But, boss, you could blow our–'

'It's still only three am and I'll be careful. Just be ready to let me in.'

The roads were deserted as Mariner drove to the Manor Farm estate. After parking his car in a cul-de-sac close to the entrance, he locked it and continued on foot, staying close to fences and hedges along the way. Under cover of a high fence he stopped at the end of Hill Crest and stood for several minutes, waiting and watching. It was a freezing morning, his breath steamed the air and a light mist cast halos round the sodium lights. A cat padded across the road ahead of him casting wary glances from side to side, but there was no other movement. Slowly and silently Mariner proceeded along the road, pressing himself into the shadows. All the houses, including Bonnington's, were in darkness. Mariner crept cautiously up the side of the drive of number nineteen and as he got to the door it opened without a sound, drawing him inside.

'Up here, sir.' After closing the door soundlessly, Millie led him up the stairs and into the front bedroom, where in the darkness Mariner could just make out the silhouette of the night-surveillance equipment on its tripod in the window. Millie passed him some binoculars. There was a light crackle as she activated her walkie-talkie. 'DI Mariner safely admitted,' she said, and the recipient rogered and signed off.

'Who have you got?' Mariner asked, his voice low.

'Solomon and Evans tonight, sir. Poor guys; they definitely got the short straw. They're tucked in behind the bins round at the side of the house. They've fixed a temporary security light down there too, for when it all kicks off – if it ever does. You want some tea, sir?' She lifted a flask.

'I'm fine,' whispered Mariner, lifting the binoculars to scan the front of the house. 'Where's Jarrett?'

'Went to bed hours ago. We've hardly seen him since we've been here. I'm starting to think this whole thing has been a complete waste of time. Three nights now and not a tickle. The DCI will do her nut.'

'That's because it's tonight,' said Mariner, still watching the street.

'But how can you be so sure, sir?' Millie had joined him now, and they stood, side by side, two pairs of night-vision binoculars trained on the drive below.

'What's the thing that Lucy Jarrett and Rachel Hordern have in common?' Mariner whispered.

'Nothing, boss.' Millie was confused. 'That's the whole point.'

'No, I'm not talking about Nina,' Mariner said, exasperated. 'Lucy and *Rachel;* what do they have in common?'

'They're both young women. They're both married?' said Millie eventually, uncertain of where this was going.

'Exactly,' said Mariner. 'And they both–' He stopped. 'Did you see something, there, on the left?'

Millie jerked her binoculars over to where Mariner was looking. 'Are you sure? There's– Yes! I've got it! Wow. That's way too big to be a cat.'

They both watched as a shadowy figure crept along the hedge bordering the Jarretts' house, tucking in behind a large shrub.

'When's the milkman due?' Mariner asked.

'The other days he's come between half-three and four,' said Millie. 'Could be here any time.' She took out a mobile.

'What are you doing?'

'Solomon's got his mobile set to vibrate. It's the signal. God, I hope those two have stayed awake.'

It seemed that no sooner had Millie replaced the phone than they heard the distant whirring of a milk float and, as they watched, dull headlights appeared at the end of the road. 'Shit, this is it,' Millie breathed, the tremor in her voice matching the pumping of adrenalin through Mariner's own body.

Millie held out the walkie-talkie. 'You want to give the signal, sir?'

'No, this one's yours.'

The milkman was making his tortuous way along the street, hopping off the float every few yards to make his deliveries. Finally he got to number nineteen and they watched as he hurried up the drive, deposited the bottles with a clink and moved on. Step by step, the milk float chugged its way to the end of the road and disappeared, leaving behind a deafening silence. Mariner and Millie stood rigid, binoculars fixed on the shrub below. Nothing happened. Minutes passed.

'Christ, have we missed–' But as he spoke Mariner saw movement, a dark figure emerge from the shadows and approach the front door.

'Go, go, go!' Millie hissed into the handset, and instantaneously the front garden was flooded with light. Mariner and Millie thundered down the stairs to the sound of shouting and scuffling outside, followed by a strangled cry. Mariner flung open the door to see Solomon lying on the ground and Evans running towards the street and after their culprit.

'He stabbed me,' Solomon was saying, in disbelief.

'Call an ambulance!' Mariner shouted to Millie, already running. 'And stay with him. Then call for back-up.' And he followed Evans, hot in pursuit of their perpetrator.

The chase was never going to be about speed, but, in the darkness, the housing estate provided plenty of cover, and rounding the corner from Hill Crest their quarry seemed to vanish into thin air. Without adequate support it was an impossible task to search the maze of roads and driveways in the dark, and, when Mariner heard the distant sound of a car engine igniting, he know they had lost. He and Evans returned to Hill Crest empty handed and despondent, arriving as Solomon was being driven off in the ambulance. By now Will Jarrett was awake and one or two neighbours had appeared to see what the commotion was. Officers in two squad cars were awaiting instructions, but Mariner shook his head. 'It's too late,' he said.

'We'll get prints from the syringe,' said Millie. 'Solomon's sure his attacker wasn't wearing gloves. Will he be all right?'

'I'm sure he will,' Mariner said. 'We need to get to Brackleys. What time is it?'

'It's quarter to five, sir. Brackleys won't be open for hours,' Millie said uncertainly. 'Why do we—'

'Then we need to get the manager out of bed.' Mariner was pacing the pavement trying to work out what to do next. Tracking down the store manager would take time, as would getting him or her into the store at this early hour to retrieve what Mariner needed. Suddenly he stopped. 'No, it's simpler than that. We just need to get back to the station. Meet me back there as soon as you can.' And he was off running back down the street to pick up his car.

Mariner had a head start on Millie, had found what he wanted from Tony Knox's desk and was hurrying back down the stairs when he met her coming up.

'I've got it,' he said. 'All we need now is a

384

piece of luck. Come with me.'

'Where are we going?'

'You'll find out.'

Driving too fast through the suburbs, Mariner drew up in a narrow street of terraced houses.

'I don't understand. What are we doing here?' Millie asked.

'Hitting lucky,' said Mariner with some satisfaction, and Millie followed his line of vision to where a silver Honda was parked some way down the road, its boot open, while the driver loaded things in. 'I didn't know if she would still be living at this address, but for once we've had a break.'

'Pam?' Millie was mystified. 'But she's the cleaner.'

'That's a relatively new career direction for her,' Mariner said. 'Up until recently she was a wedding coordinator at Brackleys.'

'How do you know that?'

'Anna's friend Becky asked me to cancel Charles and Lottie's wedding planner, so yesterday I went to do it. On the wall there was a certificate, for planner of the year, awarded to Pamela Rasen. There was something familiar about that name, and then, this morning, it came to me. I remembered the phone call Tony made to that ballet-school mother whose child had died. Jonquil's an unusual name, and I saw it again, in the crematorium book of remembrance.

Jonquil Rasen died exactly five years ago.'

'How did you know she would turn up this morning?' Millie asked.

'Remember what Bonnington said when we asked him what was special about Wednesdays? He said, *My house is clean.* That was the day she cleaned his house, and made full use of his computer.'

'But she gave me the names of her clients and Bonnington wasn't one of them.'

Mariner shot her a smile. 'Do you really think she'd have handed you that?'

'And what about Kerrigan? She gave us him, too.'

'Of course she did; to direct us away from her. She must have witnessed the altercation with Lucy outside the health centre and used it to implicate Kerrigan. He was never on the estate at the time she said he was.'

'But why would she hold Lucy and Nina responsible for her daughter's death?'

As Millie spoke, there was a bang from across the road as Pamela Rasen slammed down the boot of her car and went back into the house, closing the front door behind her.

'Time to go and find out,' said Mariner, releasing his seat belt.

'How do we play this, boss?' Millie asked.

'Carefully,' said Mariner.

Pamela Rasen seemed remarkably composed, and not overtly surprised to see Millie and Mariner on her doorstep, even at this hour. She showed them into a compact and sparsely furnished lounge, the fireplace dominated by dozens of photographs of a young girl at various stages of development, instantly recognisable from her thick, red curly hair.

'Would you like a drink, some tea perhaps?' she offered politely.

'No, thank you,' said Mariner.

'I'm parched, do you mind if I–'

'No, go ahead. That's fine.' Now that they were here, they had all the time in the world. 'Go with her,' Mariner murmured, and Millie got up and followed Pam into the kitchen.

While Mariner waited, to the accompaniment of the kettle, cups and spasmodic background conversation, he picked up one of the pictures. He was still studying it when Millie and Pamela came back into the room. 'She was a pretty little girl,' he said, stating only what was obvious.

'Jonquil was beautiful,' Pamela agreed, sitting in the chair beside the fire and motioning for them to sit too. 'Exquisite and delicate, exactly like the flower she was named after. But she had the life crushed out of her.'

'How did it start, Pamela?' Mariner asked gently, moving across to sit beside Millie. As he nodded towards her, she surreptitiously took out her notebook and pencil. But she needn't have worried. Pamela was already lost in her own thoughts.

'She always loved dancing,' she said, of her daughter. 'Practically as soon as she could walk she used to skip and dance around the house all the time. She was completely un-selfconscious you know. For her ninth birth-day we took her to see *The Nutcracker*. From then on she had her heart set on being a ballet dancer. So we enrolled her at ballet school to have proper lessons.'

'Nina Silvero's school,' said Mariner.

'It was a big mistake. Jonquil's dad and I knew that she might never be a professional dancer, but Nina Silvero had to come out and say it right in front of her. "I really think you're wasting your money," she said to me while Jonquil was standing right beside me. "She's too big and clumsy to ever be any good at it." Imagine saying that in front of a young child? I wanted to hit her. I wish I had.'

'And how about Lucy Jarrett?'

For a moment she seemed puzzled. 'Ah, Lucy Copeland and Julie-Ann Shore; Jonquil idolised them. They were the coolest girls in her class at St Felix. Anything they had, she had to have too. She thought they were so sophisticated. She knew that they called her "little fat Rasen"; they did it to her face, even though she wasn't really fat. And she laughed along, even though I knew it really hurt her. That was when she began to want to lose weight. She was heartbroken when she couldn't be a cheerleader, but she knew that if she stuck to her diet she could fit into the costume and they would have to let her join. That was when it really started. At first it was all right. She just began eating lots more salads and cutting down on potatoes and biscuits. She shed a few pounds and you could see her confidence skyrocket. We encouraged her too at first, because it seemed to make her so much happier about herself. But then, before we knew it, it had become an obsession. She was weighing herself every day before she went to school; ecstatic if she'd lost a few ounces and desperately upset if she had gained any weight at all. And if she had put on weight then she would hardly eat all day. By this time she was routinely cutting out meals and we were doing everything to try to persuade her to eat. Even though she looked like a skeleton, she was still convinced that she was "little fat Rasen".

'The doctor wasn't much help. She prescribed high-calorie drinks but somehow we had to persuade Jonquil to drink them. We couldn't afford to send her to any of these fancy clinics so in the end she was admitted to All Saints.'

'The psychiatric hospital,' said Mariner, shocked.

'It was terrible seeing her there, with all those frightening people; our sweet little girl who had done nothing wrong.'

'How long did it go on for?'

'More than ten years, until her body couldn't take any more. Her vital organs gradually shut down. For the last few days she was on a life-support machine and we had to make the decision to allow the wonderful little girl we had brought into this world to slip away again.'

'It must have been a terrible decision to make,' Mariner said quietly.

'Bob always blamed me.' She was wringing her hands. 'He said I shouldn't have encouraged the ballet, that I should have been realistic with Jonquil right from the start. But she was nine years old! What kind of age is that to shatter a little girl's dreams? We grieved separately and then he left me. For a while my job kept me going but then the factory closed and I had to look for something else.'

'You worked at Longbridge?'

Pam shook her head. 'Carter's paints in West Heath. I was Mr Carter's PA for twenty-three years. When I saw the wedding planner's job it seemed perfect, as if it was meant to be. I was a good organiser, and, if I couldn't plan my own daughter's wedding,

I could plan other girls' weddings for them instead. I thought it might help, but instead it made me angry and resentful–'

'And then Rachel and Nina Silvero walked into the store.'

Her laugh was brittle. 'Nina didn't even recognise me. I'd had my hair done differently and I hadn't aged as well as she had of course. I'd had rather more stress in my life.'

'She'd lost her husband,' Mariner pointed out.

'It's not the same as losing a child. They were so smug and full of themselves. My daughter lay cold in the ground and they hadn't a clue.'

'So, once you had their address and phone number, you started following Nina Silvero and making nuisance calls.'

'I was going to have it out with her. The first time I rang I was going to tell her who I was, and what she had done to Jonquil. But when she answered the phone I couldn't go through with it, I couldn't speak, and that was when I heard the anxiety in her voice, and it just came out: *I'm going to make you suffer like she suffered.* It made me feel powerful and in control, so the next night I did it again, except this time I didn't speak at all. Next time she and Rachel came into Brackleys I could see that it had affected her, and somehow it made me feel that I was getting some kind of justice for my little Jonquil. I wanted to make her endure what Jonquil had, to feel persecuted for no good reason.'

'And when did you decide to take things further?' Mariner asked.

'To kill her you mean? I saw in the paper that she got her MBE. An MBE for killing my daughter and I knew the time had come. I thought I'd help her celebrate.'

'So you went round to her house.'

'Yes. I'd read a lot about poisons by now and I knew that was how I wanted to do it. I took round the bottle of white wine.'

'With Martin Bonnington's fingerprint on it.'

'Oh.' She didn't know. It had been an accident. 'I almost took champagne, but I knew you'd think that was odd. Nobody drinks champagne alone, do they? It was the only bottle I had in the house; the one Martin had given me for Christmas. I doctored it before I went. Bob used to collect model soldiers, you know, the sort that you paint? But he used to make such a mess so I'd got him some paint stripper specially from work. I knew that it contained acid, and that it would do the trick quickly. I wanted to watch Nina Silvero die as I had watched my own daughter die, right in front of my eyes.'

'So you just turned up on the doorstep?'

'Yes, Nina was surprised to see me, but too polite to turn me away of course. We went into the kitchen. I could tell that she wanted to get rid of me as soon as possible. I insisted on opening the wine, and that was when I reminded her that we had met before. She remembered Jonquil then, of course, and even asked after her. To her credit, she seemed quite shocked to learn that my little girl was dead, but she played down her own part in it. Said she had only done what was kind. Kind? What would she know? The atmosphere was a little uncomfortable by then, but the wine was poured so I proposed a toast, to mothers and daughters, and she drank. It went perfectly.'

'How could you stand by and watch someone die like that?' Mariner was horrified.

'Experience, Inspector. I'd done it before, except that in Jonquil's case it had gone on for years. Have you ever had to stand by and watch a loved one slowly kill herself and all because of a few thoughtless words?'

'Meanwhile, you had run into Lucy Copeland too.'

'I could hardly contain myself. Fate lending a hand again. No reason for Lucy to know who I was of course. They liked us to stick to first-name terms at Brackleys, because it's more personal, and we had never met before. All I had to do was confirm that she'd been a pupil at St Felix. I got to know her pretty well; that she hadn't known her husband-to-be very long and that he worked away, so it was easy to judge the phone calls. The only thing now was that following both Nina and Lucy was taking more of my time. I had a few lates at work so eventually they let me go. On the plus side it meant that I could devote all my time to them, and that was when I decided to set up as a domestic cleaner. It would allow me to be closer to Lucy. I put leaflets through some selected doors on the estate.'

'And Martin Bonnington took the bait.'

'It was just meant to be. He's a sensitive soul, Martin, and he'd told me about his unrequited feelings for Lucy so I just capitalised on that situation. He was often out while I was cleaning so it was easy to use his computer. I may look like an old fogey but I'm quite IT literate, thanks to both of my last positions.' She looked at Millie. 'I don't clean for all those other people.'

'You had to be careful not to run into Lucy,' Mariner said.

'Oh, it wasn't too hard. She was mostly out at work, and if that smart car of hers was there I'd just ring Martin and rearrange my time. It hardly ever happened, though.'

'And when did you start adding thallium to her milk?' Mariner asked.

'A couple of months ago. I'd been to Lucy's house a few times by then, just outside, sometimes before I went to work, and I'd see the milk standing there. I kept thinking, I'd like to give you a taste of your own medicine. I remembered from when we discussed the buffet arrangements that her husband was lactose intolerant, and saw the perfect opportunity. I knew all about thallium because I'd had to produce safety leaflets at work. I knew what it could do.'

'Where did you get hold of it?'

'I'd taken a few things from Carter's for Bob's soldiers. It was one of them. I read up on how much you should give and then I injected it into the milk; not too often but enough to make her feel ill.'

'And Nina Silvero's too?'

She smiled, pleased with her accomplishments. 'Yes, some strategies worked well for them both.'

'Like the anniversary flowers,' Mariner said.

'I thought it was a nice touch to add in the photograph to Lucy's.'

'And were you planning the same end for her?'

'I hadn't really decided.' Pam frowned, contemplating it anew. 'In many ways there seemed no need. The thallium was going quite nicely and her relationship with her husband was also deteriorating quite satisfactorily; I was happy to sit back and let things take their course. Jonquil's Pound Puppy was perhaps too close to home, but I wanted to make her think about my Jonquil again. I didn't think she would really remember.' She looked up at Mariner. 'It was her exam mascot, you know.' So Knox had been right about that.

While she'd been talking the tea that Pam had been so eager for earlier sat untouched, but now she reached across and picked up the cup.

'All I wanted was justice for my poor, beautiful daughter, but now I feel as if my work is done.' As she spoke those final words, she lifted the cup to her lips but too late Mariner realised the implication of them.

'No!' he cried, leaping across to snatch the cup from her grasp, splashes from it burning his hand, but it was too late. She had already taken two deep draughts and her face contorted in pain as the acid seared through her mouth and throat. For several seconds, Pamela Kasen thrashed in her chair, as the acrid aroma of burning flesh filled the air. Mariner dashed into the kitchen for cold water, but, by the time he came back it was over, Pamela Rasen quite still in her chair, her face a mirror image of Nina Silvero's death mask. Hands shaking, Mariner took out his mobile and dialled 999, and, as he did, Millie, a hand clamped to her mouth, pushed past him into the kitchen, where he heard her retching into the sink.

The doorbell of nineteen, Hill Crest rang and Lucy Jarrett went to answer it.

'Hi!' Millie Khatoon handed her flowers and introduced her husband Suliman.

'The DI sends his thanks for the invitation and his apologies,' Millie said. 'He's taken some leave and is going away for a few days.'

Two miles away, Tom Mariner was standing by the boot of his car, arranging rucksack, boots, maps and a small selection of clothes. On the front seat lay a couple of Ordnance Survey Landranger Series that covered mid-Wales, and switched off in a drawer locked inside his house was his regulation-issue mobile phone.

The publishers hope that this book has given you enjoyable reading. Large Print Books are especially designed to be as easy to see and hold as possible. If you wish a complete list of our books please ask at your local library or write directly to:

Magna Large Print Books
Magna House, Long Preston,
Skipton, North Yorkshire.
BD23 4ND

This Large Print Book, for people
who cannot read normal print,
is published under the auspices of

THE ULVERSCROFT FOUNDATION

... we hope you have enjoyed this book.
Please think for a moment about those
who have worse eyesight than you ...
and are unable to even read or enjoy
Large Print without great difficulty.

You can help them by sending a
donation, large or small, to:

**The Ulverscroft Foundation,
1, The Green, Bradgate Road,
Anstey, Leicestershire, LE7 7FU,
England.**
or request a copy of our brochure for
more details.

The Foundation will use all donations
to assist those people who are visually
impaired and need special attention
with medical research, diagnosis
and treatment.

Thank you very much for your help.